Anthony Gilbert and The Murder Room

>>> This title is part of The Murder Room, our series dedicated to making available out-of-print or hard-to-find titles by classic crime writers.

Crime fiction has always held up a mirror to society. The Victorians were fascinated by sensational murder and the emerging science of detection; now we are obsessed with the forensic detail of violent death. And no other genre has so captivated and enthralled readers.

Vast troves of classic crime writing have for a long time been unavailable to all but the most dedicated frequenters of second-hand bookshops. The advent of digital publishing means that we are now able to bring you the backlists of a huge range of titles by classic and contemporary crime writers, some of which have been out of print for decades.

From the genteel amateur private eyes of the Golden Age and the femmes fatales of pulp fiction, to the morally ambiguous hard-boiled detectives of mid twentieth-century America and their descendants who walk our twenty-first century streets, The Murder Room has it all. **>>>**

The Murder Room
Where Criminal Minds Meet

themurderroom.com

T0352514

Anthony Gilbert (1899–1973)

Anthony Gilbert was the pen name of Lucy Beatrice Malleson. Born in London, she spent all her life there, and her affection for the city is clear from the strong sense of character and place in evidence in her work. She published 69 crime novels, 51 of which featured her best known character, Arthur Crook, a vulgar London lawyer totally (and deliberately) unlike the aristocratic detectives, such as Lord Peter Wimsey, who dominated the mystery field at the time. She also wrote more than 25 radio plays, which were broadcast in Great Britain and overseas. Her thriller *The Woman in Red* (1941) was broadcast in the United States by CBS and made into a film in 1945 under the title *My Name is Julia Ross*. She was an early member of the British Detection Club, which, along with Dorothy L. Sayers, she prevented from disintegrating during World War II. Malleson published her autobiography, *Three-a-Penny*, in 1940, and wrote numerous short stories, which were published in several anthologies and in such periodicals as *Ellery Queen's Mystery Magazine* and *The Saint*. The short story 'You Can't Hang Twice' received a Queens award in 1946. She never married, and evidence of her feminism is elegantly expressed in much of her work.

By Anthony Gilbert

Scott Egerton series

Tragedy at Freyne (1927)
The Murder of Mrs
  Davenport (1928)
Death at Four Corners (1929)
The Mystery of the Open
  Window (1929)
The Night of the Fog (1930)
The Body on the Beam (1932)
The Long Shadow (1932)
The Musical Comedy
  Crime (1933)
An Old Lady Dies (1934)
The Man Who Was Too
  Clever (1935)

Mr Crook Murder
  Mystery series

Murder by Experts (1936)
The Man Who Wasn't
  There (1937)
Murder Has No Tongue (1937)
Treason in My Breast (1938)
The Bell of Death (1939)
Dear Dead Woman (1940)
  aka *Death Takes a Redhead*
The Vanishing Corpse (1941)
  aka *She Vanished in the Dawn*
The Woman in Red (1941)
  aka *The Mystery of the*
  Woman in Red

Death in the Blackout (1942)
  aka *The Case of the Tea-*
  Cosy's Aunt
Something Nasty in the
  Woodshed (1942)
  aka *Mystery in the Woodshed*
The Mouse Who Wouldn't
  Play Ball (1943)
  aka *30 Days to Live*
He Came by Night (1944)
  aka *Death at the Door*
The Scarlet Button (1944)
  aka *Murder Is Cheap*
A Spy for Mr Crook (1944)
The Black Stage (1945)
  aka *Murder Cheats the Bride*
Don't Open the Door (1945)
  aka *Death Lifts the Latch*
Lift Up the Lid (1945)
  aka *The Innocent Bottle*
The Spinster's Secret (1946)
  aka *By Hook or by Crook*
Death in the Wrong Room
  (1947)
Die in the Dark (1947)
  aka *The Missing Widow*
Death Knocks Three Times
  (1949)
Murder Comes Home (1950)
A Nice Cup of Tea (1950)
  aka *The Wrong Body*

Lady-Killer (1951)

Miss Pinnegar Disappears (1952)
aka *A Case for Mr Crook*

Footsteps Behind Me (1953)
aka *Black Death*

Snake in the Grass (1954)
aka *Death Won't Wait*

Is She Dead Too? (1955)
aka *A Question of Murder*

And Death Came Too (1956)

Riddle of a Lady (1956)

Give Death a Name (1957)

Death Against the Clock (1958)

Death Takes a Wife (1959)
aka *Death Casts a Long Shadow*

Third Crime Lucky (1959)
aka *Prelude to Murder*

Out for the Kill (1960)

She Shall Die (1961)
aka *After the Verdict*

Uncertain Death (1961)

No Dust in the Attic (1962)

Ring for a Noose (1963)

The Fingerprint (1964)

The Voice (1964)
aka *Knock, Knock! Who's There?*

Passenger to Nowhere (1965)

The Looking Glass Murder (1966)

The Visitor (1967)

Night Encounter (1968)
aka *Murder Anonymous*

Missing from Her Home (1969)

Death Wears a Mask (1970)
aka *Mr Crook Lifts the Mask*

Murder is a Waiting Game (1972)

Tenant for the Tomb (1971)

A Nice Little Killing (1974)

Standalone Novels

The Case Against Andrew Fane (1931)

Death in Fancy Dress (1933)

The Man in Button Boots (1934)

Courtier to Death (1936)
aka *The Dover Train Mystery*

The Clock in the Hatbox (1939)

The Body on the Beam

Anthony Gilbert

An Orion book

Copyright © Lucy Beatrice Malleson 1932

The right of Lucy Beatrice Malleson to be identified as the author of this work has been asserted in accordance with the Copyright, Designs and Patents Act 1988.

This edition published by
The Orion Publishing Group Ltd
Orion House
5 Upper St Martin's Lane
London WC2H 9EA

An Hachette UK company
A CIP catalogue record for this book is available from the British Library

ISBN 978 1 4719 1050 0

www.orionbooks.co.uk

To Una with love
Here is a murder well within your scope,
Love—treachery—mysterious pearls—forged letter,
A body dangling on a knotted rope—
Since crime must be, the bloodier the better.

CHAPTER I

1

DURING the spring of last year the police were greatly perplexed by a violent death occurring at No. 39 Menzies Street. This district has a certain rather unenviable reputation; secretaries of societies existing to protect young girls from the pitfalls of city life counsel their clients against taking rooms there, though the more honest of them add that some of the houses are respectable. No. 39, however, did not come in this category of exceptions. Menzies Street is one of those ugly thoroughfares that make an impulsive heart sick; it consists of a double terrace of very tall featureless houses, split up for the most part in apartment-suites of two rooms and kitchenette, use of bath, or bed-sitting-rooms, those indescribable places of which it has been justly said that their occupants use them for sleeping and when they wish to go into the sitting-room remain where they are. For all its subdued appearance of furtive poverty, a fair amount of money changes hands in this street each night. For the rest, it is fortunate the lighting is so defective; otherwise it might be surprising to discover the identity of some of its occupants at a comparatively late hour of the evening.

2

To begin with, the crime attracted little attention. So many murders of women and girls had taken place recently that they were becoming something of a commonplace, and the death of the type of woman who lives in Menzies Street was nothing to trouble about unduly. She was, moreover, a woman in whom no one appeared to take any personal interest, and a cynical public observed it was amazing there weren't more of these affairs, considering the rag, tag and bobtail of a dozen nations that passed nightly in and out of a hundred secret rooms. The first person to take an intelligent interest in the affair (beyond the very alert police constable on the beat) was one Inspector Field, who realised that whoever had committed the murder had not been, as some suggested, under the influence of drink at the time. Frenzied for the instant he doubtless was, but he had been in full command of his senses. The disposition of articles in the room and the care taken to obliterate all possible clues to identity, proved that. Providence sent Field to the local station on another count at the time of the murder, and it was he who accompanied P.C. Oliver to the house and examined Mrs. Trevor, the undesirable landlady. She had been there for a good many years, and all manner of rumours were current as to the enormous profits that had accrued to her during her tenancy. It mattered nothing to her that the house was shabby, unpainted and even unsound in bad weather. Her rooms were never empty and she could insist on her lodgers taking breakfast that she provided, at a profit of at least 150 per cent. On the morning of that notable Thursday, the 27th March, she came up to the first floor with a tray for her lodger, Miss Florence Penny, and scratched on the door; she had a peculiar walk that was almost silent, and she never knocked honestly or frankly as pleasant people do. When no one opened the door she put down the tray and furtively rattled the knob, but there was still no response. Then she battered on the panels with a soft closed fist while, from behind other doors on the same landing, voices in varying strains of annoyance besought her to give it a rest or put a sock in it. Mrs. Trevor expressed herself coarsely and freely, but without violence; it was her normal language and meant no more than a refined woman's " What a nuisance! " Failing to obtain any response, she at length kneeled down and applied an eye to the keyhole. She saw, first, that the key had been removed from the door, which surprised her, as it seemed to show that Miss Penny was not in. Then she saw something else, a strip of pink silk, probably part of a nightgown, apparently suspended in mid-air.

She rose slowly, scowling with fury. She had no doubt as to what had happened, and knowing her world, realised

2

that sudden death in a house is accounted unlucky, and probably foreshadows further tragedies, violent or self-sought. There were girls here who would be looking for fresh quarters any day now, if she could not hush matters up. But before she could come to any decision as to the best thing to be done, a door farther along the passage was flung wide, and a young woman appeared.

She was bare-footed, wore a short petticoat, had a brush in her hand and a cigarette dangling from her lips.

" Hullo, Ma, what's the trouble? Lady Vere de Vere? Why you bother about her so I can't think."

Mrs. Trevor's scowl blackened. " Can't get no reply," she said heavily.

" Gone out, I expect."

" She don't go out before she's had her breakfast; and anyhow she wouldn't go, unless she flew through the window, without my seeing her."

" P'raps she's been out all night," suggested the girl, whose name was Roona Meredith. " Wouldn't be the first time. And I wish to God," she added savagely, " I could find a chap who'd take me to an hotel now and again, instead of coming back to this blasted place night after night. I'm sick of the sight of the wallpaper."

" Well, all I can say is she come in last night about half-past ten, and I never heard her go out again. I heard her, standing on the steps, talking to some chap, for a long time; then a taxi drove off and the voices went on, so I thought he'd be coming in. And sure enough, after a minute, I heard footsteps and then her door shut. That's what makes me think it's funny her being locked in there now."

" Oh, well," said Roona carelessly, " p'raps this chap had too much of her high-and-mightiness, and put a knife in her. Remember Rosie Lane? A nasty mess they found her in in the morning. And they never got the chap neither. One thing, I will say it 'ud brighten things up a bit for us girls."

She disappeared and came back again with a bright blue dress that she pulled over her head. Then, pushing past Mrs. Trevor, she knelt down and looked through the keyhole.

"Strewth!" She got up again. "That's her all right. I can't see her face, but a nightdress doesn't hang itself on a line of its own accord."

"Unless it's been washed," suggested Mrs. Trevor, coldly.

"You don't wash your feet along of your nightdress," returned Roona in impudent tones. "Well, Ma, you'd better beckon to the nice young man in blue on the other side of the road."

Mrs. Trevor's idea, however, was to evade all possible notice, and she proposed to go quietly along to the station and, if possible, get an un-uniformed official to accompany her back. But as she opened her gate the police constable who patrolled the beat at this hour met her face to face. There was some curiosity in his.

"Anything wrong?" he asked.

"I don't know."

"If you want the police . . ." he began, and then an upstairs window was opened and Roona thrust out her head.

"So you've caught him," she observed conversationally. "He'd better come and break down the door, I should think." Her tone was one of pure malice. She detested Mrs. Trevor; she had hated the woman she now believed to be hanging in the next room.

Fearful of further ostentation, Mrs. Trevor had no choice but to re-open the gate and let Oliver follow her into the house.

Florence Penny's room was probably the best in the house; it was large and finely proportioned, though the various ignoble usages to which it had been put left it shabby and somehow misshapen. There was a deep alcove in which a bed had been placed; there was a dressing-table, a wardrobe, a scarred writing-table, an arm-chair and a plain bedroom chair. The floor was covered with linoleum and two or three mats. Of these one that normally stood beside the bed now lay some distance off.

4

doubled over, as if it had been kicked out of place. Except for that, and a certain confusion of the bed-linen, there was little sign of a struggle having taken place. The most peculiar feature of the room was a long beam that stretched its complete length. Oliver, who was ambitious and alert, looked at it with interest.

"Wonder what made an architect put a beam there," he reflected. "He couldn't be trying to give an old-world appearance."

Mrs. Trevor retorted sulkily that all the houses in the road were built like that. They were old houses.

"Not so old as that," returned Oliver sceptically, stepping forward. It was from this beam that the body hung, the body of a young woman with dishevelled dark hair, wearing a pink night-dress. Her face was dreadful to see; swollen and discoloured, pointing unmistakably to the manner of her death; the mouth sagged open to reveal a blackened tongue, the eyes were staring. Her feet hung only a few inches above the floor; they were bare, nor was there any sign that she had just discarded her slippers. Indeed, by stooping a little, Oliver, who was above average height, could see them far under the bed, as if they had been kicked there, before she got beneath the clothes. A small solid oak affair, a tall stool or a low table, as you chose to regard it, lay on its side near the body, that was suspended by a length of rather dirty-looking worn cord. Oliver, as has been said, was ambitious; a suicide offered little scope for showing his abilities, but he was determined that even this comparatively insignificant affair should be efficiently handled. He must see to it that nothing was touched, no extraneous finger-prints made on the various shining surfaces by which they were surrounded and nothing removed. He said sharply, "Take care. Don't touch that bed-post. No, nor nothing else neither. Any idea why she did it? "

Mrs. Trevor, furious at the inevitable scandal, eager to blacken the name of the dead woman who had brought it upon her, said in a low bitter voice, " How should I know anything about her? Nobody did here. Thought herself a cut above the rest of us, she did. God knows why. But Roona, the girl along the passage, she'll tell you the same. Hardly get a word out of her most of the time. Sweeping in and out like a duchess she was. Never expected to live like this, she'd have you know. When her ladyship deigned to speak to you, that is."

Oliver discounted her jealousy and venom; obviously Florence Penny was comparatively a stranger, in the sense that no one knew her. And at the bare notion that she might be a mystery his interest increased. His eyes had been eagerly searching the room, and now they lighted on an envelope set on the long rickety writing-table. This was addressed to "Whoever May Find This." The envelope was a cheap one, and several like it were subsequently discovered in the drawer of the table. Inside was a sheet of buff-coloured paper, also taken from the drawer, containing a few lines written a little shakily, as though the writer had been nervous and physically unsteady.

"I do this because I must. I have made my last appeal, and he has refused me. I know no one else to whom I can turn, and if I cannot find the five hundred pounds at once I am faced with worse than death. This is the second time he has failed me.—F. P."

Oliver was still sufficiently susceptible to experience compassion; to the young there is something tragic about a life so empty of hope that it is not worth keeping. His curiosity was quickened by the dead woman's mention of five hundred pounds and the consequences of her failure to find it, and her indication of some man who had played an important part in her life, finally driving her to this strait. Restoring the paper to its envelope, he replaced it on the table. Then he walked back to the body. He remained so long looking at the dreadful dangling creature that Mrs. Trevor, malicious and on the defensive, inquired sarcastically, "Writing a poem on it, are you? Well, you've got queer tastes."

Oliver turned at once. "We'd better be getting along," he observed.

"Not even going to cut the poor thing down?"

"Not yet." He insisted on her leaving the room in front of him; it was impossible to lock the door, which he had burst with his shoulder, but he asked for some tape and some tin-tacks and he made a rough-and-ready sealing of the death-chamber before leaving the house. He hammered the tacks in so hard that the seals could not be tampered with without his knowledge. Then he observed, "I'm going along to the station. Haven't got a telephone, have you?"

Mrs. Trevor agreed that she hadn't. Oliver nodded and left her. "Something odd there," he reflected. "I don't know what's behind all that, but it's more than just a tart tying herself up to a beam. I suppose the old harpy will have spread the news all over the street by the time the Inspector gets there."

In point of fact, Mrs. Trevor would have concealed the facts had this been possible, but Roona bearded her as soon as the constable left the house, and dragged from her all the story.

"Gone and hung herself on the beam," the landlady exploded. "Just what she'd like to do, getting my house a bad name. A rotten girl, I always said. Well, what's a girl so quiet for if she hasn't got something to hide?"

Roona went upstairs and discussed the matter with a girl on the next floor, June Silver. Neither had liked the dead woman, both considered her "a swank-pot" for no reason they could see, and both were desperately keen to know the events that had led to the final tragedy.

"Us girls has a precious dull time most of the year," June agreed. "Wonder who she really was, dear."

It was a question that was to trouble Detective-Inspector Field also, within a very few hours.

3

Oliver, relating the story to Field, was pulled up with a sharp, "Any reason to suppose there's anything more to it than a simple suicide? I've often wondered more of these women don't do away with themselves. It's a hell of a life, and they're half-starved one day in three. Anyway, I shouldn't have supposed existence in Menzies Street offered many attractions."

"There's two or three things," said Oliver a little diffidently, "little things, I know, but they don't quite square with her putting herself up there. First of all, she locked the door and took the key out of the lock. Where was the sense in that? If you don't want to be disturbed you keep the key in. Besides, when the key's out, any one·can look through the hole, and Menzies Street isn't the sort of place I'd leave key-holes empty in, specially if I was going to drape myself over a beam. But it isn't just that. Where's the sense? Why should she think of taking it out? Then, she isn't wearing anything on her feet. She'd been to bed to judge from the look of things, and she'd kicked the slippers right underneath. Well, if she was going to get up and lock the door and write a note, she wouldn't want to go about without shoes on, would she? I mean, there's only lino. on most of the floor, and the room's none too tidy; dare say there's a tidy few pins scattered about. And there was something odd about the stool, too. You see, supposing she was standing on it, and then kicked it away, some one would have heard for one thing, and no one seems to have done. It was a precious heavy stool, and she'd have had to give it a good kick to get it out of the way. There aren't any bruises or anything on her feet—and, well, it seems to me that stool's too high. Still, I suppose they'll be able to show if there's any marks of bare feet on it. It's a shiny surface. And lastly, there's the cord. I haven't touched it yet, but it's not new. It looks to me as if it's been used quite a bit, but not lately. Dirty-looking, you know. It might have been round a box." He paused and bit his lip in chagrin. "I never thought to see if there was a box in the room it might have come off. But—well, it seemed to me if she'd really stood on a stool as high as that and then dropped that cord would either have broken or been a good deal more frayed than it is."

Field remarked dryly, "You seem to have noticed a good deal."

"Well, it seemed interesting," apologised Oliver inadequately.

"You'd better come with me," Field added, taking up his hat. "I suppose they can manage a relief for you. We may be some time." So the two walked the short distance to Menzies Street while Oliver answered one or two additional questions put to him by his superior.

Mrs. Trevor was waiting in the hall, like a lean, lascivious cat lurking in an alley. She had plastered quantities of mascara on her eyelashes and this had run down and mingled with the crude colour on her cheeks; her lips were artificially reddened, her hair had long ago been dyed. She gave out a kind of odour of corruption. Field shuddered inwardly at the sight of her and said he would let her know when he wanted her. Then he and Oliver unfastened the strips from the door and entered the room.

The first thing Field did was to walk close up to the body and examine the condition of the cord.

"You're unquestionably right about that," he remarked. "It isn't particularly stout in the first place, and, as you say, it's been used and got considerably frayed. There's another point. As you also observed, that was quite a long drop, and the cord ought to be rove so tightly round the throat you'd have to cut it to get it off. But if I had that body in a horizontal position I could unfasten the rope without a knife. That was a bad mistake."

He sent Oliver downstairs to telephone from a box just across the road to headquarters for a police surgeon to come and make his report, and for the photographer to take the usual impressions of the room before anything was disturbed. Meanwhile, he turned to the bed. The clothes were dragged all ways, streaking on one side to the floor; in the pillow was a deep indentation, too deep, thought Field shrewdly, to be merely the hollow made by a sleeping head. It seemed more probable that some one had pressed a head forcibly into it, keeping it there for several moments. On the pillow-case were three black hairs; a glance was sufficient to prove that they came from the dead woman's head. On the crumpled under-sheet lay a handkerchief twisted into a rag. Field took it by the corner and spread it out; it was small, made of inferior linen, bordered with cheap lace and decorated with a florid " F " in one corner. The detective examined it under a powerful lens, when it was possible to make out the marks of perspiration that showed a struggle of some violence had probably taken place, though if, as he suspected, the woman had been attacked as she lay in the bed, she would not have much opportunity of defending herself. The condition of the bed supported his theory of violence, and in the circumstances it was natural that the remainder of the room should be comparatively untouched. Field began to reconstruct the crime in his own mind. X, the murderer, had stood beside the bed on that blue and red mat now doubled over in the middle of the room; Oliver had already discovered from Mrs. Trevor that this normally stood beside the bed. Some lunging movement or sudden effort on X's part had caused him to fling his whole weight forward, no doubt at the moment when he began the horrid process of throttling, and this had caused the mat to slither across the floor. Judging from the distance it had gone, Field thought probably the woman's opponent had been a man of at least average physique. It was possible, by lying full length on the ground and examining the surface of the floor, to trace the path of the mat on the unpolished surface.

Field next examined the tumbled bedclothes and here he came upon a round pink bead, an imitation pearl, partially crushed and concealed in the folds of the upper sheet. A fragment of pink knotted cord adhered to the bauble; what had happened was plain enough. The woman had been wearing a necklet of pink pearls when she went to bed; it might be her peculiar habit or she might have forgotten them; there would be no question here, Field realised, of an evening bath or even its meagre substitute in the bright pink china basin that stood on the washhand-stand. The murderer must have acted in a panic or a flurry of rage, or he could surely have found half a dozen casual remarks, any one of which would have persuaded her to remove the necklace. No amount of search revealed any further part of it, although later he searched the ground beneath the window and inquired of the road-sweepers if they had discovered such a thing in the course of their work.

Having finished with the bed, Field turned back to the rest of the room. The bed stood behind the door, facing the fireplace, and only the foot of it came into the room, the rest being in the recess. The room presented a queer anomaly. It might have been furnished by two quite dissimilar minds. The silver on the dressing-table, though a little tarnished, was real and good; each article had a chased F in a diamond shaped design; there was a powderbox of quite unusually good cut glass with a silver lid; but the powder it contained was cheap and highly scented. This powder sprinkled the mirror, but unfortunately bore no fingermark; in a pin-cushion of dark blue velvet, encircled in silver, were stuck various brooches of tawdry appearance; other ornaments, lockets and bracelets were carelessly flung on the table; none had any value or betrayed any taste. The mantelshelf presented the same puzzle; for the most part the ornaments were what any intelligent officer would anticipate finding in such a room; a yellow camel, a child in a pink china hat swinging on a gate; some blue vases embossed in gilt filled with mauve everlastings; a plaster statue of a peasant lad and another, execrably modelled, of a nude figure of a woman. Yet, amid this tawdry slovenliness, were a charming little Spode jug, a model of Psyche, a small bronze Madonna of exquisite workmanship, a jade-handled knife. These last betrayed less an ample pocket than a careful and educated taste. The walls supported the usual futile pictures, gift mezzo-chromos in cheap frames, an original painting of flowers in a blue jug, some Kirchner girls in various stages of undress, an enlarged photograph of four kittens, a vulgar print from a second-rate French journal tacked up by four pins, and scattered helter-skelter among these, four or five attractive etchings, in narrow black wood frames,

of rustic scenes. A village with a pump in the centre of
the road; a church with a tall spire standing back from a
little row of houses; a pond with cows feeding; a bridge;
trees in a lane in winter. Field examined these with some
care. They were not, he thought, brilliantly executed; yet
the man who did them had enough of the spirit of true
art to compel a second glance.

On the chairs the dead woman's clothes were carelessly
spread; not betraying too fastidious a cleanliness or any
taste, bright-coloured for the most part, and trimmed with
lace and ribbon. Her wardrobe revealed a medley of
shabby frocks, and one that appeared new, a powder-blue
frock with a coat to match, the latter trimmed with grey
fur.

"Been through hard times lately, and just made a bit,"
was Field's summing-up. "She might have got a bit for
some of those ornaments, and she'd certainly have raised
a fair amount on the dressing-table silver. I suppose she
had some reason for not wishing to part with that. I dare
say she bought that frock for a special occasion. This looks
like it." This was a large black chocolate box, tied with
mauve ribbons that stood on the chest of drawers. It had
come from a French confiserie in Bond Street and was quite
empty. In a small, half-concealed cupboard by the window he found eggs, butter, a piece of pie, a small uncut loaf.

"She didn't intend to do herself in last night," thought
Field sceptically. "She'd just been buying her breakfast.
Let's look at the letter."

This was interesting, but for the moment led him nowhere. If his murder thesis was right, as he was increasingly
sure that it was, that had been forged by some one who
knew her circumstances. It should be possible to show
whether she was really trying to wring five hundred pounds
from a man and if she had been with such a man the
previous night. It pointed to one or two obvious conclusions, such as—that the murderer had known Florence
Penny well enough to be cognisant of her affairs and to
be able to imitate her handwriting. He hunted everywhere
for something in her handwriting with which to compare

the note, but found only a greasy smeared little list of cosmetics that she purposed to buy. The writing on this slip of paper was so rubbed that comparison was impossible, and he knew he must wait for that. The writing-table, however, gave him other information. It contained a small bottle of cheap ink and a bright green penholder. Field took up the latter thoughtfully and drew a cat's face on a slip of paper he took from his pocket. This he blotted on a scrap of paper from his diary and compared the effect with that of the letter, that had also been blotted. They appeared much the same hue; there was, however, always the possibility that an expert could detect some difference in the quality of the ink. The writing on the envelope had not been blotted. Putting down the pen, Field saw that his hands were stained with ink and examining it further saw that any one using it would be in a like condition. He came back and examined the hands of the dead woman. There was no trace of ink upon them, nor any signs in the room that any one had tried to wash away ink-marks. The towels were folded on their rail and the sponge almost dry. Had she used any of these, Field was convinced they would be lying willy-nilly as she happened to drop them.

He had not yet exhausted the clues the room had for him. The weather had been unusually warm of late, and though a fire was laid in the grate it had not been kindled. Upon the table, however, as on the floor surrounding it, he found innumerable feathery flakes of ash, where some one, presumably the murderer, had carefully burned a number of papers. The stumps of several matches, charred and crisp, lay in an ash tray that had an embossed view of Cambridge upon it. But there was nothing to show that the girl had not burnt the papers herself, except the condition of her hands, that were quite free from any marks of ash.

Field had now examined everything in the room, except some books that stood on a ledge, books that were as incongruous as the etchings and the miniature statue of the Madonna. They were well-bound and had probably never been read. *Blake's Poems*, Richard Jefferies' *The Open*

Air, a book on Old London, a pocket edition of two or
three of Kipling's books, and a very charming little book
of 18th century woodcuts. Inside each on the fly-leaf was
written "Fanny" and a date in 1923, but nothing to show
from whom they came.

Field now examined every cranny of the room in his
search for the key, but not finding it came to the conclusion
that the murderer must have carried it off with him, and
it might now lie at the bottom of the Thames or in a ditch
or drain anywhere. He had just come to this reluctant
conclusion when a bell downstairs rang imperiously and
Rogers, the police surgeon, with a companion, came
upstairs and knocked on the door.

4

Between them Field and Rogers cut down the body and
lifted it on to the bed. A more detailed examination of
the rope knotted round the dead woman's throat confirmed
his suspicions. It was too loosely tied, though probably
as tightly as would be possible without the additional
tautness the drop would give it; nor were the abrasions on
the skin, as he realised even before Rogers told him so,
consonant with death from hanging. She had been strung
up possibly as long as half an hour after death, which had
taken place at midnight. In addition, there was a long
scratch at the back of the neck, caused, Field thought, by
the violent breaking of the bead necklace; and there was
also on the abdomen an extensive bruise, without, however, sufficient discoloration for it to have been caused by
a heavy weapon or even a deliberate, furious blow. Rogers
said that most likely the murderer had been standing by
the bed when his foot slipped on the mat and his whole
weight was thrown forward on to his victim, the knee
striking her in the abdomen and causing the bruise. An
examination of the finger-nails of the deceased proved
negative, which further convinced Field that the attack had
been unexpected and she had had little opportunity of
defending herself, as otherwise he would have expected
to find traces of skin or hair under the nails, where the

woman clawed at her enemy in her death-struggle.

Next he examined the cord; this was frayed in two or three places, pointing to the fact that it had been used for fastening a box; there were also unfaded places, and by careful measurement Field was able to show that these represented the portion of cord that had been knotted. In a corner of the room was a wooden box banded with metal, the type of box used by families for storing silver or linen when on a journey, and it was obvious from the measurements the detective made that the cord had been taken from this. The box was empty, except for some old newspapers, and had probably not been used for some time. Whoever had removed the cord had carefully dusted the box on the top and sides, though not underneath; the fact that this stood very close to the mirror yet bore no trace of powder, which it must inevitably have done had it not been polished very recently, added to the weight of his evidence. He was disappointed at this development; he had an implicit faith in the value of dust from the detective's point of view, and though he subsequently had the dust on the rope examined it taught him nothing.

There was nothing in the room that he could hope to link up definitely with any particular individual, no button or pin shed in the struggle, no scrap of material caught on a nail, no dropped pencil, no footprint and, so far as he knew at present, no finger-marks. But that he would learn later. While a subordinate was taking meticulous photographs of the room and every surface that might retain a fingerprint, Field examined the wood of the beam. It struck him as being very soft, and later, after the body had been removed, he experimented with a sack of a precisely similar weight to the corpse, slinging it on a rope and then examining the place where it had hung. He found that the drop made a quite definite ridge in the surface of the wood. He repeated the experiment in a spot as near as possible to the one where the body had hung, with the same result. But that came later.

Now he examined the scattered ash. Some of this was blotting-paper, and some, as he proved, was paper similar to that in the drawer. The murderer might have been burning incriminating correspondence passing between him and the deceased, or he might have spent some time attempting to forge a letter that would pass muster, and these ashes might represent his failures.

All these points convinced him that the murder was one of impulse. Had X planned it he would have provided his own rope, would not, probably, have chosen this means of committing his crime. He fried to put together his impressions of the man. He must be a man of personality and of cool brain, yet capable of violent loss of control. As soon as the news of the death was broadcast, there was a chance that some one would remember seeing a man leave the house some time after the murder; but Field did not count seriously on this; he knew that a dozen men might have been on the spot none of whom would care to acknowledge his presence in that compromising neighbourhood.

Going over the ground he had already traversed, Field, lifting a cushion from the arm-chair, thought he detected a certain stiffness inside the lining, and ripping it open, discovered two articles that were destined to play important parts in the subsequent investigation. One of these was a Post Office savings book in which the sum of fifty pounds had been entered the previous week. This was the only entry in the book, and nothing had been withdrawn. The other article was a wedding ring. That in itself would have postulated no mystery; women who occasionally spend nights away from home are apt to find wedding rings useful; but it was the quality of the thing that struck him. As a rule these rings of convenience are broad, brassy affairs, bought cheap for the occasion. But this was fine, light, and obviously gold. Moreover, it fitted the dead woman's finger to perfection. It was, in fact, all of a piece with the pictures, some of the ornaments, the silver on the dressing-table and the etchings on the wall. Field couldn't make much of any of them as yet.

He could, however, make a good deal out of the savings book. He knew that the average run of women who live ·

16

in Menzies Street cannot entice fifty pounds out of any client, and his immediate thought was blackmail. What he had already gleaned of the dead woman's history from the room and all it contained led him to believe that this fifty pounds was not the result of months of patient saving and hoarding. Besides, why wait till it had reached such a sum? In that neighbourhood money was safer in the Post Office than in any purse or drawer. The letter bore out his contention; Florence Penny had been able to wring fifty pounds from her victim, but an attempt to glean ten times that sum had ended in tragedy. The suggestion of a sum so out of keeping with her general scheme of life made him consider a second effort of blackmail, this time with her for its victim. The letter, of course, he must assume to be a forgery, but no doubt it was consonant with all that had gone before, and the position of which it spoke was a true one.

Before he locked and left the room he came to stand beside the bed and, removing the cloth that covered it, looked for some time into the dead woman's face. He was a man of keen imagination and insight, and he often used psychological deduction to help him to arrive at his conclusion. This face, he reflected, once those hideous disfigurations were sponged away, must have been an extraordinarily interesting one. Experience had moulded it to a cheap cynicism, a recklessness, a hardness that robbed it of charm. But originally she must have been a woman of unusual attraction. Even now there was a beauty in the moulding of the bones of brow and throat and cheek that no disfigurement could altogether destroy; the eyes were dark, fierce, careless; they would have redeemed any face from insignificance; and, before greed and folly and hardness had blotted it out, there must once have been gaiety and generosity there. An expressive face at all events, thin, eager, a little secretive. The chin betrayed her by being weak and common, but probably that had been scarcely noticeable ten years ago. She was not tall, but very finely and slenderly built, with the appearance rather of a deer, springing and arched.

Rogers came and stood beside him for a moment. He was a blunt, unimaginative man, and from his point of view the case presented no difficulties. Field put a sudden question and Rogers laughed.

" Not she. A girl who's lived for any length of time in Menzies Street knows when to come in out of the rain."

Field nodded; he hadn't really supposed there could be any question of a child, but the notion suddenly occurred to him.

" Think you'll be able to prove anything?" Rogers went on, and Field replied, " Presently. So far I only know she was murdered and that there were two people here last night. See those two cigarette stubs? One's a cheap brand, the other probably is bought by the hundred and can't be had by the man who wants a bob packet. Ready? " He turned to the photographer who had been taking patient pictures of every shiny surface, sprinkling the dark ones with a light powder and the light places with dark.

The latter nodded. " Though my impression is that whoever did her in went round rubbing up everything he touched," he added.

5

Mrs. Trevor was waiting in the hall, but before he questioned her Field went out of the house and examined the window sashes, panes and fittings, borrowing a tall ladder to do so. None of these showed the slightest sign of any attempt to enter the house from the outside. He came to a stand on the pavement and examined the place with his eyes in greater detail. Originally these houses had been built for well-to-do people with large families; they were tall, flat, and had been designed by a man devoid of imagination; they had no porches, no stucco ornaments, and the customary phrase, " the wall of a house," applied to them in full measure. The windows were flush with the walls from basement to attic; each house burrowed deep into the bowels of the earth, and had a stone area protected by railings once a cheerful green, but now a dirty indescribable rust-colour; in place of the neat-capped maids and cooks who used to spend their days there, whispering behind the railings when opportunity offered, with milkmen, bakers and constables, lived the drab, secretive landladies, to whom the lives of their lodgers were generally an open book. Many of them had been in the profession themselves, and had only abandoned it through the pressure of competition, advancing years and an inability to face every kind of weather. Field had realised already that Mrs. Trevor was one of these.

It was obvious, he thought, that even an acrobat would find it next-door to impossible to leap from the railings, slender, pointed and too close together for a foot to wedge itself on the horizontal rail, to a window-sill. Even more impossible would it be to escape in a similar fashion, though, once inside the house, there seemed no reason why the assailant should not have left by the front door. The sill of the window was only three inches wide and sloped downwards towards the area; nor did the frame give any handhold, presuming the windows to be shut, as they were at present. There being no porch, it was similarly impossible for an intruder to leap from the top step, that was enclosed by the same green railings as the area; nor were there any recent scratches on the paint. In any case, the road was patrolled by a policeman in the course of his beat, there were people passing up and down during the late evening and early morning, and to attempt such a feat would be to court publicity.

All of which brought Field to another conclusion, namely that the murderer had entered the house by the front door.

CHAPTER II

1

MRS. TREVOR was of little assistance to them. She answered Field's questions with asperity and obviously had no desire to help him. She seemed to resent his very presence in her house.

Field asked about the dead woman's letters. Mrs. Trevor said she had very few.

"Saw her friends most of the time, I suppose," she snapped. "And then she'd telephone. Might ha' been born in a telephone box, I used to say. Yes, there's a 'phone just opposite. I don't have one here. I've better things to do than listen to a pack of silly hussies chattering all day."

"You knew nothing of her affairs?"

"I'm not one for gossiping much with my lodgers, not when they make it clear they don't want my company. Most of them'll stop to have a bit of a chat now and again, but not her. You'd think Menzies Street was a bit of a bog she'd stepped into by accident and she was only staying here long enough to wipe the muck off her shoes. It was only just now and then she'd change, and then she'd talk the hind leg off of a mule. Temperamental, I always thought. Bright as bright one day, and down in the dumps the next. I tell you, when I first thought something might be wrong, I was sure she'd done away with herself. I've heard her say life wasn't worth anything, and it didn't matter whether you were alive or dead, there wasn't a God, and no one cared anyhow."

"Did she often unbend like that?"

"Well, every once in a while, you know. Then she'd bring out some chocolate or a shortbread and share it out and talk big about what she'd known and how she never thought things 'ud come to this. And next day she'd be as close as a rat-trap again."

"Did she ever say anything definite?"

"Well, I do remember her saying she'd once had a flat in town, as different from this as chalk from cheese. And men! My word, she was bitter about them. The things she'd say. . . ." She smiled in a kind of hideous admiration, and Field, who had no desire to hear Florence Penny's views on men, asked, "You can't tell me of any particular visitor she had here?"

"It's not for me to interfere with my lodgers or the friends they like to have, so long as they don't upset the rest of the house," said Mrs. Trevor with an assumption of dignity that gave her somehow a tipsy appearance. "No, as I say, I don't hold with pressing yourself on people that don't want you."

" Quite. Now, can you remember any letters she had recently? "

" Can't say I do. But, of course, she had lots of friends, mind you. Always out, she was."

" And sometimes she brought them back here? But you never saw them. I see." Then he asked about the other lodgers. Mrs. Trevor named them, " though she wasn't any more friendly with them than what she was with me. None of us knew any of her friends. Sharp as a fox she was. It isn't often that any of my lodgers has friends that I don't catch a glimpse of, but if any of the girls knew 'em better than me I shall be surprised. She didn't care to mix with them nor with the fellows they knew."

" Did you see anything of her last night? "

" Heard her come in about ha'-past ten."

" Alone? "

" I can't say as to that. There's so many feet goes in and out and up and down these stairs."

" How do you know it was she coming in? "

" I heard her outside; my rooms are in the basement, and I could see through the window. A taxi had just driven up and out she got along of a man, and then the taxi drove away. I didn't think much about it; I could hear 'em talking, and wondered why they didn't do it inside, much more cosy, but I had a friend of my own in last night, so I didn't pay much attention."

" You didn't see whether one or both came into the door? "

" Well, what d'you s'pose he got out here for? Admire the door? "

" Did you hear any special sounds from her room? "

" No, nothing special. There's always sounds of some sort in a house with a lot of lodgers in it. But, as I say, I'm in the basement; I wouldn't hear much upstairs."

" If a stool were overturned, would you hear that? "

" Well, I wouldn't notice it if I did. You expect a bit

of fun when a man and girl get together. Why, if I was to get up and starting looking about every time a chair went over, I'd never need one for meself."

" Your friend was here when Miss Penny came back? "

" Yes. I happened to mention it. (Field afterwards saw the woman in question, who confirmed this statement without helping him in any other way. She had been on the other side of the room and had seen nothing.) An 'aughty piece, I said to her, though goodness knows she doesn't look it now, strung up like a parcel or an umbereller."

" How long had Miss Penny been here? "

" Matter of a year or so. Always paid regular, too, and what more can you ask? "

" Do you know where she came from? "

Mrs. Trevor shook her head. " Not likely. What business is it of mine, so long as she pays in advance, and don't try and borrow money off of me? "

" You didn't catch sight of any addresses on her boxes, for instance? "

" All new labels, they was, stuck down tight. She'd only that big box and a shiny hat-box and a little case."

" She never spoke of the place she had come from? "

" Not to me."

" Did you ever notice any particular postmark on her letters? "

" Now and again she'd get a letter in a man's writing, but I wouldn't know it again. Came from London, that did."

" Did you ever see any letters of hers? "

" Ones what she wrote? Not me. Posted 'er own, if she wrote any."

That was all he could get out of her, and he went upstairs to see the other girls and women lodging in the house. Only two of them were of any use, and with these he spent two hours patiently listening to their incoherent " And what I thought was . . ." and " I said to myself, Well, my dear, we all know what that means . . ." in the hope that one or other would let drop some hint, probably unawares, that would put him on the trail. He waited like a motionless ant-eater, ready to dart out his tongue at the first signal. Even these two—the Roona and June mentioned earlier—could tell him very little. Fanny Penny— they all called her Fanny—did not appear to have any relations, or at all events none whom she ever mentioned or with whom she kept in touch.

"But you know," remarked Roona, frankly enjoying herself, "what I've always thought was that she married when she was pretty young and had a bad time, and that's why she's got such a down on men."

"Why should you think that?"

"The way she'd talk of husbands. Rotten bad she thought they were. And once when a girl here called Louie Cross got married to something that had got born as a lobster and went wrong in the making, she said she needn't think she was made for life. Having a husband wasn't the same as having everything else, and so Louie would find out."

June, who was smaller, fairer, more gaminesque altogether, nodded, with shining eyes; she wore a scarlet kimono over a ragged petticoat, and was very much painted. It was obvious that she didn't like Fanny, thought her conceited without cause and standoffish, the unforgivable sin.

"What I always say is," she observed earnestly, "if we girls don't stand together, what are we going to do?"

"And Miss Penny wouldn't respond to your friendly overtures?"

"Respond?" exclaimed Roona. "Hear that, June? Ever seen a dog turn over a bone in the gutter and put up his head and march off? That's Miss Fanny Penny for you. Many's the time I'd have liked to have smacked her face, and I only hope some of her friends did it for her."

June was less antagonistic. "Well, yes," she acknowledged. "You couldn't call her matey, but you know, Roona, there was something about her. I dunno what it was. Not her looks, because she hadn't got any. And she hadn't got any manners either. But the boys she took up with—well, there was something different about them. I mean, real gentlemen some of 'em. I've seen her out with them."

"Would you know any of them again?" interposed Field sharply.

"Oh no." June had a Cockney accent that lengthened the shortest words into a second syllable. "Well, I mean to say, you just see a fellow for a minute, can't expect to remember him again." Why, she thought to herself, she wouldn't even know all the men she'd picked up, let alone Fanny's.

"Made something out of 'em, too," added Roona, speculatively. "Mean to say, she might look a bit off, as she did till just lately, but she never came down on her beam-ends, like the rest. Always something in her purse and never anything to give away—I guess that was her motto."

"Well, there was Paula," suggested June, in a dispassionate voice.

"Who was Paula?" questioned the patient Field, when it became obvious that they did not propose to enlighten him.

"Paula was one of the girls, and she got taken by the cops once. 'Tain't safe to cross the road after the shops are shut these days. Anyway, they got her and she was fined three quid. Gave her a week to find the money, like they generally do, and it so happened all the next week it poured like the flood, and she got a shocking cold, something shocking it was, and didn't hardly like to venture out. Well, of course, they'd have put her inside if she couldn't find the money, and it so chanced we were all on our uppers at the time, and blest if at the last minute, when she was sitting snivelling on the stairs, out flounced my lady and shoves the three quid into her hand. 'Take it and stop talking about killing yourself,' she said, in a rough sort of way. 'Though I dare say it wouldn't make any difference to any one if you did.' We was a bit surprised, and I suppose we showed it, for Fan said, 'Oh, well, always makes me feel mad to think of any one being shut up. I know I'd go off me chump.' Might ha' bin in Paula's shoes herself once, I thought."

"Or done a stretch," added the irrepressible Roona. "Anyhow, that's the only time I ever heard of her doing any one a good turn. And, come to that, what's three quid? We've all lost that on one another some time, haven't we? "

June was paying no attention. "You know, I've often wondered who she really was. Illegit., that's what I've always thought. Father a gentleman and mother his daddy's housemaid or something of the kind. P'raps he allows her something. I mean to say, what did she mean by her swagger friends at Cambridge, and never expecting to come to this? "

"To Menzies Street? "

"I s'pose so. What's wrong with Menzies Street? Don't look so very different as far's I can see from Mayfair, and I dessay there aren't any more tarts in it."

"What did she say about her friends? "

"Oh, the men she'd met at Cambridge, and the different kind you met in London. 'So la-ow, my dear.' That was Fanny. Well, why didn't she go back to her blooming Cambridge? That's what I asked her once."

"And what did she say to that? "

"Oh, just looked foolish and said her friends wouldn't be there no more. She'd be lonely. Well, the whole of Cambridge hasn't moved away just to please her."

Roona laughed harshly, then added, in a tone of quickened excitement, " I say, if you're really interested in Fan, I can tell you some one who might help. That's a girl we know; lives in Harlech Mansions, No. 18. She was passing remarks about her the other day, said some people had all the luck, and she seemed to have struck a gold-mine; said she'd seen her here and there with a young chap she'd never seen hereabouts before, all done up to the nines. You might try her. A proper toff she says he was."

Both girls were unaffectedly eager to solve the mystery

of their fellow-tenant, the strange pale girl with her smouldering eyes, her sudden flares of rage, her long periods of reticence, her queer pride, her watchfulness, her moments of unguarded admissions.

"There was something about her," June went on thoughtfully. "I dunno what it was, but somehow men liked her. We mightn't, but you must admit she could take 'em off any of us. You know what I mean, Roona."

Roona nodded reluctantly. "Yes. Something exciting, in a way mysterious, if you like. . . ."

"That's right," June backed her up. "And come to that, she was mysterious. Never knew where you were with her. And if she hated men, it wasn't that they wouldn't take any notice of her. What they call sex-appeal, I spose."

"What I should call personality," reflected Field, as he left Menzies Street with the address of Miss Maggie Bream, 18, Harlech Mansions, in his pocket. "That's why she interested people as those chattering hussies never will."

He went first of all to the local station, and asked to see the constable on midnight duty the previous night; he was not at the moment available, and Field left a message for him to come to New Scotland Yard that evening. Then he telephoned the Yard asking them to put through an inquiry about the dead woman. Had they any particulars? Had she ever served a sentence of imprisonment?

It was now half-past two, and Field turned into a tea-shop and ordered coffee and a piece of cake, while he put together such scraps of information as he had been able to elicit. It was his belief, as it was Mrs. Trevor's, that women only maintain silence about themselves when there is something of importance to be known; when there is nothing, they are at pains to make much of the veriest trifle. And so the very fact that no one appeared to have heard anything of the deceased convinced him that she had a "history" in the criminal sense of the word. Unlike Roona, he found Fanny's assertion that she had known a number of men at Cambridge who would by this time be dispersed a most reasonable and probable condition. There is only one other town in England where it is equally easy for a personable young woman to become acquainted with men in a different social stratum, and that place is Oxford. Field placed the dead woman at about thirty or thirty-two. She might have been serving in some Cambridge shop, behind a counter or a tea-table, possibly even in a bar. Here, with her air of vitality and mystery, she would easily attract the attention of undergraduates, the most impressionable of all creatures. Supposing a liaison to have followed, possibly with a promise of marriage on the man's part, that would explain the ring and her bitterness about men in general. All this was pure conjecture, but it gave him a basis on which to work. Paying for his light meal, he went to Harlech Mansions, where he had to cool his heels a further thirty minutes while he waited for Miss Bream to return. But the fruit of his interview with her was worth ten times the delay.

There was no need for hedging, since already the reporters had begun to surge round No. 39, and the news would be in the evening press.

" Well, now," cried Miss Bream, excitedly, when Field had explained the position, " I thought she was riding for a fall when I saw her all dolled up like that. What I've always said is, never trust a gentleman. A gentleman don't think a girl has any feelings if she wasn't born in his street. Thinks she's lucky to be having a coupla days at the seaside in his lordship's comp'ny. Well, when I see Fan in a dress that was so little of it it seemed a pity to spoil a good piece of material to make the shoulder-straps, I thinks, ' She's riding for a fall.' "

" When did you see them together and where? "

" Well—Friday night it was."

" Last Friday? "

" Yes."

" You're sure? "

" Quite. Because I was there myself. And seeing I'd been wating weeks for my friend to be able to get seats for us . . ."

" Where was this? "

" The Prince John—you know, that new theatre by the Park. ' A Kiss for George,' that's what they're playing. You must have seen the ads. in letters about two foot high all over London. Can't take a bus or go in a blinkin' train without seeing something about it, let alone every feller called George trying to put his slimy arm round your waist and making his silly jokes. Well, my friend and me, we'd been trying to get seats for that—we weren't with the nobs down below; he's not a gent. my friend isn't—and we had to wait three weeks to get these seats. Why, they say you can't even get stalls the same day. Well, I was settled down nice and comfy and was having a look round the house when blest if I didn't see Fan down in the stalls with her fancy fellow."

" Would you know him again? "

" Oh, yes, I should say so."

" What was he like? "

" Oh, proper little Lord Fauntleroy. Dark hair, quite a toff, morning suit, though, though she was wearing something new; black it was, so I could see she was fishing in deep waters; the other kind likes something a bit brighter. And ermine over it. At least, it looked like ermine, but it's wonderful what you can do with household pets like cats and rabbits these days. Spending his money on her, too, he was. Stalls to start with, third row; best place in the house a fellow once told me; all the bloods go for the third row. And then chocolates and coffee—and she didn't let him stir from her side start to finish. Well, I thought, if she plays her cards right, she may be lucky. But I don't know. He had a funny sort of look as if for two pins he'd chuck the whole thing up. Well, I know what Miss Fanny's temper's like when she's upset—something chronic it is, honest—and I thought she better look out for herself. But I suppose she managed all right, because I saw them again just by chance this time, a few nights later. . . ."

" When? "

" Monday that was. Monday's a bad day generally; you know, every one fed up and spent all their money. They were having dinner in a place in Verulam Street called The Man with Three Legs. She looked as nice as nice in one of those new two-piece suits, blue with a fur collar; made her look—well, not pretty, you know, you couldn't say Fanny was pretty—but quite sort of distinguished. And she'd been looking a bit shabby lately, I thought."

Field reflected for a moment on the impossibility of such a woman as Fanny Penny retaining privacy; even the contents of her wardrobe were noted and commented upon as much as if she had been the speaker's sister. Then he realised that there had been in her room no sign of the black evening dress or ermine wrap; high-heeled shoes there were in plenty, flung pell-mell under the bed, smelling strongly of benzine, but the only evening gowns had been a pink georgette and a coffee-coloured lace, both on their last legs. He knew that it is a common device for such women as Fanny and Maggie Bream to go to one of several dress shops in a certain quarter of London and hire a frock for a particular occasion, and he supposed Fanny had done this.

Another thought struck him. " Could you see the box of chocolates or were you too far away? "

" You couldn't have been far enough away to miss them. Those didn't come off any tray in the theatre. Great big black box with mauve ribbons; cost a guinea if it cost a bob."

That was definite proof that he was on the right track. " Will you try and describe the man in detail? " he asked.

She tried; her eagerness was almost revolting; for himself he experienced a keener need to explore the interrelationship of character and motive that had called a situation into being than the bare skeleton of the facts. The description was unsatisfactory, as it was bound to be. To say that a man is tall and dark is to describe several millions, and to say he is interesting but not what the speaker would call handsome exactly, means nothing at all, since all people have individual standards of beauty and the things that interest one mind are negligible to another. But she could give him other facts that were eventually to prove of much assistance.

"He went home in a taxi, and her with him, of course," she said, with an aggrieved air; he saw that she blamed the dead girl not for her manner of life, but for engineering it more successfully than she herself had done. "At least, I saw them talking to the commissionaire after the show. They were a bit late because Fan had lost something—broken her beads or dropped an ear-ring. I don't know which, but when every one else had gone out of the row she began looking on the floor and he looked, too. An attendant came to see what was wrong, but I think they found it—at least, I'm pretty sure Fan wouldn't have left the place without—and then I saw them outside. She was in a bitchy sort of mood, and he was talking to the commissionaire and looking rotten. I couldn't see what Fanny thought she'd make off it. A fellow doesn't go buying you tickets and drinks and taxis if you don't do something to make him feel you're worth it. But p'raps he'd told her this was the end of it or something. Anyway, I heard the commissionaire say, 'Yes, sir. In one moment. I'll get you one,' and then my friend wanted to know what I was so interested in 'em for, so we moved on for the tube. No taxis for us."

Field glanced at his watch as he came away from the Mansions. It was already four o'clock. He had looked in the papers and seen that there was no matinee at the Prince John that afternoon, so it seemed improbable that the commissionaire would be yet on duty. He wanted, however, to see the booking-clerk, to whom he gave his card.

"I want a little information, in confidence," he said. "You're playing to pretty crowded houses just now, I understand."

"Full to the neck," said the clerk comprehensively.

"If a man wanted stalls, would he be able to get them on chance?"

"Not a hope here. I don't know about the agencies."

"Who has the third row of the stalls?"

"Whitemans of Bond Street. Took over a whole block from the first night. They know how to spot winners."

Field noted the address, asked for the commissionaire, learned he would not be on duty until six o'clock that day, and put one more question.

" What about the taxi-drivers? Do they roll up in the evening, or are they on tap all day? "

" Nothing for them to do here in the afternoon, when there's no matinee on. We're too far out of the line of theatres and galleries. They'd be wasting their time. They'll come along later. You'll find plenty of 'em to-night."

" The same gangs each night? "

" More or less."

Field went next to Whitemans, but here he could obtain no help at all. He agreed that it was unreasonable to expect them to produce a description of a man who had walked casually into the office and taken his tickets with him; their records showed that these seats had not been sent by post, nor had they been booked by telephone, when a name would have been supplied. Field had not banked on getting any information here, and in any case it was only a side-issue to trace the identity of Fanny's companion.

When he returned to the Prince John Theatre, Peters, the commissionaire, was at his post, and eagerly looking out for him. He seemed anxious to give information. He was a tall, solidly-built man, elderly, with a slow manner, but remarkably quick in movement. Field postulated his problem.

" I want to find out anything I can about a couple who were here at the Friday night performance last week. A youngish couple of about thirty. He was tall and dark, in a lounge suit; she wore a black evening frock and an ermine wrap. They came out a bit late, because she'd dropped a glove, and she seemed put out about something. He asked you for a taxi, and you said you'd get one in a minute. That's all rather vague, but does anything recur to your mind? "

Peters responded at once. " Now, it's a strange thing, sir, but I do 'appen to remember that couple. There was something about 'em; they stuck in your memory. He was such a pleasant-looking sort of gent, and her—well, I dunno. She meant trouble anyway; you can tell the type. 'Ad a tiff, I suppose. Anyhow, she was as black as thunder, and he lookin' as wretched as a man can be after seeing a show like ours. I thought once she might be 'is missus, but I don't think she was. No, she was some young woman he knew, got hold of him, if you ask me, and p'raps she was trying to jockey him into marrying her. Well, I hope if he'd had any thoughts of that, he's changed his mind by now."

" Did you gather what the trouble was? "

" Well at that minute she was raising blazes because neither him nor me could take a car out of our coat-pockets for her ladyship to step into. ' I told you to get a car,' she said spitefully. I thought it was a bit queer with an ermine wrap and all that they hadn't got a car, but I dessay she's an expensive dresser. And 'e 'adn't got the look of a rich man, some'ow. You can mostly tell."

" What was she like? "

" Something that's gone all shrivelled. Know what I mean? Not a bad-looking piece, though too thin for my taste. I'd as soon 'ave a broomstick, and anyway, it ain't got a tongue. Lor, the way she talked to 'im. And 'im never saying a word back. It was that made me think for a minute she must be 'is wife. But, if you ask me, 'e'd 'ad some before, and didn't want a shindy in public. Gave me half-a-crown for getting him a driver that pretended not to notice he'd come across the road for another fare. Well, no rich man does that. Wouldn't be rich if 'e did."

Hope stirred in Field's breast, though his voice was cool enough as he asked, " Would you know the driver again?"

Peters shook a dubious head. " Can't say I should, sir, not with all the men coming and going here."

" Do you remember where he drove them? "

" Well, I don't, sir, and that's a fact. The truth is, I didn't give the man directions. Didn't have time. The old girl I'd diddled out of a taxi was dancing on the pavement half dotty with temper, and just then I see another coming along, and, of course, I had to collar that, and put her in it, and by that time the first taxi was out of sight."

" Would you recognise the young man again if you saw him? "

But the commissionaire was cautious. " Sorry, sir. I couldn't say Yes to that. This is a police case, ain't it? "

" Yes."

" Then I daren't risk it. I might say Yes to the wrong man; they all look pretty well alike these days, tall and dressed the same, and no hair on their faces nor nothing. Very pleasant spoken gentleman he was, though I know that's nothing to go by. Some of the nicest gents are just the ones that take your watch or put a knife in your ribs. But no," he came back to Field's original query, " if you ask me, could I pick him out again, No. It 'ud be on me mind for the rest of me life, and I'm carrying enough trouble as it is. Got a wife with melancholy—that's what the doctor says—and two boys out o' work. How's that for a peck of trouble? "

Field agreed that it was stiff and went away to look for the driver of the cab. He had to wait some time, because it was still too early for the theatres to start, and there were very few cabs on the rank; most of them were cruising about in the neighbourhood of adjacent hotels and corner houses, with a wary eye for fares. He had not thus far had anything that could be called conspicuous good luck to assist him in his search, and therefore was the more grateful when he discovered a man who recollected the couple.

" Not that it was them so much," the latter explained to Field, " as the old geezer that had thought it was her taxi and then found it wasn't. I should say the young fellow was pretty well finished; mean to say, he looked a decent sort of chap and might as a rule have let a lady that age have the cab and waited for another. But he just stood as mum as a mouse and let the young woman get in, and followed her, sort of dazed-like. I wonder if the old woman got another cab? "

Field reassured him on that point, and continued his examination.

Pryke (that was the driver's name) adopted leisurely methods, and he had the unfailing delight of his kind at finding himself involved in a police case on the right side of authority.

" Yes," he repeated meditatively, " she wasn't arf giving 'im what-for, and I didn't see why she should go on doin' it on the pavement for all the world to 'ear. Besides," he winked at Field, " a man in that state—and 'er tongue never stopped all the time she was in the cab—don't 'ardly notice what 'e pays. And I know these old women. Give you a good show of their false teeth and think it's as good as sixpence."

" Do you remember where you took your fare? "

" I do. It was all of a piece, if you know what I mean." Field confessed that he didn't.

" With her rowing him and him looking so miserable. Oh, I knew there was something pretty wrong. If you ask me, I thought she was breakin' it off. And if she was, some men didn't know their luck, that's all I can say. Just think of 'aving a temper like that about the 'ouse for the rest of your natural! But you want to know where I took 'em. They hadn't given me no address when they got in, and I thought I'd drive a little way till he got less flustered. I could 'ear 'er goin' on at 'im all the time and suddenly she takes up the communication tube and fair hoots down it. Made my blood curdle, I tell you. Made me jump, too, but she's the sort of woman that wouldn't have any consideration for your nerves, driving in traffic and all. ' Put me down at the nearest tube station,' she says, and we were near Oxford Circus then, so I drew up and out she got. She went into the station and he paid my fare and went sort of hesitating after her. I don't know if he was trying to make it up or what, but the next minute he came out looking like a kid that's been belted, and started walking along, not caring-like, though it had begun to rain. I drew up alongside and says, ' 'Ere, sir, don't you want a cab. This ruddy rain . . . You'll get

34

fair soaked walkin'.' And 'e looked up at me as if 'e
'adn't realised there was another 'uman creature in the
world, and says sort of short and queer, ' No—no. I want
air.' Well, in a way I understood 'im. Any man 'ud want
air after that sort of an evening. But 'e was on my mind
a bit, if you understand. I wouldn't ha' bin surprised to
'ear 'e'd gorn and pitched 'imself under a train. I've seen
fellers like that before, and they're pretty well reckless.
Don't seem to care about nothing. I did just creep along
close up for a bit—'e was going no end of a pace 'imself,
rushin' along as if 'e 'ad to get to the end o' the world
by midnight—but then I heard a voice calling ' Taxi ' so
I turned round and didn't see him no more. But it's funny
you should come asking after him. It worried me all
night; why, I even began to wish I'd told that other feller
I'd finished me day's round and was goin' back to me
garridge, and then I might ha' kept an eye on him. You
silly moke, my wife says, worrying like that about a man
that could buy you and half a dozen cabs and not notice it.
You think a bit about your 'ome and less about these toffs
wot ain't no ruddy use to you. Well, I began to think she
was right, but all the same I couldn't get his face out of
my mind. Fair 'aunted me, it did. Well, what did 'e do?
Shove 'imself under a train or make a hole in the river? "

" I don't know. I'm trying to find him."

Pryke became more melancholy than ever. " You take
my word for it, that's wot 'e done. Blimy, I knoo I ought
to 'ave kept my eye on him. Wot you might call a regular
'unch I had about him. But this other chap 'ad the sun
in his eyes proper, and that always means a bit extra. And
whatever the toffs may tell you, things ain't a beanfeast for
us drivers these days. Fares are lower, I know, but you
don't get the tips you did. Folk count their change, if
you'll believe me, sir, and don't mind asking for change
from 'arf-a-crown for a two-bob fare. Straight, they do.
It wasn't like that in the old days, but these folks that
wave their umberellers as if you was there just for them,
they ain't been brought up to taxis. They don't understand. Enough to make you turn Conservative, I say."

Field, who had listened patiently, found room for another question.

" In what direction was he walking when you last saw him? "

" West from Oxford Circus. I say, wonder if 'e did do 'imself in. Dessay."

" We don't know," Field reminded him.

" Well, but then you don't really know nothink, do you? " said Pryke practically. " I know you ain't found 'im yet, but they ain't found for a week or more sometimes. Sometimes never." He nodded lugubriously, pocketed Field's tip without a smile, as though feeling it would be unbecoming in the circumstances, and implying that his distress and apprehension blinded him to its generous nature, and watched the detective disappear.

2

There was still time for further inquiries before he must give up work for the day, so Field turned first of all in the direction of the little restaurant*so oddly named, " The Man with Three Legs." Here he proceeded to interview the commissionaire, the manager, and various waiters in the hope of proving Maggie Bream's story. But he met with no satisfaction. The restaurant was one of a type common to the neighbourhood, frequented by young men and women who generally contrived to look more artistic than they were, with narrow purses and an odd taste in dining companions. It was unlikely that any particular couple would be noticed unless there was a scene; men taking their typists out to dinner often brought them here, where they felt themselves unlikely to encounter acquaintances, or, should they be sufficiently unfortunate as to do so, a mutual policy of silence would be observed. Field supposed that the young man had come here for a similar reason. He had to leave the place, after a good many questions had been asked, no wiser than he came.

He also made inquiries at the confiserie in Bond Street, but, as he had anticipated, it was impossible to identify one among scores of men buying boxes of sweets there.

So Field turned back to the Yard. Here Jenkins, the constable on duty in Menzies Street the previous night, was waiting for him. He was a man in the late thirties, dark, rather slow, but obviously candid and anxious to appear intelligent. He was efficient in a rather unenterprising way, and any criminal with imagination would get the better of him.

He acknowledged that he was patrolling Menzies Street and its district at the time of Fanny's death, but could add nothing that helped the detective.

" How far does the beat extend? " Field wanted to know.

" Tenterden Square one day, Paulton Terrace the other."

" So when you're on duty it would be quite easy for a man who didn't wish to be seen to watch your movements, and as soon as you were out of sight get to work on his own account? "

Jenkins looked puzzled. " It isn't possible for a man to be in two places at once, sir," he pointed out, gravely.

" My point precisely. There are times when Menzies Street is right out of your sight. Even if you looked over your shoulder you wouldn't see it."

" That's the way the beat is, sir."

" Quite. Can you remember—did anything happen to make the time stick in your memory—where you were about midnight? "

" I wouldn't like to be sure, sir."

" I was afraid you wouldn't. Now, did you see any one coming in or out of No. 39 that night? "

Jenkins said he was afraid he couldn't recollect. There always were a number of people going in and out of that house, but Mrs. Trevor was a careful woman and didn't have rowdy tenants. Unless there was a great shindy you didn't interfere in a road like that, and there hadn't been a shindy last night. He was convinced that no man could have scaled the railings, leaped the area and got through the windows. For one thing, it couldn't be done, and for another he'd be bound to be seen by some one.

Field felt it was unreasonable to be disappointed in the lack of evidence. He hadn't really expected any help.

He asked about the inquiry he had put through that morning as to Fanny's past record, but nothing was known of her. Nor did a photograph assist matters at all. The expert on inks told him that the letter purporting to come from the dead woman had not been written with the ink on her table; but it was a quite common blend that might be used by almost any one, the product of a well-known firm of fountain-pen makers. No fountain-pen had been found in Fanny's room, so that this formed one more link in the chain in favour of murder.

But he was disappointed when the man who had taken the photographs assured him that none of them revealed a single fingerprint; Field had hardly realised how much he had counted on getting this sort of evidence. But the fact that the stool was devoid of footprints added weight to what was already a certainty in his own mind. There weren't any footprints on the stool, because Fanny had never stood on it.

He put through another inquiry as to men who had been reported missing or found drowned or otherwise deceased since the previous Monday, but none of these descriptions tallied in the least with those given him by his former witnesses.

That was the end of the work he could do for that day.

CHAPTER III

1

INTENT on following up the slenderest clues, Field returned next morning to the flat, where he inspected the etchings afresh. It was barely possible, he decided, that the man who had made them was known to some of the London dealers, and, taking the smallest, he determined to go the round of the trade, leaving no stone unturned in his effort to trace the artist.

He also examined, in greater detail, the blue coat and dress that played so prominent a part in the identification of the dead woman. There was no tab sewn into the coat, as he had expected, and he realised that very likely Fanny had bought the articles second-hand from some shop where cleaning and possibly dyeing made a garment look practically new. The thought of dyeing made him take out his knife and carefully cut the seam of one shoulder; here the colour was paler in shade, and Field knew that the coat's original colour had been white or fawn. That opened a vast field for speculation, but it narrowed again when he remembered the evening dress and ermine wrap. He knew the district he must search where demi-mondaines can hire clothes for a special occasion, and he determined to go through this neighbourhood with a tooth-comb until he discovered the evening dress and mantle. Very likely the blue dress had come from the same place, though he couldn't dogmatise about that.

He dealt first of all with the etching. This he took to B——, the well-known dealers, who examined it and declared they knew nothing of the artist. He was an amateur, and though his work was delicate and distinctive, it was not sufficiently finished for them to find a market for it.

" C. H.," added the representative, thoughtfully, and bending his head, Field saw that what he had hitherto taken to be part of the design was in reality a cunningly concealed monogram. No other dealer to whom he went could give him information, and at length he abandoned the search and proceeded on the quest after the coat.

He could understand Fanny not retaining the wrap and gown; in such a neighbourhood and for such appointments as would come her way they would be ostentatious, a needless extravagance; and he agreed with Roona that she had passed through a time of financial precariousness before the fifty pounds appeared in the Post Office. He had already inquired as to the manner in which the money had been paid in, and had learned that it was five ten-pound notes. The clerk who had made the entry remembered Fanny and identified a picture of her; she had been struck by her shabby appearance in view of the amount she was depositing. Until, however, he was able to trace some man intimately connected with the dead girl, this information did not help Field forward, as the numbers of the notes were not forthcoming. The quest for the frock took longer than he had expected, and it was late evening before he ran it to earth in a shop with a single window and a flaring " Astarte " over the doorway. The manageress was tall, sheathed in black satin, admirably soignee and so painted and powdered that she bore scarcely any relation to a human being at all. Indeed, she resembled one of her own futurist models, and Field twisted a derisive lip at the old women of both sexes who spoke of such creations as seductive.

" I could be more easily seduced by a cauliflower," he reflected grimly, as she tried to evade his questions. Only when she realised that he represented the police did she reply frankly. She had had experience of official methods before, and had learnt her lesson.

" It isn't a practice of ours to hire out gowns," she explained with some hauteur. " And, of course, we didn't hire out the model, only a copy. But Miss Penny was an old customer, and made another purchase at the same time. . . ."

" A two-piece blue suit," agreed Field, and madame nodded.

" She explained that such a gown and mantle would be beyond her means, but that she urgently required it for one night. These are difficult times for all of us, one does not care to disoblige an old customer—but I should not like it to be said that that is our habit."

Field left that alone. " How long have you known Miss Penny? "

" Oh, quite a time."

" Five years? "

Madame looked startled. " Oh, not so long as that, I think. I couldn't be quite sure. . . ."

" Won't your books tell you? "

" Well, if I were to go through them . . ."

" Do," said Field heartily. " I'll wait."

Madame, looking annoyed and taking no pains to

conceal the fact, turned over the leaves of a dilapidated-looking ledger, muttered, counted on her fingers for some mysterious reason Field could not understand, and presently said, " About a year, I think."

" What addresses have you for her? "

" Menzies Street. No. 39."

" She's been there, then, all the time you've known her?"

" Oh, yes. She says she's got ever such a nice flat there."

" I see. Has she ever hired anything before? "

Madame said No very emphatically, but he was not convinced. However, it really mattered very little. He left the shop without having greatly advanced his knowledge. He was simply piling up evidence that it had been Fanny whom his various witnesses had seen in the theatre and the restaurant. He had hoped to get another address for her through " Astarte," whence he could trace her previous history.

Walking towards Tottenham Court Road Station he turned over in his mind the extra scrap of evidence he had accumulated. At all events he knew he was on the right track, and he was a cautious man, leaving nothing to hazard. One proof was good, two were better. But he still had to learn something concrete about the man who had been her escort on both occasions; so far he had not got the shadow of a clue to his identity.

Pondering the matter that night, he thought his best plan would be to go to Cambridge and see if any one there remembered the girl. If he could not trace her movements from this end, he might from that. Next morning he caught a train that deposited him at Cambridge shortly before noon, and began again to try and trace the man by means of the etching. The first two picture dealers could tell him nothing, but a third said he recollected having a similar piece of work offered to him some years earlier, though he could not fix any approximate date. A young man from one of the Colleges had brought it—he did not remember his name or that of the College—and had seemed disappointed when I told him it would be valueless from a dealer's point of view. Though he admitted to

Field that he had been struck by a certain individuality and poise in the craftsmanship.

It seemed to Field this was going to prove one of those heart-breaking cases where a horse is perpetually led to the water, and at the last instant shies and refuses to drink. Having traced his man to Cambridge, he found a gate up across the road. That chance recollection was the sole fruit of a busy afternoon.

The next day was Saturday, and Field devoted it to trying to trace Fanny at the local shops and tea-houses. He went patiently from one to another, the photograph of the dead girl in his hand, making meticulous inquiries, tactful, courteous, tireless, but never with any result. He realised that Fanny might have been the daughter of a lodging-house-keeper, might even have been a maid-servant, and it was manifestly impossible to examine the householders of every building in Cambridge for information of this kind. He obtained a postal guide to the town and looked for the name of Penny, but without result. Pennys there were, true, but none of these was any relation to Fanny. The whole day passed in a round of inquiry, and at its close he was no farther advanced. The afternoon was gloomy, with fine stinging rain, and he wondered for a dreary moment, sipping badly-made coffee, why the uninitiated supposed a detective's life to be one of excitement and colour. This tedious round of examination and cross-examination, of fitting a case together detail by tiny detail, the perpetual necessity for eliminating the superfluous, the long suspense, the disappointment and the weariness of motive, all these at times were irksome to a degree. Yet, inwardly raging at the barriers that appeared to enclose him on all sides, he was bound, that moment of impatience past, to acknowledge that for a man of his temperament, the work held an undeniable charm. When you had discounted all the lost time, all the obstacles put in your way by foolish, conceited or hysterical people, there was a fascination in piecing together just such a problem as this. His mathematical brain rejoiced in it; he liked the pleasure that, he resolved, he would presently experience, of seeing the relevant pieces go into their right place in the pattern. As a child he had loved jig-saw puzzles for the same reason, early discarding the simple ones of fifty pieces and demanding always larger and more elaborate patterns; and he was unlike most children in that he never clamoured for an interesting puzzle; the result was nothing but achievement. He turned from the pictures of Vikings or horse-racing, where the pattern assisted the struggler, back to seascapes where every piece looked alike, blue seas, blue empty skies and a white shadow that might be a distant frigate on the ocean or the wing of a gull on the foreshore. By the time he had disposed of the disgraceful coffee he had forgotten that spasm of irritation and dissatisfaction; this was, he assured himself, the type of case he most preferred; this would not easily resolve itself into an affair of suicide or in some hysterical idiot coming to confess; it was a problem, and for the moment its intricacy mastered even his feeling about the players in it.

2

The next day being Sunday, and all shops being closed, he determined to take a walk and clear his mind. There was always a possibility that the exercise would quicken his senses; it was his normal cure for a stunted imagination, and though he did not forget that the girl who reported Fanny's speech might be mistaken and Fanny mightn't have said Cambridge at all, while the ash-tray could have been picked up at a charity bazaar, he felt this morning more optimistic about the whole affair. He could even experience sympathy for the young man upon whose trail he was; it was poor luck for him to have this sort of thing dug up several years afterwards, when as likely as not he had forgotten the girl's name.

After last night's rain the day was clear and cloudless; the sky, pale and luminous, was like the polished interior of a cup of porphyry, a smooth cool blue with a glint of silver where the faint clouds met the horizon. It was too early for the swallows, but the blackbirds were all out.

They perched on the gutters of houses and sang with such vehemence that he could see the palpitation of the small soft breasts where the wind ruffled their feathers. Against the clear sky he saw miniature towers and steeples, and occasional tall pointed roofs; the city had not the antiquity of Oxford, but it had an elegant and academic charm of its own. A missel-thrush sang loudly from the branch of a budding lime tree, and Field paused a moment to listen. In the gardens the sparrows were industriously pecking off the buds of the primroses; while against the farther distance rose a faint film of smoke that produced an effect, not of dismal gloom, but rather of a veil against the cool space it shadowed. Field walked for several miles through the low open country, meeting hardly any one at this early hour. He had deliberately forsaken the roads where young men on motor cycles went whizzing by; and after so much tramping of pavements the turf was pleasant beneath his feet. He had walked for about three hours when he came to a stile at the end of a field and, crossing that, found himself on the verge of a small village called King's Sutton. It had a delicate air in the fresh noonday light; although the church clock struck twelve as he lingered, few people were on the move; the old bell was tolling so gently that no one heeded it but one or two of the older inhabitants, wearing black dresses and hats and carrying prayer-books. A kind of charm lingered over the place; it was like a village in a fairy-tale. In the market-place, as Field rounded a curve in the road, was an old pump and opposite the pump a forge. When Field saw those he forgot his dallying and the pleasure of the morning, as sharply as if some one had caught him by the elbow and jerked him back to attention. For the scene was familiar; he had never to his knowledge been in this village before, but he knew the effect of that slightly crooked steeple, the overhanging roof of the forge, and the precise position of the pump. And he knew where he had seen all these before. In one of those etchings signed C. H. that hung in Fanny Penny's room.

Now he was convinced that his original suspicion was

right. C. H. had been an undergraduate, and he proposed immediately to put off his return to town until to-morrow and search the records of the University for a man with those initials. It was a tremendous undertaking—heaven only knew how many C. H.s there had been in 1923, but the fact that he had dabbled at etching might help. A tutor might recall him, or one of the College servants. The hope was a slight one, but he told himself he must bank upon it. Turning left from the pump, he commenced to walk down the single narrow street. The houses, cottages for the most part, came first, a long straggling row with gardens in front, and beyond them the shops, built on a square. Field read their names, above their blank shuttered fronts. Butcher, General Stores, Tobacconist and Newsagent, Bootmaker, Dairy Produce, and then a second start shot through his blood. The corner shop was a picture-dealer and frame-maker. Without hesitation he approached and knocked twice on a green shabbily-painted door in the wall. Painted over the shop was the name " Welling—Arthur Welling." He it was who opened the door; he was only partly-dressed, a shirt stuffed into his trousers, his hair unbrushed. He looked surly and was neurasthenic as a result of his war experiences. Field mentioned the Yard, watching his man narrowly, as though he might determine the source of his persistent anxiety, but Welling only nodded. Whatever his fear, it had nothing to do with the law.

He explained his position. " I'm anxious to trace a man who made etchings of this village some years ago. His initials are C. H. That's rather vague, I know, but perhaps you can help me."

Welling looked suspicious. " I don't know," he said, preparing to shut the door. " C. H. Not much sale for etchings here."

" Have you any at all? "

" Just a few. Not that we sell them, of course, but I took them over with the rest of the stock. They haven't got any name to them, though, that I remember."

" I should like to see them, if I may."

Welling grumbled that it was Sunday.

" I know. But we have to get on with our job whatever the day of the week. What are the etchings like? "

" Oh, just what you'd expect. The church and the pump and cows in a field. As if the folk living here want to buy pictures of what they can see for nothing any day of the week."

" Does no one buy them? "

" We've sold a few of the smaller ones," Welling acknowledged, " but not to the people here. But folk passing through. We're a sort of exhibit, we are." His smile was bitter. " It's the church that does it. Regular museum that is. And there's a house here dates from 1600; supposed to have one of the oldest stained-glass windows in the country. That's older than the house by a long chalk; taken out by its owner and buried for God knows how many years, and then dug up again. One bit of coloured glass looks the same as another to me, but there's folks with so much money, in a country where there's thousands starving or living on the edge of it, to pay to see a bit of glass like that."

" You say you have some etchings, but you don't know the man who did them. Did you buy them outright, then? If not, what about the artist's commission? "

" I didn't buy them, and I don't pay any commission either. I haven't been here above four or five years. I took these over with the stock. The small ones we did manage to sell, but the big ones no one wants. I put 'em in the back of the window. Fine Original Etching—that sort of thing."

" Who had the shop before you did? " asked Field.

" My father-in-law. But after he had his trouble he turned it over to me and Sally. Said it was worth a lot. Well, it gives me a job, and now we sell pottery and medals and such like it pays its rent. But if it wasn't for my wife having the tea-shop at the corner, we wouldn't make two ends meet. But folks like their stomachs better than their minds, so she does well enough. You'd hardly believe how many people she can get in the season. Too

near Cambridge, you might have thought. But no. Motor
out here, some of 'em walk, I dare say. Dunno, I'm sure.
But you'll see plenty of cars outside in the yard in the
summer, and folks don't seem to mind what they pay. We
store up then for the winter when like as not we don't see
a soul for days on end. They're the people that buy our
china models and your water-colours and your hand-tinted
photographs. We sell post-cards of the church, too. Oh,
it's a living of a kind."

He had at last unlocked the shop door and produced
from a rather dusty pile an etching larger than any Field
had seen in Fanny's room. Instantly Field recognised
the original sensitiveness that had distinguished the other
pictures. And, examining this carefully, he found the
monogram in one corner.

" I suppose your father-in-law would know who C. H.
is? "

" He might. But he's a bit touched-like now. There's
his missus, of course. Like an eagle, she is. I never see
her but I feel she's wanting to put that great beak of hers
into my neck. I'm not surprised at anything that happened with them, not at the old man going silly or the girl
leaving them the way she did."

" What did happen about the girl? Did you hear? "

Welling's mouth took on a peculiar curve. " You
couldn't believe everything that old fishwife told you,
though you can't doubt she did go off with the young
fellow. I never saw him myself; I wasn't married to Sally
then, and I was only here off and on. But the old man
knew, if she didn't, they'd never hold a girl like that for
ever. No, I don't remember his name. Some young chap
from one of the Colleges, I heard. But no one—not even
my wife—will speak of her now."

" What's your father-in-law's address? "

" Jesmond Cottages, Brickhaven. Up north that is.
Went up there after he got rid of the shop. And if you
ask me," he added fiercely, reverting to his earlier grievance, " the place was barely paying its way before Fanny
went off. It isn't likely that 'ud make so much difference."

" What's Mr. Penny's Christian name? "

Welling didn't appear to notice Field's familiarity with the surname, that had not hitherto been mentioned. He only said, " Joseph." And then, as if the words were torn from him from some secret sore place in his life, he went on, " Proper little bitch that girl was. I'd have taken a strap to her if she'd been mine. Why you liked her you couldn't have said, once you'd stopped doing it. But for the time—oh, I dunno—but she seemed to go to your head. Never knew what she'd be up to, neither. Smiling as sixpence one night, and like as not hit you over the head with an umbrella the next. And lie! I never heard such a liar. But the funny thing was you didn't seem to mind. I can't explain it. It was something about her; had a sort of life most women haven't got. Sally hasn't, though she is her sister. Made you feel warm and as if something was going to happen, just to be with her. And if you felt down on your luck she'd put new heart into you, not by anything she said—God knows she never wasted any feeling on other people's troubles—but just by being so full of fun. Seemed silly to grieve. And nothing to look at neither. Just a thin sallow sort of girl, straight black hair, not a bit the sort you'd expect a man to want. But for a time she could have had any man she set her heart on. But she couldn't hold 'em. Tired 'em out, I suppose."

While he was speaking, the man's face had changed; he seemed suddenly younger and more supple, as if the bare memory of that ardent girl kindled in him a reciprocal flame; then, under Field's eyes, the spark died down and the bitterness returned. Field looked away. He realised now what underlay that dissatisfaction; and his interest in the dead girl who had exercised this peculiar fascination over diverse types of men, swelled like a sail ballooning in the wind. Now he was on her track, though he never failed, when exaltation threatened to overthrow his balance, to put the drag on his mind, and remind himself that he had only tracked down a liaison with a young man seven years ago, who might easily prove to have nothing to do with the murder.

Field reached Newcastle next day, and discovered Jesmond Cottages to be small solid buildings, workmanlike and hideous, erected in pairs. In front of No. 2 grew a neat bed of white marguerites and veronica. There were short white lace curtains at the windows and a red geranium in a green pot on a bamboo table. It sounded, from Welling's remarks, as though Mrs. Penny wore the breeches here, a position that would instantly explain Fanny's rebellion without excusing it; for no mother could have held that reckless, alluring type for long. Her face was in his mind as he opened the gate and walked the few steps to the front door. Sponge out the marks of exhaustion, dissipation and bitterness, and he knew what Welling meant. For a brief season she would be irresistible. That quality of life cannot be gainsaid, though there are few men who can respond to it for more than a short time. It demands a vitality of the spirit that not many possess.

The door of the little house was opened by a forbidding-looking woman with her sleeves rolled above her elbows, and her arms steaming. Field realised that he had brought her from the wash-tub, and that she had mistaken him for the rent-collector. Then she thought he was trying to sell her something, and would have shut the door in his face had he not instantly mentioned Fanny's name. That made her stop, aghast, incredulous.

" I've only one daughter," she said harshly, " and she lives near Cambridge. A married woman, she is."

" Speaking from a legal standpoint you have—or had until Wednesday last—a second daughter, Florence. She's dead now. . . ."

It seemed impossible to be anything but abrupt with such a woman; nor had he any fear of wounding her in a tender place. If ever he had seen hate in a mother's eyes, he saw it in Mrs. Penny's now. She only said, " She has been dead to us for seven years."

Field asked for her husband. She laughed, a short, savage sound that chilled him. " You can see him, but he won't help you. He's never been in his right mind since Fanny went."

Field followed her into a small square room furnished as a parlour, with a long narrow couch in horsehair, a velvet armchair with a straight back and a cottage piano. In the velvet chair a man was sitting, so old that it seemed impossible for him to be Fanny's father. When he glanced up, however, with the surprised expression of a child, half-excited, half-alarmed, Field saw that the eyes had no age in them; they were surprisingly bright and were not, as he anticipated, vacant; it was simply that they did not hold that quality of memory that one expects in a man of experience. Like a child's, they were expectant and attentive. Moreover, they were indubitably the eyes of a happy man.

His wife said harshly, " Joseph, here's a gentleman come about your daughter, Florence."

The old eyes brightened into pleasure. " Oh, Fanny? My daughter, Fanny? A lovely girl, sir." He paid no attention to his wife's enraged, " Don't be a fool, Joseph. It was Sally that had the looks," but smiling and shaking his head, continued, " You don't understand, Kate. You've never understood. It isn't just the colour of a girl's cheeks or the size of her eyes. It's what lies behind the eyes. Oh, I miss her, I can tell you. I don't seem so cold when Fanny's here."

" You haven't set eyes on her for seven years."

" Oh, she comes in her own way. You don't know. Like a wind or a bit of honeysuckle. She was never like other girls. Always a mystery—like a wood, I used to think, full of surprises, full of pretty things, too. . . ."

Field realised the futility of such a conversation and went out again, with the grim-visaged Mrs. Penny, whom you couldn't think of as a bereaved mother. He asked her if she could arrange to attend the inquest, and she said No. She hadn't considered Fanny alive to her since she went off in that immoral way with her young man.

" What was his name? " Field asked.

With native shrewdness she realised the unpleasant publicity that might surround her own name if she gave him his information, and answered that she preferred to forget. Field threatened her with a subpœna, realising that she would know too little of the law to recognise the weakness of his position. She understood when she was defeated, and said stonily, " Charles Hobart."

" The undergraduate who did those etchings of King's Sutton? "

" Yes. And I wish he'd been dead, or my daughter had, before he brought them to us."

" Your husband sold them for him on commission?"

" That was the idea, but he didn't sell above two or three, and the commission worked out so small. There's probably some left in the shop still."

" Did any of you know him before he brought the pictures? "

" Never seen him. He just came in, when the big men in Cambridge wouldn't look at him, to see if he could coax a few shillings out of unlearned folk like us. Not that my husband was taken in. No, he said, from the beginning, there's no sale for that kind of thing. I'm sorry, sir, but every one's buying post-cards these days. They're like drawings themselves, and only twopence and go into your pocket."

" What made him change his mind? "

" Oh, Fanny, of course. Jumped up from behind the counter and says how pretty they are and how she'd love one, and won't her father please buy one for her. He was a noticeable-looking sort of young man," conceded Mrs. Penny grudgingly, " and she didn't see why she shouldn't have her bit of fun with him as well as the rest of them."

" You don't know his College? "

Mrs. Penny didn't. To her all Colleges were alike, and in her mind she linked them up with such establishments at Pitmans and Clarks, whose names she had seen in staring brass letters across the fronts of tall buildings. She naïvely supposed that their names weren't written across the Cambridge Colleges because no one could afford to have it done.

" When did this happen—this affair . . ." he hesitated.

" When did she go away with him? Haven't I told you? Seven years ago. They hadn't met above a dozen times,

I shouldn't think. I always did think it was a mistake to have a girl like that in the shop. Men couldn't keep their eyes off her. And my husband couldn't be there all the time; he'd be making frames down below. And it was no use me trying to do it all, and if ever I couldn't find a thing and asked the girl, she'd turn round and answer me as saucy as saucy."

" Did you hear nothing of her since she went away?"

" There came a letter from Brighton where she was living in sin with this man—oh, as bold as brass she was, and no talk of being married—and after that I told her she needn't write. And she never did. What happened to her?"

Field explained as gently as he could. She had sat down while she was talking, and he saw the involuntary movement of her hands in her lap. Those treacherous tell-tale members, of whose power for betrayal man is seldom aware, hung loosely together, the fingers just touching, the expression of an inward weariness and disappointment she would have indignantly denied with her lips.

Her mouth, indeed, was indomitable. " She made her own bed and she had to lie on it in the end," said Kate Penny. " It was the same with her always from a child. My cousin had her for a time, but she wouldn't keep her. Made trouble there, and said she didn't want to have a girl in her house having a baby with no marriage lines to show for it."

Before he left Field managed to obtain a photograph of the younger Fanny, that he might need in tracing her subsequent career from the day she left her mother's house. It was one of those odd, old-fashioned pictures taken probably in some seaside booth when she was about sixteen. She had long hair flowing down her back, and a cheap white blouse fastened with a flamboyant brooch. But something in the pictured face, its gaiety and mobility, the happy curve of the large mouth, the sparkle of the eyes that even a cheap apparatus had not been able to dim, discovered even to this casual onlooker an excellent reason why a young man, susceptible to beauty and charm, should have been swept off his feet. She was like a magnet then; and he wondered what the intervening years had held for her that at two-and-thirty she should be so bitterly disillusioned and dismayed.

CHAPTER IV

1

FIELD had no difficulty in getting information about Charles Hobart. He had been at Cambridge from 1920-1923. He had not distinguished himself scholastically in any particular direction, but hadn't been a dunce. He played racquets and was remembered as a wet-bob of some distinction. The authorities could not tell Field his present whereabouts, but believed he was abroad.

"And if he is, that's the end of that trail," thought Field.

His next move was to inquire of Hobart's old school, in case he had kept up with them. Here also he met with the news that Hobart was believed to be abroad, but that his uncle and one-time guardian, Sir Gerald Hobart, still paid his nephew's subscription to the school magazine, which was sent to the baronet's rooms in Jermyn Street. Sir Gerald, Field learned, was a shrewd, keen-witted man, a bachelor, popular, and having an inquisitive finger in a good many pies. Field went to Jermyn Street and was interviewed by a man who was almost too good to be true, so exactly like a film butler did he appear. He told Field that his employer was at Cannes, and added, " I don't know if you're another of them, but it was only a motor accident, and I understand Sir Gerald is practically recovered."

" I didn't know there'd been an accident of any kind," retorted Field, pleasantly.

The man took on a shade more vitality. " Oh, yes, there was a rumour that he had been badly injured, in fact, that he had been killed. We had the press round, but I was able to assure him that I had heard nothing, and the next day I had a communication from Sir Gerald himself ordering me to send him certain things, as he had been involved in a motor accident and injured his knee. I wrote him that there was some talk of his being dead."

" What did he say? "

" Like their damned impudence. Sir Gerald hasn't any use for the papers, bar the midday edition. But, of course, a gentleman like Sir Gerald is always news. The press rang up his paper to say they'd better hold up the information until it was confirmed. In quite a stew, if I may say so."

" I'm not the press," Field assured him. " I merely want the address of Sir Gerald's nephew, Mr. Charles Hobart. I suppose you don't know . . ."

" No, sir."

Parsons showed an odd reluctance to giving the detective Sir Gerald's address, urging that all letters would be forwarded without delay. But when Field said in a brief voice that discouraged argument, " I'm going over to see him," he unwillingly disgorged it.

Field caught the night boat and found himself on French soil on one of those white, chilly mornings that frequently usher in April. The more he thought of the approaching interview, the less he liked it. He knew Sir Gerald's type, the sort of man who considered a policeman part of the landscape, and the detective only a policeman in his Sunday suit. The notion that one of these creatures should actually ask for his nephew's address for the purpose of raking up an old scandal would put him in an apoplectic rage.

" Though, if the fellow's really abroad, there's no reason why he should make heavy weather," argued Field with himself, waiting in the lobby of Sir Gerald's hotel, and handing his card to a page.

The interview went off very much as he had imagined it. Sir Gerald was a tall, handsome, choleric man who made no attempt to hide his feelings. In his eyes Field was a " low feller," glad to turn over any stinking heap of garbage for the sake of a little gratuitous publicity. Field let him exhaust his first indignation; he couldn't so much as suggest the sympathy that any human being must feel for the unfortunate Charles, who was going to be hauled over the coals, most probably in public, for a misdemeanour he had very likely forgotten by now.

" Fatuous! " exploded the elder Hobart. " And most disgustin' impertinence. Mean to tell me that because some wretched woman's been killed in London you're goin' to try and drag my nephew into it? Why, the boy's been abroad for six years."

" Is he abroad still? "

" No," said Hobart sullenly. " He's not. He's been back for six months."

" Do you know where he is? "

" He's stayin' at my rooms in town."

Field silently cursed Parsons, and wondered if the man was acting under instructions. If so, it made things look bad for young Hobart.

" Ah, a pity I didn't know that," he murmured. " I needn't have troubled you."

" What do you want the boy for at all? Are you tryin' to make out he did it? "

" He'll have to account for his movements that night," Field acknowledged.

" Oh, I dessay he can do that. That all? "

" I'm afraid not. You see, we know nothing whatsoever about this Miss Penny beyond the fact that she's been murdered, that she left her home several years ago with your nephew, while the years between his going abroad— six, I think you said—and the years she came to live in Menzies Street are an absolute blank to us. We must get hold of any one who may be able to put us on her track. Your nephew may remember her making some definite plan when they separated. . . ."

" Never heard anything so damn' silly in my life," said Hobart contemptuously. " D'you suppose a man like my nephew is goin' to keep up with a girl like that because they had a week at Brighton together when he was a young fool at Cambridge? "

"We can't afford to leave any avenue untried," said Field.

"And you're goin' to drag all this into the papers, I suppose? What about his feelin's? Haven't you any natural decency? Why, I believe the fellow's on the verge of getting married."

Field's brain registered, "Motive. Glaring," while Hobart continued to say quite unconstitutional things about there being too many of these damned women anyway, and what the devil was coming to a country that made all this fuss when one of them got herself triced up by some blackguard she'd brought home, he didn't know. But beneath all that bluster Field discerned a genuine alarm for his nephew's security.

Lying wakeful at about two o'clock the following morning as the boat made her peaceful way towards English shores, Field was struck with the idea that probably Hobart had by this time telegraphed to his nephew warning him what was in the air. Long before the detective could hope to reach Jermyn Street Charles would have determined what story to tell—provided, of course, that he couldn't show at once he had nothing to do with the affair—and then all the knots would be tied a bit tighter. At this stage Field was surprised to discover he was seriously thinking of Charles Hobart as a guilty man.

2

Parsons opened the door of the Jermyn Street rooms, as wooden-faced and imperturbable as ever. Field was annoyed at the man's obstinate silence on the occasion of their first meeting. If he hadn't lied about Charles Hobart's whereabouts, saying he knew nothing of them, Field would have had the first innings. As it was, heaven only knew how the Hobarts, uncle and nephew, mightn't by this time have tangled up the position.

Field came to the point at once. "Is Mr. Charles Hobart in?"

No expression flickered over the man's face. "Mr. Hobart is out."

"I'll wait for him."

"Mr. Hobart is away."

"Then give me his address."

"I can't do that, sir, but I fancy he'll be back in a day or two."

"Don't be a fool," said Field, impatiently. "Don't you realise you're dealing with Scotland Yard. You've made enough trouble for yourself as it is by saying you didn't know where Mr. Hobart was. You don't want to put yourself in a criminal position."

"I take my instructions from Mr. Hobart," said Parsons, unaffected by this display of officialism.

"I'm afraid the law is superior to a private employer," Field warned him.

"And Mr. Hobart said particular not to give his address to the police. That," Parsons condescended to explain, "gives the reason for my haction."

This, thought Field, his ill-temper evaporating on the instant, is damned interesting. And aloud he asked mildly, "Why do you suppose that was?"

"I couldn't say, sir." Parsons looked bored, and began to shut the door; Field wedged his foot in the opening.

"None of that. And you'd better let me in. That's better." The door closed behind the pair and Field found himself in a fair-sized hall, well furnished without any suggestion of a fastidious taste. Hunting prints were ranged along the walls, with an occasional college group. A deep sofa and a low chest furnished the place. "Now answer me a few questions," Field observed. "Where, first of all, is Mr. Hobart now?"

"Staying with his sister."

"Where's that?"

"Fernden."

"That's no more use than a stomach-ache," said Field curtly. "Fernden might be the name of a villa on the Great North Road. Where are you forwarding his letters?"

"He left instructions that, as he would only be away a few days, he did not wish to have any correspondence forwarded."

" Does that mean you don't know the address? You're behaving very stupidly you know."

Parsons reluctantly disclosed it. " Mrs. Warren, Fernden, Harringford, Wilts."

" When did he go? "

" On Thursday morning."

" Was it a long-standing engagement, or did he make up his mind on the spur of the moment? "

" I heard nothing of it until Wednesday night, or Thursday morning, early, to be correct."

" Did he say why? "

" No, sir, but I rather think it was force of circumstances."

" What circumstances? "

" That," said Parsons, " he did not confide to me."

" But you drew your own conclusions? " Field's voice had lost its rasp, was smooth and silky.

" In a manner of speaking."

" Then suppose you tell me what happened, or what you think happened. What about the night before Mr. Hobart went to Fernden? "

" If I remember right, that was the evening he was out till late, or as I said, early, and I had a friend or two of my own in for a game of bridge."

" Contract? " murmured Field.

But no irony could destroy Parson's icy composure. " Certainly. There is very little pleasure in playing a game that has become demoddy among the upper classes."

" And what time did your friends leave you? "

" At about a quarter before eleven. Mr. Hobart had said he did not expect to be late, and that generally means about eleven o'clock. Rooms," added Parsons, musingly, " have their good points. There are not many stairs, not by comparison with a house, I should add. But they do not have two exits. That, I may say, I find a great disadvantage."

" I'm sure you must," agreed Field, cordially. " What time did Mr. Hobart return? "

" I should say, as near as I can recall, about one o'clock.

I should not care to make that statement absolutely on oath, you understand, but I should say about that hour."

" You don't think it might have been nearer midnight? "

" No. I myself retired at midnight; I had been interested in the photographs of some gentlemen in a periodical, gentlemen known to Sir Gerald. And I was in my first sleep—and I seldom sleep immediately upon retiring—when Mr. Hobart returned and awakened me."

" I see. So it must have been about one o'clock. Did he call you? "

" I heard him, and came to see if there was anything I could do. It was understood that if he was not back by, say, half-past eleven, I could retire to bed."

" And was there anything? "

" He asked me for a drink."

" And you gave it to him? "

" I did."

Parson's tone as he made this reply was so peculiar that Field asked, " Was there anything so very strange about that? "

" Mr. Hobart had never come home in such a state," said Parsons, coldly.

" What sort of a state? "

" A state of very great excitement. Not, understand, what you might term pleasurable excitement. Far from it. Distraught is what I should have called it myself. Something on his mind without a doubt, I told myself. I waited to give him the opportunity to unburden himself, like Sir Gerald does sometimes, but this he was disinclined to do. But I did venture so far as to say to him, ' I do hope, sir, nothing is wrong.' "

" And he said? "

" He made a most peculiar answer. That is to say, I don't consider it was addressed to me, just him speaking to himself, if you understand me. ' Wrong, Parsons?' he says. ' There's a mort of things wrong in the world, and the worst of 'em all are those things that can only be put right by another wrong.' "

" What did you make of that? "

"I didn't make nothing of it. It wasn't intended that I should. I hope I shouldn't try to see sense in anything a gentleman like Mr. Hobart says at one o'clock in the morning, coming back all of a lather like that. And anyway, as I told you before, that wasn't said to me really, and I wouldn't demean myself to go listening to a gentleman's conversation with himself at that hour. All I said was, 'I expect you'll be getting along to the feather now, sir,' or something of the sort, and he said, 'Yes, how late is it? Oh. How quickly time passes, doesn't it? I hope you've had a pleasant evening, Parsons,' he said. I said, 'Thank you, sir, I took the liberty to entertain two or three of my friends at a hand of bridge. Most entertaining.' And he said, still as if he was speaking to himself, 'It must have been.' And then quite suddenly he swung round and told me he'd be leaving town to-morrow, that is, on Thursday last. 'Don't send on any letters,' he said, 'and don't give me away to any one, not even the police.'"

"What made him mention the police? It sounds a little unusual."

"I think, sir, it is just a phrase."

"One he was in the habit of using?"

"I really couldn't say."

"But you hadn't heard him use it before?"

"No. He wasn't in the habit, as you might say, of making light conversation for my benefit."

"He wasn't, perhaps, a very conversational employer?"

"I shouldn't expect it," said Parsons more coldly than ever.

"Did the phrase startle you at all?"

"I can't say it did. I merely memorised it for future use among my own intimates."

"You had no reason to suppose, either from anything he let drop then, or from any word or action of his afterwards, that he meant the words in their literal sense?"

"Certainly not."

"Quite. Now one more point. Should you say, if you were being questioned on oath, that Mr. Hobart was at all the worse for drink at the time?"

"No," said Parsons in a more thoughtful voice, "I'd be more inclined to say he was in some sort of dilemma. Had a disagreement with a lady, perhaps. I've noticed that gentlemen that have had the misfortune to disagree with a young lady, especially after dinner, are inclined to come back rather in that mood."

"I see. And—was there any special young lady in whom he was interested?"

"I couldn't say definitely, but he's been getting a lot of letters from a lady this past two or three weeks."

"Have any come since he went away?"

"No. There's been nothing of importance."

"You never saw the lady?"

"I wouldn't like to say Yes to that neither, but one day when I happened to be standing at the window, I thought I saw a lady watching the house in a very peculiar way. I went back to my kitchen and when I returned she was still there."

"She never came here?"

"Not to my knowledge."

"I suppose you're out sometimes in the evening?"

"Well, one evening in a week, of course. . . ."

"So she might have come then. But this is pure supposition. You couldn't pick her out again?"

"I didn't see her face properly," protested Parsons. "I only meant it was all of a piece with his being so jumpy and all that."

"How long has he been staying here?"

"A little over a month, since Sir Gerald went away. I think he was at a club before then."

"And have you heard anything from Mr. Hobart since he went to Fernden?"

"Nothing."

Field decided there was nothing more to be learned for the moment, and risked Parson's wrath by offering him a handsome tip. Parsons, pocketing it with a secret grin, thought less of its value than the fact that he had a rich yarn to spin his friends to-night. He wondered what that young chap had been up to.

3

Field meanwhile went to inquire the trains to Harringford; there was one soon after lunch that would reach its destination at six o'clock. It would not be possible to return the same night, and as soon as he arrived Field made arrangements at the local inn to get a bed. Fernden was some distance from the village, about two miles, and, a market being held in an adjacent town that day, no cars of any kind were available. Field walked across the bare fields and up a steep hill until the house itself came in view. He had time to realise that it was comfortable, solid and well-kept. A fair amount of money there. Then he remembered the dead girl's letter and her mention of five hundred pounds. He knew that even people who present an appearance of prosperity to the world are often desperately hard put to it to raise five hundred shillings in an emergency, let alone twenty times that amount.

CHAPTER V

1

THE big library at Fernden contained a quantity of books rarely taken from their bookshelves, a good many comfortable chairs, and even more articles testifying to the sporting tastes of the hosts and his guests. When Field started out on his two-mile walk from the station there were gathered in this room several men and two women; these included Warren himself, a thin, polished, cynical man who wondered what pleasure his vivacious wife got from entertaining this heterogenous house-party—a regular beehive, he called it—and decided characteristically that it all redounded to her social credit, or she wouldn't have done it; Charles Hobart, a tall, dark young man, not what you'd call good-looking exactly, as Miss Bream had said, but with a keen, expressive face that was now well in shadow; Scott Egerton and his wife, Rosemary; and two or three high-spirited young men who were wrangling over a wireless set in one corner.

The general topic of conversation was vaudeville. It was less a discussion than a casual utterance of sentiment on the part of any one who had sufficient energy to speak.

"I like the vulgar items," said a young man called Beresford, in a placid drawling voice. "I find 'em inspiriting." And he chanted softly:

There was me and the missus and half-a-dozen kids,
And nothing in the bottle but the bung.

Rosemary laughed. "Barrie was quite right; it's natural to be vulgar. And if we can't be vulgar by proxy I don't see how we're ever to accomplish it at all."

"Seeing the sort of men we've married," capped Mrs. Warren neatly. "They are frightfully respectable." Her glance wandered from her husband, cool, bored, debonair, in a long chair by the window, to Scott, equally cool and imperturbable, but not in the least bored, sitting near his wife. "You've nothing to say to that, I suppose," she added challengingly.

Beresford spoke before Egerton could reply. "Oh, don't ask him. He couldn't possibly agree with any sentiment so uncivilised as the one we've just persuaded Peter to put a sock in. As a true constitutionalist, by adoption and grace, how can he support anything that tends to lower the public respect for the great institution of marriage? Backbone of the Empire and all that. One of these days, Scotty, they'll put you in the British Museum as a flawless specimen of the upper middle classes in the year of grace 1930."

Mrs. Warren said speculatively, "I wonder why it is people always regard marriage as something comic—unmarried people, I mean. Married ones don't."

Her husband opened one eye to murmur, "Of course not."

"What do you mean?" They turned towards him with the spontaneous unanimity of feeding sheep.

"What I say. Married people don't rag about it because either marriage is so rotten you can't forget about it, or else you're so much accustomed to it you don't remember you are married. Like that fellow in Kipling's yarn who had gone about naked for so long he didn't even realise he was naked. And burst into tears when he saw himself in a mirror."

No one liked to take up so obvious a gauntlet, and Beresford said hastily, "What does Charles think?"

Charles said, "Oh, quite right," in so serious a voice that most people laughed; but Egerton, whose eyes happened to light on the grave face, shadowed by the curtain, received a curious impression of tragedy. Before the laughter had died down the door opened, and a girl came in. She was clearly very young, so young that no one felt it necessary to show her any ceremony; she pulled out a straight-backed chair from the table, and sat down without saying anything. She was thin and dark, small and delicate of build, and all her life found its expression in her black eyes. Despite her obvious immaturity, her movements were singularly assured and controlled. She had no difficulty in disposing of her limbs, nor did she feel any embarrassment or awkwardness because no one spoke to her. Indeed, she herself spoke very little at any time. She had to a superlative degree the lovely quality of silence; it was like something tangible surrounding her, enclosing her from the companionship of the other people in the room. Her mouth, soft and deep in colour as a peony, smiled faintly, as though she were amused by some remote jest; but if you could see her eyes, which at this moment were veiled, they were bright and dancing, full of the vitality so noticeably absent from word and gesture. Her name was Lucy Egerton, and Scott was her half-brother, and a dozen years her senior. The pair had seen little of one another since she was a child, her education having taken place under the ægis of her French mother's sister, now living in Italy. Egerton sometimes wondered what sealed thoughts passed through that luminous eager mind of which he was now and again permitted a glimpse. She looked to him even younger than her nineteen years, and in spite of the happiness of his married life he felt a momentary spasm of jealousy for the man who could unclose that bright treasure-chest of a personality that would to the end conceal its final secret for the sheer mischief of tantalising a lover.

She had not been among them many minutes before Charles Hobart turned and, with a murmur they could none of them distinguish, passed out on to the wide verandah. Gradually the other members of the party followed him or left the room, until at length Scott and his sister found themselves alone. As soon as the door closed behind the last, Lucy stood up, delicate as a flower, and crossed to her brother's side.

"Break your lifelong rule for me," she said, and he discerned anxiety under the disquieting brightness of her gaze. "Be indiscreet for just five minutes."

"What do you want me to say?"

She did not hesitate. "Scott," she asked in perplexed tones, "why doesn't Charles ask me to marry him? Doesn't he know I would?"

Egerton, a little taken aback by this candour, said, "Why should he be sure?"

"He must know. I recognised him immediately we met. You can't be mistaken over things like that."

"Oh, yes, you can," said Egerton harshly, speaking from a depth of experience.

"Well, I'm not," said Lucy simply. "And I'm convinced he feels just the same as I do. But something's gone wrong. I think it must be something that happened before we met. You don't know anything that would prevent him. . . ."

Egerton shook his head. "I don't. But then he's been abroad so long. None of us really knows much about him."

"You don't suppose he's so foolish as to mind because I have so much money and he so little?"

"It is the sort of thing men care about," Egerton acknowledged.

"Oh, some men. But not Charles, not to let it come between us. I wish I could be sure. If it were only that, I could put it right at a word. But it might be something else. I should only embarrass him horribly then."

"Don't say anything," Egerton urged. "Charles isn't

a speechless fool. He's able to propose like any other man."

"That's just what he doesn't seem able to do. Oh, Scott, I'm so unhappy."

She felt the pressure of his hand on her arm; there wasn't anything he could say.

"There may be some other woman who's proving tiresome," Lucy went on, in a small, restless voice. "If he only knew, he needn't be so afraid. I should understand."

"I'm not sure you ought to understand so well as that," Egerton murmured, a little dismayed at the position.

She seemed astonished. "But it's so easy to make a mistake and so hard very often to get back to the right road again. Besides, think how much worse for him than for me. When I was small I used to think I ought to be punished for the little things I didn't much mind having done, and forgiven for the sort that make you ashamed."

Egerton, newly aware of her youth and a kind of rare innocence that was oddly touching, said in urgent tones, "You are sure, Lucy? There's nothing worse than making a mistake in these matters. And so many of us do it."

He saw from her expression that, no matter how much she might regret her decision in coming years, there would be no moving her now. That smile, the spontaneous amazement when he spoke of the possibility of a mistaken love, the young assurance, warned him that he was wasting time, and he only said in a less calm voice than usual, "Well, take care, anyway."

Lucy laughed clearly, so clearly that the group on the verandah stopped talking for a moment to listen to her. "Care?" she repeated. "I don't mind taking a risk. It's a risk getting born and I never wanted things to be safe. I'm not like you, Scott. You count your steps, don't you? I'm prepared to jump in the dark and then see where I am when I've got there. That's my mother's fault and she didn't live to regret it."

Scott thought of the dark, impulsive young mother who had not lived long enough to regret anything much; but before he could find anything to say they were interrupted by a servant who said, " I beg your pardon, sir, but there's a gentleman wants to see Mr. Hobart."

2

Sir Gerald had not written or telegraphed to his nephew to prepare him for Field's arrival. He was a man who disbelieved in interfering where he could not help; he knew nothing of the matter and considered Charles should be capable at thirty of managing his own indiscretions; and even if he had written he could only have said something of this kind—" There's a fellow from the Yard trying to track you down about a woman you ran off with seven years ago who went to the bad and has just been murdered by some johnny who probably knew what he was about, and they want you to lend a hand "—a position so absurd that he couldn't be concerned with it.

Charles was taken completely by surprise. There had been newspapers at Fernden, of course, during the past few days, and he had read them; but he had only looked at the political situation, on which he could argue endlessly with Scott, who was a Liberal, as opposed to Charles's Conservative tendencies; the world of sport and the theatre news; while the women read fashions and books, and they all were amused by Gluyas Williams. But the police news didn't interest any one especially, and even if they had read of the death of a woman in Menzies Street it wouldn't have occurred to them to discuss the case. It wasn't the kind of thing that intrigued the household at Fernden.

Charles's first terror was that Fanny had tracked him down after all. He had given rigid instructions to Parsons not to yield his address to anyone, but the man must have been over-ridden, for no one else knew his whereabouts. When he saw Field's calm, stocky figure a quick dread overwhelmed him. Better by far to have stood the racket in town than to have brought it on himself in the same house as Lucy stayed in. Field saw him restrained, white, haggard, and obviously on his guard, and realised that here was a man with something to conceal. His first words, though he didn't know it, confirmed Charles's fears.

"I've come in connection with Miss Florence Penny of 39 Menzies Street," Field began, "in the hopes that you may be able to give me some information."

Charles's face, that had hardened with the mention of the dead woman's name, changed now and a perplexed look replaced his defiance.

"Information?"

"Yes. She was found dead in her room on the morning of 27th March."

If Field had expected a surprise he now got it. The perplexity disappeared in its turn, but what took its place was not alarm or crafty concealment but an open relief. Field thought, Is the fellow glad we've come into the open at last? knowing that criminals can frequently endure anything but suspense. Or did she have some hold over him, and he's innocent but thankful she's out of the way?

"We've traced her history up to the time you and she left Cambridge for Brighton," Field continued. "And there our trail breaks off. Perhaps you can tell us what happened after your separation."

"I went abroad and stayed there for six years," said Charles unemotionally.

"And she?"

"I don't know. We didn't correspond."

"And when you parted you've no idea where she went or what she did, or even if she was provided for?"

"Oh, she was provided for to a certain extent. I settled on her some property I inherited from my mother, that brought in about a hundred a year. I thought I'd done all that was required of me in the circumstances."

"What were the circumstances?"

Charles hesitated, then said slowly, "Not the usual ones between man and wife. She wouldn't rely wholly on what I gave her; even if she didn't go back to work herself she had other supporters."

His face was impenetrable now, as if it had been glazed; his voice had an impersonal quality, too, as if the Fanny and Charles of whom he spoke had died six years ago, and this resurrected man had nothing in common with the disfigured dead woman.

" You say other supporters. Did you know of any specifically? "

" Not by name. There was a man—surely it isn't necessary to go into these very unsavoury details? But it made it impossible for me to continue my married life. . . ."

A shock of dismay and self-disgust swept over Field. So that was the explanation! He had wondered why a man who appeared neither a fool nor a weakling should allow himself to be intimidated in this fashion by a woman with no claim upon him. But marriage! He wondered why it hadn't occurred to him.

" Where were you married? " he questioned.

" At Brighton. Then we came to London and separated within the year."

" What year was this? "

" 1923. We parted in 1924 and I went abroad. My uncle got me a billet. Have you seen him? "

" Only to get your address. You know, you're not compelled to answer anything. I ought to warn you of that."

" But anything I say will be used against me; and if I don't answer now you'll find some way of pulling me out of my shell. Thanks for the warning. Is there anything else? "

" I'm afraid there's a good deal more. You never tried for a divorce? "

" I couldn't at the time. For one thing, I hadn't the money; for another I was taking a job that would only be open to a bachelor and if I'd filed a petition I'd have lost my job. I didn't think at that time I should ever want to have a second shot. I was glad of the chance to get away."

He answered Field's questions with a greater readiness now, and there was an element of recklessness in his bearing. This stranger had come bursting into the sore intimacies of his life, and he could hope to preserve no privacy and sanctify no grief.

" Who knew of your marriage? "

" The various landladies from whom we rented rooms; people with whom I worked. That's all, I suppose. I wasn't seeing my own friends at that time."

" You didn't tell your uncle? "

" He wouldn't have recommended me for a bachelor's job if I had."

" Or any of your friends? "

" No."

" You had some special reason for that? "

" It was Fanny's suggestion really. She'd broken with her people, refused to write, said she never wanted to see them again. Then we talked of my people, and agreed to wait a little till I was in a better position. I had a very small job at that time, and I think Fanny thought they wouldn't look at her any too kindly when they saw what our marriage meant—I mean, the sort of neighbourhood where we had to live—and Fanny doing most of her own work. Oh, they wouldn't have understood. Besides, I think she was a bit afraid of meeting my uncle. Afraid he'd notice first of all our social differences; she felt that if we could meet my folk in more prosperous circumstances, they'd change their tune. I must say," he added candidly, " I think she was right."

" And this—position—between you had arisen before you got the offer of the work abroad? "

" Oh, yes. Otherwise I'd have turned it down. But we'd agreed to separate in any case; neither of us wanted a divorce; I only wanted to get away, and she was one of those women to whom marriage is nothing more than a name and an inconvenience."

" So far as you know, she went to live with this man you've mentioned, as soon as you parted? "

" I dare say. In fact, yes. He was some one she'd known before we were married. I never asked questions about him. It wasn't my affair by that time."

" How did you manage about the transfer of the legacy? Through a lawyer? "

" No. I gave my bank the necessary instructions; they were to pay her the interest to whatever address she gave them; and she had the right to draw the capital, if she wished."

" Did she ever do so? "

" Yes. About two years ago."

" How do you know that? "

" She told me . . ." He stopped, as if suddenly aware of the trap into which he had fallen. Then, with a gesture of helpless despair he went on, " Oh, you were bound to find out, I suppose. Yes, I've seen her several times since I came back."

" Did you seek her out? "

" As a matter of fact, I got hold of a private investigator to try and discover if she were alive or dead. He couldn't trace her, but by sheer luck we came face to face one evening, and she told me at once that she needed money. I didn't think I owed her anything, as I told you, but she pointed out that we hadn't any legal deed of separation and that I was liable for her upkeep. Above all things I wanted to avoid an open scandal; I gave her whatever I had on me at the time, five or ten pounds, and hoped that would finish it. But she trailed me back to my club, and alarmed me by coming next day to inquire if I was in and could be seen. A few days later my uncle offered me the run of his rooms in Jermyn Street, and I moved in as unobtrusively as possible, but she found me. I'd see her loitering on the opposite pavement; she'd follow me like a dog, and I'd find her opposite me in buses. It was driving me half-crazy. I felt I could put up with anything rather than have the facts given to all my world. And the second and third time we met she said she wanted to be acknowledged as my wife. Of course, I refused. I said considering what had happened it was a ludicrous suggestion; and then she reminded me what people say about a man who deserts a wife after a year and leaves her inadequately provided for. Well, as you know, in these press stunts it isn't what a man's done that matters but what you can suggest he may have done. She'd have got a fistful of public sympathy and I shouldn't have dared look a man I know in the face." His gaze travelled beyond Field's head to the wide country, lying serene in twilight on the farther side of the window-pane, as if he envied its calm liberty, and was more than ever aware of walls enclosing himself.

" Did you see anything of her after your refusal? "

" Oh, yes. I saw her several times. She used to write to me, too, every day. I burnt her letters, but she scared me a bit. I couldn't see any way out."

Field marvelled at what was either colossal courage or equally colossal blindness. Couldn't the fellow see his own peril?

" So you never came to any agreement? "

" Never. And now you say she's dead. . . ." He looked for a moment like Christian when the bundle fell from his shoulders and he gave three leaps for joy. Then he sobered again. " How was it? " He seemed only now to be recognising the implications of his wife's death and the presence of a Scotland Yard officer in the room. " Dead! " he muttered. And then again " Dead! "

" It appeared to be a case of suicide," said Field, watching every gesture and inflection.

Charles surprised him again. " That's all my eye and Betty Martin. Why on earth should she commit suicide? She held all the cards in her hand. She'd nothing to gain and everything to lose by taking her own life. I'm afraid that cock won't fight." He was silent for a moment, then asked what it had been.

" Strangulation."

" Oh. And you think I had a hand in it? Of course. What a fool I was not to realise that all along. I must seem infernally slow. It all fits together like a jigsaw puzzle, too."

" Does it? " asked Field. " Would you care to make a statement as to your movements on the night in question? "

" I don't know which night it was."

" The 26th. Last Wednesday week."

Charles said slowly. " The night I had dinner with her."

" Will you tell me in fair detail what happened that night? " And added the usual warning.

" I had arranged to take her to dinner and we were to

continue our endless discussion as to the future. Neither of us intended to yield a step, and I couldn't see why we should waste another evening. But I had to conciliate her to some extent, for fear she should discover my sister's address and go rushing round the family with the news. I hadn't spoken much of my sister. She'd been abroad at the time of our marriage. That night we went to a place in Soho called Martino's. A queer place, a bit continental, but very safe if you don't want to meet people you know. And we had to talk. We met about eight o'clock—Fanny was rather late—so we didn't leave till about nine. After dinner she asked me to come back with her, but I swore I wouldn't enter the house, and after some discussion we chartered a taxi and drove down to Richmond. You remember that night, one of those miraculous evenings you get occasionally just before Easter. We drove through the park. It was about half-past ten when we got back, no nearer a solution than when we'd met. My original idea was to drop her at Menzies Street and take the taxi on to my uncle's rooms. But she made such a commotion on the pavement that I had to pay the taxi off."

" And you went on talking where you were? "

" Yes. She asked for a cigarette and I lighted it, and then she asked me once more to come in. She said it wasn't safe to discuss your private affairs in a neighbourhood like that, and that every wall was full of ears. And if any one realised the truth I might be blackmailed by a dozen people in the morning."

" She'd given up asking you for money, then? "

" Oh, no. She asked for five hundred pounds, said she must have it or something worse than death would happen. Of course, it was out of the question. The hundred pounds I'd given her already had drained my resources to the uttermost."

" I haven't heard of the hundred pounds before. What was that? "

" That was the previous week. She said she was desperate and must have the money, and I found it for her. But I couldn't repeat the experiment. When I told her

that she turned perfectly white and said, ' But I've got to
have it. By hook or crook.' "

" Did she tell you why? "

" No. It wasn't any use my asking questions, I couldn't
do anything."

" So that you parted on hostile terms? "

" Yes, I suppose so."

" And when you left her—what time would this be? "

" Oh, I didn't stay more than, say, five minutes. It
would be a little after half-past ten."

" And you went straight back? "

" No. I didn't. I felt I couldn't rest. I was in a
cul-de-sac, and I couldn't get out. More, I couldn't see
any way out. I walked—just anywhere. I turned down
one road and up another, just for the sake of moving.
I couldn't even give you an accurate itinerary of the route
I took. I remember walking by the river for some time
and hearing Big Ben strike, though whether it was eleven
or twelve I couldn't say. It was nearly one, I suppose, when
I got back. Parsons might remember. He's my uncle's
man who's looking after me while my uncle's abroad."

" And all that time you didn't meet any one you knew? "

" I didn't recognise 'em if I did. Besides, you must
remember I've been abroad for years. And my marriage
cut me off from most of my contemporaries before that.
I scarcely know any one in town."

" You didn't stop to ask your way, have a drink, go for a
ride on a bus even, hail a taxi? "

" No to all those."

" Was there any one in Menzies Street when you parted
from your wife? "

" No. I remember looking because she spoke of our
being overheard, and I said there was no one within
earshot. And I don't think I ran against many people
later, or else I instinctively took the quiet streets. I
remember thinking how empty London was. As a matter
of fact, I suppose the theatres wouldn't have emptied by
then, and even when they did most people get taxis or cars
or go by tube. Or they go on somewhere. There wouldn't

be a great number wandering about the streets. Though, of course," he added, " there may have been some one at a window in Menzies Street who saw me go."

" There may," Field agreed politely, but his sceptical heart thought most probably not. Menzies Street was too commercially-minded to waste time over street quarrels, even if it hadn't been sated with them long ago, though he didn't want to humiliate Charles further by telling him that.

" And it was when you got back, still having come to no conclusion, that you decided to come down here? "

" Yes. I thought it would give me breathing-space for a day or two, and perhaps I might be able to find some way out. It seems absurd that an act of madness when you're twenty-two can ruin your whole life."

Field forebore to comment. But he asked, " Had you taken any one into your confidence? "

" No."

" Not even a lawyer? "

" No."

" Did it not surprise you to hear nothing from your wife after you arrived here, though she'd been writing practically every day when you were in town? "

" I'd told Parsons not to forward any letters or give my address to any one. I thought she might get it by a trick and that would be more than I could stand."

" Quite. Now, you've seen a good deal of your wife lately. Did she ever speak much of her personal affairs, beyond the demands she made of you? "

" I can't say she did. That seemed to take up all our time. Besides, if she had other troubles, no doubt when she was reinstated as my wife, with sufficient financial backing, any other troubles she had would disappear automatically."

" Not necessarily. Did she ever hint to you that she had some one preying on her? "

" What? Blackmail? "

" It's quite conceivable. You acknowledge that your wife's life during your absence was practically a closed book to you. Almost anything, given her temperament and opportunities, may have happened then. Did she say why she withdrew the capital you made over to her? "

" She said she started a business, but it failed."

" That may be true. One can't tell. But what you've said about her declaring that if she didn't have money she would be face to face with something worse than death impresses me. We've already had evidence of a kind that she was terrified of the bare thought of imprisonment. Suppose she's got some one bleeding her, with that threat in the background. I don't say so, it's merely an idea. I suppose you can't throw any light on such a position."

" I can't," said Charles dully. " In fact, I think it's pure hypothesis and not a bit likely to be true. If she'd been in that position I'm convinced she'd have told me. It would have been such a weapon in her hand. Because she wouldn't hesitate to describe herself as my wife in the courts, and she must have known that I'd have moved heaven and earth to prevent that. No, I think she thought she'd got me in a cleft stick and I couldn't refuse anything. She was always very—grasping, shall I say? Money, as money, had a peculiar significance for her that it hasn't got for the majority of people. She liked to handle it and count it; she hated to spend it, if it was hers, though she was extravagant enough at other times." He coloured as if he had been unwittingly betrayed into a treachery he had not contemplated. But Field clung to his thesis, though he admitted candidly to himself that it was probably quite a side-issue. But it was hard to see how any woman of even moderate intelligence could make demands for money when she hoped to be accepted as the wife of a man like Charles Hobart. She must see that nothing would more completely ruin her prospects. Charles meanwhile was ridden by a fear that Lucy's name would be swept into this sordid, chaotic stream. And he remembered Egerton, who wouldn't exactly appreciate the position for his sister. Too late Charles saw that his only hope had been to confide in that resourceful and reliable young man; it couldn't have made the position worse, and conceivably Egerton would have found the way out he himself had sought in vain.

Looking up he was slightly surprised to see that Field was still there; he had forgotten about him. Now he said, almost indifferently, " I can't quite figure it out, you know. What would be the idea of killing the goose that laid the golden eggs, since I gather you're inclined to think there's a third party behind all this? "

Field felt irritated at such obtuseness. He didn't at that stage suspect any one but Charles. But he replied, " Impulsive murder is the commonest kind there is."

" Still, a grievance has to go pretty deep to involve crime on that scale."

" The experience of most of us doesn't back that up. The most absurd disagreements sometimes lead to the worst crimes, just as people fight like wild-cats over quite inessential things, like the date they saw a certain show or the colour of some one's frock at the Archbishop's garden party. Impulsive murders are frequently committed for reasons that in cold blood would be ludicrous if they were less tragic."

3

But Field was wrong about Charles's obtuseness. As a matter of fact, that young man realised his peril so thoroughly that he couldn't do more than stare hopelessly at it. He couldn't even flare up at the anomaly of his situation, couldn't even feel bitter against the dead woman. He had the sense of reaching the end of something, finding himself in a cul-de-sac. So far he hadn't a particle of fear. He was almost dead to feeling.

As soon as Field had gone, he went to look for Egerton, whom he found knocking the balls about in the billiard-room. He supposed every one else had gone up to dress; anyway there was no sign of them anywhere. The ease with which he had discussed the situation with Field had now deserted him and he was tongue-tied and aware only of a desire to couch his information in the most crude and savage terms. Egerton, skilfully potting the red, asked in a casual voice, " Your visitor gone or is he staying to dinner?"

" Oh, he's gone for the moment, but he'll be back to-morrow or possibly the day after."

" I see," murmured Egerton, and Charles found that maddening composure more than his tattered nerves could bear.

" You don't see, damn you," he shouted. " You wouldn't be so infernally superior if you did."

Then he calmed down as rapidly as he had exploded. " Sorry," he muttered. " Matter of fact, I've had a bit of a shock."

" Take your time," said Egerton, chalking a cue so that he need not look at Charles's convulsed face.

There was a minute's silence. Then Charles said, " He's going to arrest me for murdering my wife last week."

He didn't know how he expected Egerton to take that, but all Egerton said was, " And did you? "

That cooled Charles down as nothing else could have done. " Did I? What do you take me for? "

" Oh, you can't tell," Egerton assured him. " I once met a fellow who'd killed his wife. She teased him till he couldn't stand it, and he gave her a shove and she went over and cut her head open on the corner of the fireplace. Died two hours later. They brought it in manslaughter and he had seven years. But he was an awfully nice chap. That kind of thing makes you re-mould your judgments, so far as you admit that any human being has the right to judge another."

" Suppose I said Yes to your question? " asked Charles curiously.

" Then we shouldn't have to waste time looking for a mythical murderer."

" As a matter of fact, I didn't. What I've told the police is absolutely true."

" And what did you tell the police? "

Charles repeated his story, and Egerton nodded thoughtfully at the end.

" Well? " demanded Charles. " Aren't I right about the next visit?"

" Most probably," Egerton agreed. " It's a nasty piece of work, and you can't show you're innocent. None of us can do that for you." He leaned over the table and began a masterly break that attracted even Charles's jaded interest.

" Oh, played, sir. You're a clever chap, Scott. What's the next move? "

" For us? Oh, we must find the real criminal, of course."

" You talk as if that were as simple as buying something off a barrow."

" It shouldn't be impossible. The murder was committed by a human agency, and it wasn't you. It may be a long job, but we ought to be able to do it."

Charles said savagely, " What fun it's all going to be!" And then, " Will they drag Lucy into this? "

" Unquestionably, I should say. I don't mean the police, I mean the press. I dare say there's betting going on in the servants' hall already as to the date of the wedding. That's inevitable in a house like this. And, of course, the village will revel in that. It'll supply a spice of excitement and romance (God help us) to a rather sordid murder. Of course, all the evidence is circumstantial. . . ."

" It couldn't very well be anything else," observed Charles gloomily. " There aren't, as a rule, witnesses to a murder. You're bound to act on deduction and opportunity."

" Precisely. And, as you say, that's what they'll do. And, of course, there's motive."

" And to spare," supplemented Charles. " If they bring in Lucy's name, they've only to show that nothing short of Fanny's death would make marriage between us possible. . . ." he broke off there, colouring with embarrassment and humiliation. There wasn't the slightest reason

79

to suppose that Egerton would welcome him as a brother-in-law with his record.

"Tell me a little more about her," said Egerton. "Your wife, that is. When were you married?"

"While we were at Brighton."

"Was that part of the original plan?"

"No. I was ready for anything. But, to do her justice, she never wanted marriage. She wasn't made for it; her moods changed too quickly. It was one man to-day and another to-morrow night. I wasn't sufficient of a chameleon to hold her three months."

Egerton asked in an expressionless voice, "And why did you marry her, if she felt like that?"

"Because of the way I felt," returned Charles violently. "We lived there together about a fortnight. It was my first experience of that kind of thing, and I felt pretty ghastly about it. It seemed to me that if we were sincere enough to be living together at all, we ought to be married and take the chance. Even then I had a job talking her over."

"But she married you eventually because it was the only alternative to losing you altogether?"

"I suppose so. I was crazy about her at the time—you know how it is, was glad I hadn't much money so I could earn it all for her. I'd no notion at that time what a damned lot we should need."

Egerton passed over all that. "How long did it last?"

"Ten months. Then I came back one evening and found her with another chap—in my room—my—oh, Scotty, you don't know what that's like, even when you don't care so much any more. And she was so devilish calm. She honestly didn't mind, thought I was a fool to make a scene about it. I think it had been going on for months. It was some one she'd known before me, she said. I didn't care. I suppose I ought to have tried for a divorce, though that wouldn't help me much now. I know your views and Lucy's on that point. But anyway, I couldn't stand the thought of one's private life, that sort of private life, being given to the public . . . oh, I've read other men's stories, and pitied them, poor devils. And then I got this chance to go abroad and I leapt at it."

" We shall have to hope for the best," said Egerton platitudinously. " Some one may have seen a fellow leaving the house that night. It's no use hoping for anything from the police, because the Yard will have put them through the mill. But perhaps a taxi-driver was cruising about . . ."

" Or some respectable member of society who'd rather see a dozen men hanged than let his wife know where he was in the small hours," suggested Charles composedly. But though he had his voice under control, his face, that was ravaged with anxiety and white as paper, betrayed him.

4

That evening Charles took his brother-in-law into his confidence, and offered to clear out.

" Why? " murmured Warren imperturbably. " We shall be quite a show place in a day or two. Wouldn't be at all the thing for you not to be on the premises. Besides, where could you go? Back to y'r rooms, where Parsons will be agog to watch the latest developments? Or to the local inn, where they'll talk of nothing else? One thing," he added reflectively, " you'd get a deuce of a lot of free beer."

CHAPTER VI

1

FIELD went back to his inn and spent a cheerful evening with the landlord, who seemed glad of a bit of company. He let the conversation wander round to the party up at Fernden, and the landlord said in a hearty voice, " And there's another little matter coming out soon or I'm a Dutchman. Riggin' another garland before midsummer, I shouldn't wonder," for the landlord had once been a seafaring man.

" Really? " smiled Field. " Who's that? "

" That young Hobart. Going to marry young Mr. Egerton's sister, if you ask me. A nice couple they'll be, too. The long and the short of it." He laughed appreciatively. " Funny quiet little thing she is. But got a way with her. Came upon her in the woods round Fernden a week or two back, whistling and calling till I thought she was a blackbird herself. And they was coming down all round her like the birds in the picture the new rector put up in the church. Not," he added hastily, " that I care for all the things rector does." From his tone Field judged that he was a man who never looked inside the church unless he found himself marooned there on a wet day. Probably he only knew of the St. Francis picture by hearsay.

" Poor devil! " thought Field, letting the landlord ramble on while he himself pondered Charles's predicament. " Pretty wretched outlook for him, I should say. Of course, it's only circumstantial evidence, but that's hanged plenty of men before now. I've got Parsons's evidence; that fits in neatly enough with what Hobart himself told me, so he seems to be telling the truth up to a point. He might have said he was back at eleven. A fiver would have squared Parsons all right, and he could have 'phoned while I was getting back. Besides, he hadn't time to make up a yarn, and I don't think he's such a fool that he doesn't see how things are."

He went back to London next morning, going first of all to Martino's Restaurant, where he asked for the manager. To him he explained his position.

" Would it be possible to identify two people who dined here on Wednesday, the 26th? " he asked.

The manager looked a little doubtful. " If there was not anything notable about them, sir, there is no reason why we should remember them. Did they come here often? "

" I gather they didn't." He produced photographs of both, but the manager only shook his head. He did not recall them at all, nor did the commissionaire, nor any waiter.

" The lady wore a blue dress, and a blue coat to match, with a grey fur collar," Field urged, certain that Fanny wouldn't have let that stay unworn in her wardrobe where her other clothes were so shabby, " and very likely they were quarrelling."

The commissionaire brightened into interest. " Si, si, signor," he cried eagerly, forgetting that he was only supposed to speak English. " Now I think I do recall them. The young man is tall and dark—yes? And she is tall, too. And with a temper! Ah!" He spread his arms and puffed in an exhausted manner to show the effect Fanny's temper, even in retrospect, had on him.

" What happened? " Field inquired keenly.

" She was angry with him, signor, for bringing her to so small a place. If," again a magnificent gesture of indifference, " if the signorina require a large room, why does she not go to the Corner House? That would be large enough for her eh? "

The manager, who had been listening intently, here seized the opportunity to air his opinions of the English bourgeoisie.

" That is them all the time," he assured Field emphatically. " They require utmost value for everything. I see it here every day. Never a drop of wine left in a bottle, not often so much as a crust of bread. And their theatres," he continued enthusiastically, apparently regarding Field as an attentive audience, " oh, these endless plays. But if they are let away before eleven o'clock they feel they have been cheated, they have not had three-and-sixpence-worth of amusement—only, perhaps, two-and-nine. Well, signor? "

Field said unsympathetically that he didn't go to theatres and asked the commissionaire, " Did this couple take a taxi after dinner? "

The commissionaire said No, they hadn't. They had walked to the corner talking, oh, so quick, he said, so loud. That young woman, she had a voice. He had heard it until the corner was turned.

" Could you hear what she said? "

" What should they do now. That was it, signor. It was too late, they thought, for a theatre. It was a little minute past nine. I heard her say that he should come home with her, and he said No. Signor, he was right. I have seen that type before—many times. A spider, that is what she was, a spider. Once let her get so fine a fly into her net, and never, never will she let him go."

" Could you hear anything he said? "

" Only that he will not go. When she say Yes, yes, yes, he say, Never, never, never. But I do not know, signor, if in the end he agree. It is difficult." He sighed voluminously.

" That's all you heard her say? "

" Only that she has her rights. No, he say, and no again. Such as she—what do they know of rights? "

" A good deal, very often," remarked Field grimly. " Did you see what happened? "

" They had turned a corner, signor. Perhaps, after all, he went. . . ."

Field agreed. Perhaps he had. But how the deuce he was ever going to prove anything in a case where he hadn't got any witnesses was more than he could guess. He only asked the commissionaire where the nearest taxi rank stood. The commissionaire said there wasn't one very close; people who came to Martino's often couldn't afford taxis. And anyway, where could room be found for a rank? The streets there were narrow, the virtuous police so ardent that they coined regulations a man had never heard, till a constable shouted them out to him, until his mind became so confused that he did whatever he was told, as he could not be expected to remember if the order was an actual regulation or no. In short—and he spread his hands for the last time and looked nobly surprised to find a large coin in one of them—there was not a rank at all close.

Field discovered the nearest one—about seven minutes' walk from the restaurant—and talked to all the drivers he could find. The stand was small, with room for no more than ten cabs. Of these, seven were on duty when Field approached, and three were out with fares. Two others were summoned while they talked, but not before Field had convinced himself that they knew nothing of Charles and his wife. The remaining three came in later, but none of them could be of any assistance. They hadn't been near Richmond Park lately, most of them not for years.

Field realised he had done all that he could for the moment. He went back to Headquarters and drafted a notice to be circularised to all cab-ranks and garages whence taxi-cabs were hired. He said that the authorities were anxious to trace a man who had driven a couple down to Richmond Park from the neighbourhood of Soho on the evening of the 26th. The circular was so worded that to neglect what was practically a police order would imply trouble, and Field was gratified but not surprised when the following day an elderly red-faced man came down to the Yard at about one o'clock.

" Couldn't get away before, guv'nor," he explained. " 'Ad a big job on this morning. But I come right along without me dinner. 'Ow's that? What abaht this 'ere couple? You ain't mistakin' 'em for the pair what was found in the park under some bushes, 'aving drunk carbolic acid, are you? 'Cos, if so, you're on the wrong track. Brought 'em both back to London, I did."

" That's right, they're the people I want. Just tell me about them, where you picked them up, what they were like, anything that you may have heard of their conversation, anything that struck you as odd about them. Carry on. Smoke? " He offered, not a cigarette, but a pouch. The driver, whose name was Nelson, took it with a mutter of thanks. His story was brief and coherent and left no doubt of its accuracy in Field's mind. He had been hailed just after nine by a young man walking with a girl in a blue coat and blue hat. The young man had offered him a quid to take them down to Richmond and back. They seemed to be quarrelling, and the man appeared glad of the opportunity of putting her inside a cab where she would attract less attention.

" Did you hear their conversation inside the cab? "

" To tell the truth, sir, I wasn't listening much. You 'aven't driven a cab all the years I 'ave without realising these stories of the romance to be picked up by a sharp man is mostly lies. Sixteen years I bin at it, and I ain't come across much romance. Most romantic thing ever 'appened to me was when a chap that was sozzled offered to fight me for 'is last fiver. I didn't 'it 'im, of course; not likely, when 'e was that blind. But it wasn't needed to get the fiver from 'im." Then, remembering his audience, he went on quickly, " But I did 'ear this; they was quarrelling all the way to Richmond. And I 'eard something she said. She said it was all of a piece with the rest of 'is shabby treatment of 'er, going away and leavin' 'er, and then takin' 'er to a third-rate restaurant full o' tarts, and 'iding 'er very existence from every one. Well, and wouldn't any gent do the same? "

" What did you make of her? " Field asked in some curiosity.

" Why, she was a tart 'erself," returned Nelson indignantly. " We see plenty of 'er sort that hour of the night. I don't know what she wanted off 'im. P'raps 'e 'ad a wife and didn't want a scene, any more than a gentleman like you or me would. Well, there it was, a lovely night, all moony and fit for lovers and so on, and the taxi there, nice and dark, and them fighting like a pair of toms all the way and back. Fair made my gorge rise, so it did. Then, when this young chap tells me to drive to Menzies Street I thinks, ' So that's about the size of it, is it? Paying the rent, are you? ' But he goes on, ' Put the lady down there, and then take me on to Jermyn Street.' But when 'e got to Menzies Street 'e made a mistake. 'E got down and give 'er 'is 'and, and do you think she was goin' to let 'im go after that? Not 'er. She kinder stood between 'im and the cab, and wouldn't budge. And she begun again till if she'd bin my bit o' trouble, I'd 'ave shut 'er mouth in a way she'd understand. ' You think it's always going to end like this, do you? ' she says. ' Oh, no, Charles '—Charles was what she called him. I remember that quite will. And 'e says, ' We can't talk no more to-night. Iv'e 'ad enough.' And she begun to laugh a bit, the way wives do. I don't know if you're a married man yourself, sir, but anyway they do. 'Oh, my poor Charles,' she says, ' what a lot of trouble it would save you if I preferred death to dishonour. Wouldn't you be glad to see in the papers to-morrow that I'd bin found 'anging from an 'ook in the ceiling?' "

" Will you swear to that last bit? " asked Field sharply.

" Course I will. It's all gospel I'm tellin' you."

" It'll all come out at the inquest," Field warned him.

Nelson started. " The what? D'you mean . . ." he stopped to stare.

" I mean life's odd. She was found hanging from the hook—to take advantage of poetical \ licence—the next morning."

Nelson was tremendously impressed. " Crikey! And to think I missed that! Was it in the paper? Well, and I always read the police news first thing after the racing, of course. 'Oo did it, djer mind me asking? You don't mean to say," his eyes lighted up, " it was that young feller? Well, I wouldn't ha' thought it of 'im. Didn't look that kind. Still, you never can tell."

" You didn't look over your shoulder as you drove away or see if they'd separated, I suppose? " Field suggested.

" They was still talking when I steamed off. She looked to me good for a quarter've nour at least. And I ain't got eyes in the back of me 'ead. I've often wondered why providence didn't put 'em one each end. Lord, the trouble it 'ud save on the roads."

" I don't doubt it. What time was this? "

" Oh, say, half-past ten."

" Did you see any one else in the road? "

" I see a taxi waiting round a corner, that's all. But the bloke had gone inside."

" You didn't chance to see the driver's face? "

" No. It was precious dark. I could jest see the taxi."

" Did you notice the colour. You wouldn't see the number, of course."

" Just an ordinary-looking taxi. Not one of them orange ones, f'r instance."

" H'm." That opened up a new field of inquiry. He decided, Nelson rewarded and dismissed, that it would be very little use to examine the drivers on the nearest rank individually; the taxi might have come from almost any part of London. So he had recourse once again to the printed circular. He wanted the names of any drivers who had taken fares to Menzies Street on that night. But he realised that with a week having elapsed since the murder it was quite probable many men would forget their precise destinations. He himself made a journey to Menzies Street and examined the cul-de-sac where the taxi had been seen by Nelson. It was obvious, since the shadow of a tall house fell across the entrance, that a man driving casually past would be quite unable to determine the features of any one in the cul-de-sac, or even if there was a man there at all. There was only one house in Menzies Street whose entrance was situated in this insignificant cul-de-sac, and here Field made further inquiries. The woman who opened the door looked at him in rather a scared fashion, and went to fetch her mistress. It was obvious that this house was of quite a different character from No. 39. The men and women who lodged here were students or typists, and lived their private lives with less blatancy and more subtlety. Most of them were out at work during the day. The tenant was a Miss Eames, who had been a dressmaker until her sight became defective, and she now made a living by running the " Penywern Boarding Establishment."

Field didn't expect this inquiry to get him very far, but if he could trace the driver of this cab it was just barely possible that he would recall seeing Fanny and Charles. The farther end of the road was up for repairs, so that all taxis and road traffic must enter from Hollington Street; it was not even possible at the moment for foot passengers to use the farther end of the road, which meant that Charles must have walked past the cul-de-sac if he had left Fanny when he said he did. And in that case he must have passed the taxi. If a man could come forward and give evidence that he had actually done so at about half-past ten, then he could be removed from the case; and it was on the chance of proving this that Field made his careful examination. He asked Miss Eames if she could remember telephoning for a taxi on the Wednesday night in question, or if any of her lodgers had had a visitor who came by taxi that night. Miss Eames said she couldn't be sure and offered to look up her books. Her lodgers' visitors were charged for meals and she could ascertain whether there had been any on the 26th. Since the taxi had been seen in the cul-de-sac at half-past ten Field did not think this would advance them at all, though he let her turn up her books, as she suggested. She came back with the information that there had been no visitors to dinner that night. That meant the visitor must have arrived after dinner. Field went away and returned later in the evening, at about six-thirty, when the first batch of lodgers got back from work. He remained in the house until eleven o'clock, by which time he had interrogated them all. None of them had sent for a taxi, none recollected being visited that evening, and several had themselves been out of the house. Field came away a good deal disappointed. The fact that this was a minor point and that he could hardly have expected to be successful, while even the solution of the difficulty might easily prove useless to his problem, did not affect him a jot. To him there were no trifles in detective work; everything was important and part of its charm was the fact that you could never be absolutely sure that some quite minor incident was not the key to the truth. Of course, the taxi had very likely brought to that neighbourhood some man who certainly would not wish to be seen there, and doubtless it had been instructed to wait round a corner until its hirer re-appeared, so as not to call attention to any particular house. In his zeal he re-examined Nelson, asking if the taxi had carried lights on that evening. Nelson said they were not kindled; he had thought himself that perhaps there was a couple inside that didn't want to be disturbed; or else the driver had a

" date " with some one in the street, which would explain his efforts to preserve anonymity for his car.

" You're quite sure it was taxi, and not a private car, I suppose? " Field asked, and to his surprise and rather to his disgust Nelson wavered. It was precious dark, he said, and he couldn't see much. Moreover, such odd cars were put on the road these days. . . . In short, he couldn't be relied upon on this point, so that Field dismissed the hope of tracking down the driver of the vehicle, and instead, armed with a search-warrant, went along to go through Charles's rooms with a tooth-comb.

He began his search with very little expectation of finding anything to link up the occupier with the murder. He examined clothes, correspondence, every nook and corner with care; on the writing-table in the sitting-room were a stamp-box, a silver box of cigarettes, a massive silver inkstand presented to Sir Gerald Hobart by the fellow-officers and mess of the regiment with whom he had fought for four years, a Bradshaw, a leather-covered book of telegraph forms and a telephone. Field examined them all methodically; the cigarette-box, as he had expected, contained a brand similar to that found in Fanny's ash-tray. But then Charles had admitted giving her one as they stood on the pavement of Menzies Street, and the second stub was perhaps one she had lighted for herself after she entered the house. A further point struck him. Two of the cigarettes were bent and broken, which was suspicious, since cigarettes kept in orderly rows in a box do not break themselves, and neither Hobart nor his nephew would be likely to smoke a ruined cigarette. While, had Parsons been responsible for their condition, he would certainly have pitched the two broken cigarettes away. Field took up the box and carefully emptied it; before he reached the final row he saw something glint and felt a smooth substance under his fingers. A moment later there lay in his hand the broken pink necklace for which he had searched Fanny's room in vain!

It was not difficult to see what had happened. In strangling the wretched woman the pearls had been a hindrance, and the chain had broken, or been forcibly broken—in view of the mark on the back of the neck Field inclined to the latter view—and later had been thrust into the murderer's pocket, since it might rouse suspicion later if the crushed necklace were found, with one or two beads missing. In his search after the death, X had overlooked the single pearl in the fold of the sheet; then when he returned, having disposed of the key which, having just removed it from the lock, he would certainly not forget, he would discover, as he undressed, the accursed necklace in his pocket. He could not go out again that night without arousing suspicion, and in any case there was probably nowhere in the immediate neighbourhood where the pearls could be safely concealed. Even for a night he would not dare leave them in his room; Parsons, excellent servant that he was, might come in to brush the coat or clear the room, and nowhere would they seem to the distracted young man to be safe. All he could think of for that one night was the box of cigarettes, and he showed wisdom in selecting this rather than a similar box holding cigars, to which Parsons might help himself. Charles would argue that the necklace was safe until the next day, when he could carry it off and lose it from the train-window on his journey to Fernden. Possibly he had been afraid of detection even while he concealed the beads, as otherwise he would scarcely have broken the two cigarettes, perhaps he expected Parsons with a drink or some letter or message he had forgotten. The next morning, in his haste to get away from London before the murder was discovered, the pearls had completely slipped his memory; he must have remembered them by this time, and be having some bad moments wondering whether Field would find them. And even so, not knowing about the single pearl found in the dead woman's bed, he might not think Field would connect them with the murder.

2

Charles, Egerton and Lucy were present when Field came down with his warrant for Charles's arrest. Charles himself did not know all the evidence on which he had been convicted, but clearly this consequence came to him without surprise. Egerton, watching keenly from the half-shadow of a curtain, was struck by a certain nobility and courage in Charles's bearing as Field spoke the fatal words. Not since he had seen Denis Brinsley's face across the width of the coroner's court some years earlier, in circumstances that were oddly similar, had he seen any man at once so vulnerable and so controlled. For a moment it was like watching the mechanism of a heart under the microscope. Then Lucy broke the spell by coming forward and, without offering her hand, saying, " Good luck, Charles. Things all work out for the best, if you mean that they shall. And now we've got a chance of proving definitely it wasn't you."

Charles uttered a kind of groan and Egerton wondered a little, as he had often done before, at the emotional insensitiveness of the female creature. Wasn't it true that even Lucy, delicately-strung though she was, inflexible as steel yet pliable as a tempered sword, couldn't realise how she turned the knife in the wound with those words? But later, no doubt, Charles would remember them with gratitude.

Charles was muttering something absurd. He was beginning to lose grip. That Lucy should have been present now was the crowning humiliation. He said something about " my life not being worth all this fuss." And Lucy said, with a sudden sweet and unforgettable smile, " Oh, but it's my life I'm thinking of. You mustn't, dear Charles, forget that."

After Charles had gone away with Field, Egerton remained staring out of the long French window on to the three terraces that fell away, one beneath the next, to the long orchard that gave place, in its turn, to the silver gleaming lake where the swans sailed in silent majesty. His mobile face was expressionless, but Lucy knew from his pose how ardent and intent were his thoughts. She said at last, " What is it? "

He turned at once, and his face relaxed. " I was

wondering whether that was true, what you said to Charles.
That it's a good thing in the end. I'm not so sure. These
months of suspense might easily prove the undoing of a
less highly-strung man."

" Then the sooner you find the real man the better,"
said Lucy coolly. " And if there's anything for me to do,
you can tell me."

" Thanks," murmured Egerton, in his dry, ironical voice.

Her face changed. She slipped a hand under his elbow.
" I believe in Charles," she said. " As soon as you've
unearthed the truth I'm going to marry him. And whatever happened, or whatever any one could say, I should
go on believing in him. And I trust you absolutely. I
know everything will be all right. I'm not even afraid."

Not even Rosemary had ever paid Egerton a compliment
like that.

CHAPTER VII

1

EGERTON went up to town next day and obtained an
appointment with Sir Claude Arbuthnot, the big criminal
lawyer. When Arbuthnot had all the information in the
hands of the police and realised that his new client could
offer him no assistance at all in the matter of proving his
innocence, he looked a little blue.

" On the face of it, the prosecution has a flawless case,"
he observed, a grim smile twisting his long upper lip.
" Certainly, no one can prove he was actually in the
house, but on the other hand he can't offer any suggestion
as to where he actually was."

" Even if he remembered the exact route he took I doubt
if we could get an alibi for him," remarked Egerton. " The
majority of people don't notice the most glaring peculiarity
in their fellow-travellers, and there was nothing particularly
noticeable about Charles that night, so far as we know.
We're faced, as usual with the alternatives of producing a
spick-and-span murderer, which would be nice but not

simple, or raising sufficient dust to get Charles off on a virtually ' Not Proven ' decree."

" I suppose it would be something for him to escape the gallows, but I'm not sure these half-hearted acquittals do their owners much good," retorted Arbuthnot, as grim as ever. " You remember G——," he named the central figure in a famous poison trial of some years ago, " every one, humanly speaking, believed him guilty of wife-murder, though there was precious little evidence either way. Still, the fellow got off, though he'd blackened his name by being fool enough to marry again within a few weeks, which turned the general public against him—but he died in great poverty and obscurity, after a brief flare in the Sunday press, about a couple of years afterwards."

" H'm. You're a pleasant prophet. Incidentally, when Hobart is released, my sister proposes to marry him. She's merely waiting for us to achieve the miracle. Oh, that's no secret. Every one who knows Lucy knows the position, down to the boot-boy. She sees no reason why they shouldn't."

" You're her guardian, I suppose, until she's twenty-one. You could forbid the banns, if you chose."

" There are several reasons why I shouldn't choose. To begin with, I don't believe in these arbitrary rights of one human being over another; secondly, I think Charles wants a little pleasant relaxation; and thirdly, it wouldn't be any earthly use. She'd abduct him, when it became obvious there was no other way of getting him. You don't know my sister."

" There seems to be a strong family resemblance," re-marked Arbuthnot. " Now, coming to the evidence. The chief point against him, and one that will hang him if we can't dispose of it satisfactorily, is the pearls."

" I've seen Charles on that point," put in Egerton. " He's positive she was wearing them that night. He said they were so blatantly artificial they made him feel worse than usual. Of course, he denies any knowledge of them in his flat."

" They're the devil," Arbuthnot acknowledged.

But Egerton was not to be so lightly cast down. " Now, there I don't agree with you," he remarked. " It seems to me the pearls help us more than they hinder."

" It would be interesting to know how you make that out."

" Without them we should be hopelessly in the dark. But some one put them in that box—and it wasn't Charles. That's the basis of our case. All we have to do is to discover who did put them there, and then, I should say, you've got the murderer under your thumb. I don't think there was an accomplice; I don't think one would be necessary or safe."

" That's certainly one to you," Arbuthnot agreed, " but don't forget that even when we discover some one who had the opportunity of putting those pearls where they were found, we may be just as far off identifying or collaring him."

" Oh, quite. Still, we can only go one step at a time. Charles's man will, with a little luck, give us that point. You know, when you don't bind yourself down to the view that Charles was the murderer, you've enlarged your scope enormously. We're allowing that the murder took place about eleven-thirty and that Charles did all the preparations for the suicide effect and got back in a little over an hour. But if it was some one else he may have spent half the night there; so we don't want to limit our inquiries to men seen in the neighbourhood up to midnight or a bit later. It's quite possible the fellow may not have left the house till the morning, to lend colour to a story he might tell his own establishment about spending the night at the club or in the train. We've got another point, which is that the murderer knew Fanny Penny, knew her handwriting well enough to imitate it. A man she'd casually picked up couldn't, I think, have done that. Also, there are no letters in the room that would help us; and since she had had letters it seems possible that X went round destroying those, too. Now, if we're right—if Field is right, that is— in assuming that not only was she blackmailing Charles, but was being blackmailed in her turn, then we've got in the picture another figure from her past life who may very well be concerned in this. Charles says he refused her demand of five hundred pounds outright. It's rather significant that she didn't offer to abate it, say, half or even less. No, I think we shall find, when we've unravelled the skein, that she had to have that money for some specific purpose, that she was terrified at the prospect of not getting it. . . ."

"Keep the threads straight," Arbuthnot advised him. "Remember she didn't write that letter. But whoever did write it knew the facts of the case. That's important. And knew all about Hobart or he wouldn't have planted the pearls in his rooms. Obviously, Parsons is our first step. By the way, do you know the other Hobart? "

"Sir Gerald? I've met him. We belong to the same club."

Arbuthnot, who was a staunch Conservative, nodded. without smiling. He thought Liberals only one degree removed from Communists, whose nests themselves had made. But he only said, " I wonder if Felix Gordon is engaged just now. To my mind, he's about the best, if the most expensive, of these private inquiry agents. We need a pretty good man if we're going to set him on the trail of a murderer about whom he knows nothing."

"Oh, we know quite a lot," suggested Egerton cheerfully. "And we shall soon know more. Field's trouble was that he didn't know who Fanny Penny really was. We do. So we can trace her back history, at all events from the time she married Hobart. And I don't see why her relations shouldn't tell us the rest. Charles takes us up to the time of their separation; when he went abroad he left this legacy for her, to be administered by the bank. Ergo, she had an address, and if and when she changed it the bank would have to be notified. Gordon can get on to the trail of her past addresses, and that should give us something to get our teeth into. There's this man who broke her married life to pieces; he may come in again, and we might get some information about him from the family."

"And you think he's the man who wanted the five hundred pounds?"

"I think it's possible. I can't say I think so definitely, because we know too little."

They remained discussing the position in further considerable detail until late in the afternoon. Then Egerton drove back to Eaton Square, and settled down to a tremendous batch of political correspondence that had accumulated during the past few days of his absence from town. He wasn't going back to Fernden; he said he would polish off his outstanding liabilities while he had the house to himself.

Callous as he sometimes thought it must appear, such crises as these keyed him up to the highest mental tension; his mind felt clear, his energy indomitable; he knew nothing of depression, of fear or of weariness. He dealt with his work in a manner that would have amazed Arbuthnot. An indescribable ardour upheld him; he had this much in common with Field, that a difficult job with a tremendous issue at stake revivified him. His vitality knew no flagging in the difficult days that followed; each blind alley, each careful chase up a cul-de-sac, only strengthened his will. Rosemary said he had probably been a bloodhound in a previous incarnation. She was far more on edge during this trying period than Lucy, who came back to Eaton Square with her a couple of days later. No one, not even Egerton, suspected the night terrors and dreams that racked her when she dared lift the curtain of restraint that protected her during the day.

2

Before Arbuthnot could set Gordon on the trail he had to see his man himself; it took him forty-eight hours to get his facts together, and when he went down to the prison where Charles was detained he half-anticipated a distracted suspect, scarcely able to give him a coherent answer to his simplest question. But Charles greeted him quietly, and replied without heat or hesitation to everything he was asked. Arbuthnot realised this as the tranquillity of an unassailable despair. Charles was convinced that he would shortly be hanged and it was because he was untroubled of hope that he could maintain his calm bearing. This tragedy had swept away all the small personal ambitions he had hitherto cherished; he could scarcely credit it, even while he accepted it, and in comparison with its implications nothing else assumed any recognisable proportions.

He repeated clearly and concisely to Arbuthnot what he had already told Egerton. He recollected the pearls, and had said on impulse that he would buy her some new ones.

" Were you in a position to buy her pearls? " the lawyer asked him.

" I wasn't, of course. I said that on the spur of the minute. I suppose I could have run to a string of seed pearls. Some imitation pearls aren't so bad, but these were terrible. I hate all this sham jewellery anyway. It's so infernally dishonest."

" You're sure she didn't break the pearls in the taxi, and ask you to put them in your pocket? "

Charles smiled faintly. " What an ingenious theory! I wonder, if I said Yes, if you could get a jury to believe that. As a matter of fact she didn't, of course. She was wearing them when we stood on the pavement talking."

" I see. Now, about the cigarettes. . . ."

" I gave her one after we got out of the taxi, and she was still smoking it when I left her."

" Do you remember which way out of Menzies Street you came? "

" You can't come more than one way just now; the whole of the other end is blocked up. My taxi-driver told me that. I wondered why he was taking us the long way round. The pavement's up and there are barriers all across the road."

" Do you recollect crossing a turning soon after you left No. 39?"

" After I left Fanny, you mean? No, I'm afraid I don't. I don't recollect noticing anything."

" Not passing a taxi, for instance, a stationary taxi? "

Charles shook his head. " Sorry to be so little use to

you." But he didn't sound nearly so sorry as Arbuthnot felt.

" Now, you'd been seeing a fair amount of your wife lately; had she spoken to you of any special difficulties, anything that would warrant the demand for five hundred pounds, when you'd only recently given her a hundred? "

" She simply said she'd got to have it somehow, and I must find it for her. She seemed a little hysterical about it, but you must remember I had seen her like that before. It didn't, to be frank, cut a tremendous amount of ice."

" She never suggested that there might be grave consequences for her if she couldn't raise it? "

" She didn't say anything beyond what I've told you. I only looked on it as an attempt to get anything she could. She felt she had been ill-used."

" She never spoke to you of any man, any one who might have an undue influence over her? "

" No."

" Now, going back to the time of your marriage—when you first discovered she was unfaithful to you, did you ever learn the man's name? "

" No. I didn't inquire. She told me it was some one she had known before we met."

" Did you ever see him? "

" I found him in my rooms once. I can't say I saw him very clearly. I had an impression of a medium-sized man with dark hair and a dark complexion."

" I think it would be as well if you told me everything you can about your wife, your original meeting with her, the marriage and so forth. I only have a quite sketchy notion of it all, and it may be that a chance detail will help us immeasurably. In circumstances like these, one can scarcely be too well-informed."

" I met her, as I dare say you have heard, in a picture shop about ten miles outside Cambridge. I had very little in the way of private means, and I was often hard put to it to meet expenses; my uncle didn't encourage my running up accounts. I decided that I had a talent for etching, and it seemed to me that perhaps I could turn a few pounds by selling my work. Of course, it was glaring with amateurisms that I didn't realise, and none of the big people in Cambridge would look at it. But you know how it is, perhaps, when you're without experience; you listen to what disappointed hacks tell you and persuade yourself that you're not looked at simply through the jealousy of men who've already arrived. So I went on outside the town, and one day I saw this shop with Penny painted over the door. I knew as soon as I set eyes on the Pennys themselves they wouldn't be good for a sou; not because it wasn't good enough for them, but simply because they wouldn't even understand what I was driving at. The big men had realised that, at all events. But what I hadn't counted on was Fanny. It's difficult for me now, remembering her as I found her when I came back from abroad, to give you any impression of what she appeared to me that day. She wasn't exactly good-looking, you didn't think about looks when you were with her; she had a quality I can't describe; she overflowed with vitality. It was like suddenly coming into sunlight. Oh, this is all absurdly inadequate and beside the point, but there was something—believe me, sir, I wasn't by any means the only man to feel it. Other men were the same, men of all ages and intellectual capacity. I saw that during the short time we were together. She had a kind of gift for living. That's the best way I can express it. And I had a desire then to get the utmost from everything, and she seemed to me something that represented the things I was after. Anyway, I didn't worry much whether they sold anything of mine or not, though, as a matter of fact, they did sell one or two small ones at ridiculous prices. I wanted Fanny; and presently it seemed that she wanted me. But when I spoke of marriage she shied; said she didn't believe in it. It was fettering an emotion that should be pre-eminently free. I might have guessed then that she was echoing what some one else had said to her. It wasn't her kind of language at all. I argued. The thought of the alternative seemed to put the whole affair on a different footing; besides, then, I wanted her for my wife. She said she couldn't, she'd seen her father mown down by matrimony. That was her actual expression, and it was extraordinarily eloquent. He certainly had the look of a man who has been overwhelmed, except when she was with him. Then he revived like roses if you put them in warm water. I don't think she kept that quality for long; I think she'd lost it to some extent even before we separated, tho' she'd lost it far, far more by the time we met again. But at all events, I couldn't move her. I promised not to try and hold her if she found marriage with me intolerable, but it was no good."

" And in the end you agreed to her terms? "

" Yes. We went down to Brighton. For a fortnight I was as happy as any man could have been. I saw she exerted a similar spell over other men, but I wasn't jealous. After all, I had her. Then one day I chanced to catch sight of a fellow I knew. Fanny was with me, and to my disgust I found myself involuntarily diving behind some building. That settled it. I wasn't going to have the thing spoilt and cheapened like that, so I told Fanny it was marriage or immediate separation, and this time I won. We were married out of hand—we were qualified for a registry office marriage; we'd been living in the place for a fortnight. We stayed down there another month, and then we came to town. I hadn't got a job and I had very little money. I think my uncle's original notion had been that I should go and talk matters over with him. I still thought I'd do that, and tell him about Fanny, but she disillusioned me. She was quite right, of course. I don't know if you've ever met my uncle (Arbuthnot recalled the choleric blue eye, the determined curve of the mouth, the ruthlessness of the grim jaw, and sympathised with the young man before him, foolish though he had been), but she made me see that it was one thing to approach him as a dutiful nephew, ready to fall in with his suggestions and quite another to appear in the role of a married man who was having a desperate time trying to support his wife, and anxious for a job at all costs. He wouldn't have approved of the marriage, either, and, of course, Fanny was wise enough to realise that. I, inconceivably, wasn't, not at that stage; however, I agreed it would be pleasant to be able to show I could get on without favours, and would put my whole marriage on a different footing. So we agreed to keep it dark for a time, until we could announce it without people saying what a fool I'd made of myself, saddling myself with a wife I couldn't keep. Fanny had one letter from her mother when we first went to Brighton, full of stinging references to the less desirable characters in the Old and New Testaments. Fanny was furious, but you couldn't help seeing her mother's point of view. Afterwards I think Fanny was glad of the opportunity to get quit of them all. They were never on good terms even when she was at home."

" How long had you been married before you began to realise your mistake? "

" Not more than a few months. I was ambitious, I wanted to get on, partly, certainly, for Fanny's sake, but also partly for my own. I had a sort of contempt for men who went under, and were always trying to borrow fivers to pay doctors' bills and so forth. I wanted to study at nights and Fanny found that dull. She wanted to go out, she didn't much mind where; any sort of entertainment amused her. We could only go to the cheapest amusements, and they soon palled as far as I was concerned. That irritated her and we used to quarrel. If we stayed at home she'd prevent my working by complaining of the drabness of her life; she didn't care at all about my work or what we might do five years hence. She said she mightn't be alive five years hence, and when I wouldn't or couldn't take her, she'd go with other men. I remonstrated about that and put my work aside, but I had hardly any money to spare, and I couldn't give her nearly such a good time as other men did. She wasn't particular as to the sort of men so long as they had plenty of money and gave her an exciting time. During the first part of this period I was still very much in love with her, and a disagreement would keep me awake most of the night and send me to work with a splitting head and all manner of ridiculous terrors in my brain. Presently I realised that she thoroughly enjoyed a scene; I think I began cooling off then. She was always casting it in my face that we hadn't enough money, and we hadn't, for the sort of life she wanted to live. Then she reminded me that she'd fought against marriage, she'd been afraid it would drag her down to this, and she wasn't cut out for domestic drudgery. So it went on till I'd been married nearly a year, and then I came back to find this other man in possession."

Charles had spoken coolly and without any pauses, but now the lawyer became aware of a certain breathlessness, a speechless effort he made to rein his mind in from following the images his words had conjured up. Arbuthnot was reminded of a death mask he had once seen in a French gallery; always lean, the face now seemed well-nigh fleshless; he succeeded, without raising his voice or using any striking phrase or gesture, without even being aware of the impression he created, in bringing home to the lawyer some of the horror, disappointment and shame that had overwhelmed him on that terrible afternoon.

" And you separated after that? " was all Arbuthnot said.

" Yes. We spent that night in the rooms—it was too late to make other arrangements—but I took a furnished room for myself the next morning and stayed there till we'd settled things up. It took about a week. It wasn't the first time it had happened; she acknowledged that. There was an evening when she sent me out, before I'd had time to hang up my hat, for some chloroform for a bad tooth; she'd locked her door, said she was in pain and I was to hurry; but I found the bottle still corked a long time afterwards. And that was one occasion of several. As you know, we didn't have a legal deed. I thought I'd done all any one could expect of me, and I was thankful of the chance to get abroad. Fanny wouldn't think of putting a spoke in my wheel; she was glad to be quit of me, I think. I don't know what plans she made after I left. I had no further communication with her till I came back here some months ago and she found me in London.

" You've no notion whether she kept up with this man? "

" None. But are you seriously going to try and link up the murder with a man she knew six years ago? "

" Why not? " inquired Arbuthnot urbanely. " Haven't the police succeeded in linking you up with her, and it's seven years since you first met? "

Charles acknowledged the reasonableness of that. He added, in reply to further questions, that he understood Fanny had lived at one time with some distant connections at some place not far from Cambridge, but that she hadn't got on with them and had therefore returned home. That bore out the information the police already had. Arbuthnot remained to test the position at various other points; he asked for the address of the last rooms Charles and Fanny had occupied before the break. It was a slender hope, but the landlady might be able to help them. When he heard the address, however, he smiled his wry, grim smile: Fate meant to give them a run for their money. Those buildings had been pulled down to make place for a super-cinema a couple of years earlier.

So there was not any way of testing the truth of Charles's story. The man who had broken up the marriage might be a pure fabrication, though Arbuthnot had to acknowledge that so far his client appeared to be sticking to the facts, inasmuch as they had been able to verify anything he said. But the position was not a very hopeful one, and he came away from the prison heartily thankful that he wasn't in that poor devil's shoes.

" He must be prevented from expanding so lavishly on his relations with his wife," he reflected. " We shall have the whole of the estimable British jury on our shoulders if he doesn't salt his speech with discretion."

It would, of course, be necessary to employ counsel to conduct the defence, and Arbuthnot decided to try and persuade Sir John Driver to undertake the case. Driver had come into especial prominence in his brilliant conduct of the case Rex. v. Cheyne, which was still spoken of, less, as a matter of fact, because of Driver's striking cross-examination than because of the dramatic break-up of the trial. Driver listened with interest to what Arbuthnot had to tell him. Then he asked in his direct way, "What's your own feeling?"

Arbuthnot, equally candid in camera, replied, "I'm still going canny. It strikes me as extraordinary that a man like that should come back, be aware of his wife dogging his footsteps, and go about among his own relations and friends and never drop a hint that he was married. No, I'll qualify that. After he'd met the woman again and realised what she was up to, then I dare say you might expect a hundred per cent. secrecy; but before that. He needn't have taken the girl into his confidence—oh, yes, there's a girl, of course; she provides the motive—but it appears he wasn't telling any one. Suppose this fake suicide had been accepted by the police, he need never have let out that he'd been married."

"How would he describe himself when he wanted to marry the other girl?" demanded Driver.

"A fellow who doesn't shrink from murder and can plan as neat a case as he did—supposing it was his job—wouldn't worry over a little thing like describing himself falsely on a marriage certificate. If he'd described himself as a widower, don't tell me that a cautious chap like Egerton wouldn't ask questions. And I don't imagine he's the kind of chap that would appreciate that sort of secret. A jury is bound to make a lot of those circumstances, and between ourselves we can admit freely that they are suspicious. Their point will be that Hobart intended to get his wife out of the way—he acknowledges that she was a drag on him socially and financially—and then marry Miss Egerton, who's incidentally on the road to being an heiress. It doesn't look well, either, that he should have passed as a bachelor for the last six years or so. Our only hope will be to show that there's a plot to foist the blame on to him."

"Which, if he's innocent, there clearly is. And if there isn't, then he's guilty. He can't be innocent and not be the butt of some other criminal."

"If. Candidly, I'm still a little uncertain. I like the

fellow's manner; he's quiet and he knows how to behave. That's partly because he doesn't think he's got a chance. He doesn't contradict himself and, which is even more important, he doesn't contradict any of the side-issue facts the police have unearthed. He's clear in his manner and he appears frank; he hasn't tried to put up an alibi, which I think he could have done, and he doesn't deny that he was with this girl until a short time before her death."

"On the other hand, he's given us very little that we can hope to prove, either as to what happened years ago or what happened last month."

"Well, as to that, he may very well be innocent and still be unable to prove any of his assertions. You must grant him that. A young couple, who lived for less than a year in dingy apartments that have since been pulled down, aren't going to find it easy to produce witnesses who remember them at all. And it's simple enough to walk about London for an evening without meeting a soul you know. It's pure luck whether you're recognised or not."

"In spite of your protestations, I think you're more convinced than you realise," said Driver, with a laugh. "What course are you mapping out?"

"I've been into it very thoroughly with Egerton, who's a long way from being a fool and has a very definite stake in the matter, and we think that if we can unearth this man she went off with six years ago it might help us. He may have some hold over her. Of course, that's not our only line of inquiry. There's Parsons; and we are going to try and trace Mrs. Hobart by following up her various addresses. We may learn more of her gentlemen friends that way. It won't be a short case, and we can't see far enough ahead yet to realise what it will involve; but we're hoping to get Gordon to do the spade work, and he'll have his own assistants. We can't do much at the moment because we're in complete darkness, but I fancy Egerton is going personally to see Hobart's man in Jermyn Street, and that may give us a thread on which to work. Of course, the inquest is postponed, though they had the funeral some days ago. I'll get in touch with you again as soon as anything fresh turns up. D'you think they'll convict if we can't produce an alternative criminal? "

" Bound to," said Driver emphatically. " Those incriminating pearls! "

CHAPTER VIII

I

EGERTON approached Parsons, whom he regarded as the most important of possible witnesses at this stage, by indirect means. He had spoken truly when he said he knew Hobart; he knew his reputation, his fiery temper, the bitter rage with which he would greet such a position as the present; and he asked him to dine at Eaton Square. At first it seemed as though Hobart did not intend to do anything of the kind. He didn't understand what Egerton had to do with the affair, and it was not until Egerton, meeting him at the Club, explained matters, that the baronet consented to be soothed.

" What the devil Charles wanted to marry the slut for," he exploded, " is beyond me. Especially as he says there was no need. God knows I never put those notions into his head. These pure young men who want to resurrect Galahad are beyond me. Why, the girl isn't even a lady."

Egerton's expression told him nothing, and Hobart realised that he was unlikely to get sympathy from that quarter. He asked if there was anything he could do.

" I think there is. You must realise that a tremendous amount of public opinion will hinge on the question of the beads. If Charles put them into the cigarette-box, he's guilty; and if he isn't guilty, that means some one else put them there, and we've got to discover who. Now, manifestly they were put there after the murder and before Field searched the rooms."

" That does appear reasonable," agreed Hobart sarcastically.

" Which gives us a period of approximately ten days, during which Charles was absent from town." Egerton's imperturbability was unshaken. "The only person who can tell us anything useful will be that man of yours. If any one came to the flat he admitted him, unless it's possible for some one to get in when he's out, as I suppose he sometimes is. But we must try him first of all."

"Are you trying to drag Parsons into this?" Hobart demanded incredulously.

"Not at all. But he may be able to give us the missing clue. I don't know what his attitude in these circumstances may be, whether he'll answer you readily. . . .?" He glanced in an inquiring manner at his companion.

"I'll bump his head off if he tries any tricks on me," was Hobart's trenchant response. "He'll tell me all I want to know. But there's one thing." He fixed Egerton with his fierce blue eyes. "Don't go getting any bees in your bonnet over this affair. Parsons isn't in it, even if he has been made a catspaw of by some ruffian."

"I never thought he was," said Egerton politely.

Twenty-four hours later he heard from Hobart again. Parsons had given him a list of his own friends who had visited him at the flat, and for the rest there was the usual number of trades-people. In addition, there was a postman and a one-legged ex-service man selling combs and toothbrushes, who had not been admitted over the threshold.

Egerton gave the list to Gordon, who went systematically through it, and reported that all the men concerned could be regarded as outside the case. Three of the five names belonged to men in similar positions to that of Parsons, and one was a chauffeur to a man in Albemarle Street. He had been out with his employer on the night of the murder, and hadn't been to the flat since. The other four men were tracked down and dismissed from consideration. Egerton then telephoned the rooms in Jermyn Street and, learning that Hobart was out, went round in person. Parsons, a little disturbed at the turn things were taking, had shed his affected manner and became a normal anxious human being.

"Sir Gerald is out, sir," he began, seeing Egerton on the mat.

Egerton nodded. "I know. But I didn't come to see Sir Gerald. I came to see you, and you're in all right." He walked past the astonished man into the hall. Parsons looked more apprehensive than ever; Egerton was going to some function and was in all the glory of top-hat and frock-coat.

He explained his position as he set the silk hat down on a table and laid his stick, a foppish affair with a handle of clouded amber, beside it.

"I hope, sir," said Parsons, awakening to a realisation of the position—he recognised Egerton's name now—"you're not trying to put me into this in any way."

Egerton reassured him. "I only want your help," he said. "Need we talk here? Is there any one in the sitting-room?"

"No, sir." Parsons led the way into a large and extremely pleasant and well-lighted room, with three tall windows facing the door. In front of these windows stood the writing-table, unchanged except for certain marks on the blotting-paper since Field examined it. Egerton leaned against this, his back to the windows and asked, "Ever go out and leave the flat empty, Parsons?"

"Well, sir, I'm bound to go out sometimes."

"Of course. What chance is there of some one getting into the flat when you're away?"

"Practically none, sir. I always lock all the rooms, and conceal the keys, and there's a special Yale lock outside. And then all these doors, as you may have noticed, sir, have bolts to them. The last gentleman that lived here had them put on. Very nervous of burglars he was."

"Must have been," agreed Egerton. "Do you go out at particular times? Regularly, I mean? Would any one be able to guess at any special time that you'd be out?"

"Oh, no, sir. And I'm not out a great deal. Perhaps for a bit in the evenings when Sir Gerald is away. Of course, when Mr. Charles was here, it was more that I'd have a friend in, perhaps."

"Yes."

He turned and looked out of the window. "Not very

easy to get in through the windows here. What about the other rooms? "

" No better, sir. I don't think it could be done. You see, we're on the front here, and any one trying to make a felonious entry would be detected at once. And at the back I don't think it could be done. All parcels and orders, tradesmen's orders, that is, come up by an outside lift. Well, nothing heavier than a baby could come up on that, and if a man tried to climb up by the fire escape, say, he'd most likely be seen."

" Still, that wouldn't be an impossible feat? "

" He couldn't get into this room from the fire escape. He'd have to come in by the bedroom, and then how'd he get out of there? It isn't just the lock, it's the bolt. And then I always lock the windows as well, and if he was going back through the window, how'd he lock it from outside?"

" I believe you're right," agreed Egerton. " It's too complicated. However paradoxical though it sounds, it's simpler than ever. We may assume, I think, that the pearls entered the house by the front door. Therefore, you must have admitted the man who brought them. Question—who was he? "

Parsons stiffened. " I don't understand you, sir. I've already told Sir Gerald all the people that's been here. . . ."

Egerton shook his head. " Just what you haven't done. Well, be reasonable. No supernatural agency put those pearls where Field found them. Either Field put them there himself, which is ridiculous, or some one did whom you had admitted to the flat. Think again. I'm sure you're a rationalist, that is, you don't believe in miracles."

" Well, to tell you the truth, sir, they always have stuck in my gullet."

" Then that proves my case. Now think, Parsons. Did no one come to attend to the wireless or clean the windows or look at the gas or check up the telephone, or . . ."

Parsons took a step forward, lifted his hands, and dropped them again. " My God, sir! "

" Yes? " Egerton tapped a cigarette on the back of his hand and looked round for a match.

Parsons stepped forward and struck one. "That journalist chap! I might ha' guessed it was odd."

"Journalist?" Egerton watched a smoke-ring rise slowly to the ceiling and there break.

"Yes. Came in with a story about Sir Gerald bein' killed out abroad. All nonsense, I told him. I didn't know then, you see, there'd even been an accident. As a matter of fact, he just lamed his ankle a bit. The chap seemed excited and said that the press had heard he'd been killed, and then asked if he could use the 'phone. Had to stop the rumour, he said."

"And you pointed out to him that there was a box just opposite? I noticed it as I came in."

Parson's face was a study. "No, sir," he said at last. "Tell you the truth, I never noticed there was one there."

"That's why the police force costs so much," was Egerton's slightly cryptic rejoinder.

Parsons looked startled. "I beg your pardon, sir?"

"National habit of overlooking obvious details," explained Egerton. "It's been there for a long time. It's almost due for another coat of paint. Well, what happened? He came in here. Did you come with him?"

"He dropped a pencil, a little gold pencil, on the floor in the hall. We both heard it drop and he tried to stop it rolling, with his foot, but he only kicked it under the chest."

"Clever of him," conceded Egerton. "So you shifted the chest while he came in here?"

"Yes, sir. And a heavy piece of goods it is. But I kept the door open, so I could hear what he was saying."

"But not see what he was doing. Did he really use the telephone?"

"Oh, yes, sir, asked for a number and all. He was talking hard when I came in with the pencil. Saying they'd nearly made a bloomer and Sir Gerald wasn't dead, and something about Old Gilly or Billy. I don't recollect the name exactly. And then he hung the receiver up and went out, taking the pencil with him."

"I see. Let's rehearse that, shall we? You go into the

hall and start moving the chest, leaving the door in approximately the position it was that afternoon. What time, by the way? "

" About half-past three, as near as I can remember."

" I see. Now, look up. Can you see me? " Parsons was by this time in the hall straining at the heavy chest. His voice came through the open door.

" No, sir."

" I thought as much." Egerton had his profile turned towards the door; with one hand he went through a pretence of using the telephone, while with the other he dropped a pencil into the cigarette-box, concealing it beneath the contents. He had laid his watch on the table, and he saw that half a minute would be more than sufficient for his purpose. He had now no doubt as to how the pearls had been deposited, but he had to prove his case, so far as he could.

" Did your visitor mention any particular paper? "

" Not that I recall, sir. Except he said it would be in the evening edition if he didn't stop it at once."

" That should narrow the field. Which day was this?"

Parsons reflected. " One moment, sir. It was a day I'd just had a letter from Sir Gerald asking me to pack him off a book he wanted. Mr. Sponge's *Sporting Tour* it was. He said, too, they were having a lot of rain. More than we were having, from all accounts."

" Have you got that letter? "

" Yes, sir. I always keep those letters, at any rate, for a time."

" Why? " asked Egerton, genuinely interested.

" Well, sir—you'll understand that I'm not speaking of Sir Gerald—but there's some gentlemen will tell you you didn't do what they asked.

" And you can produce the letter to show they're in the wrong? " Egerton's light brows lifted a little.

But not nearly so high as Parsons'. " Certainly not, sir. But it's a satisfaction to oneself to feel one wasn't in the wrong."

" I see." Egerton felt his irrepressible curiosity about

human beings lift its head. " Then you've got that letter? In the envelope? "

" Yes, sir." The man fetched it, and Egerton saw that it had been delivered on the 27th March, the day on which the murder was discovered. So that the murderer had lost no time in " planting " the pearls. He must have realised that, if anything came out, Hobart's rooms would certainly be searched.

" Very neat," murmured Egerton, handing back the letter. " Don't you think so yourself? "

Parsons looked utterly mortified. " I shan't ever forgive myself, sir. . . ."

" I should," said Egerton, clapping on his hat. " In fact, if you hadn't let the fellow in, I don't see what chance Mr. Hobart would have at all. It's all this over-caution that's the ruin of most enterprises. If the chap had been content to chance his arm—but no; he must salt the trail against some one else so thickly that even a dunderhead couldn't miss him. And I think—oh, I think he will find he has been too clever."

He took up his stick and went out.

2

Having a fair number of strings at his disposal, Egerton had little difficulty in ascertaining the telephone calls sent from the Jermyn Street establishment on the 27th March. As he suspected, none of these had anything to do with a newspaper. Nevertheless, being in his way as dogged as Field, he determined to obtain counter-proof of his contention. He went to the London office of each newspaper publishing an evening edition. His name was sufficiently well known for him to get an audience without delay; but, as he had expected, no rumour as to Hobart's death had ever reached England.

" Most stories that go through the office fetch up here," observed the editor of the *Morning Record*, taking up his house telephone and talking with incredible speed to a subordinate. After a moment or two he shook his head at Egerton.

" All my eye and Betty Martin," he observed. He tried to make Egerton talk of the police blunder in the Hobart case, but Egerton would only become expansive on the subject of the blunder in the *Record's* morning leader, and after a few minutes' pleasant vituperation he took himself off. The same answer was given him in each office. There were not, fortunately, many offices to try, since the number of evening papers had substantially decreased during the past ten or fifteen years. He pondered the position as he walked back.

" Of course, he didn't actually use the 'phone at all, only made use of it. He kept the hook down while he poured all that rubbish into the mouthpiece for Parsons's benefit; he must have wedged the hook or put the ear-piece down on the table for an instant while he did his sleight-of-hand with the pearls, but since he was alone in the room for the moment that wouldn't be difficult.

" And now," decided Egerton, turning in at Eaton Square, " Gordon can have his innings."

3

Gordon had already set to work, following another trail. He went to the bank where Charles had deposited his wife's inheritance and asked for the manager. A hint to the effect that he represented law and order, though not precisely as the clerk on the other side of the counter imagined, brought him a speedy interview, though Holt, the manager in question, was afraid he could not be of much assistance.

" We never had a great deal to do with Mrs. Hobart," he explained, " and nothing at all during the last two years or so. After her husband went abroad she remained where she was for about a year, and we sent her her allowance each quarter. We never heard much of her, but at the end of the year she came up to see me, and said that in future she would call for her money. She had an idea her letters were being tampered with, and she didn't want strangers to learn any of her business. As a matter of fact, I dare say the truth was that she didn't see why any

one should know she had the money at all. I offered to
have her letters sealed—there wouldn't be many of them—
but she wouldn't agree. I didn't much care about her
appearance, and I knew about the husband. I could do
nothing but fall in with her suggestions, and after that
for about two years she came up each quarter, drew her
cheque and disappeared again. I've sent for the books,
and I shall be able to tell you the exact dates. So far as I
remember she'd been calling for her money for two years,
as I say, when we got a letter from her, saying she'd be
glad to have the cheques sent in future care of Mrs. Browne
at an address in Maida Vale. This went on for about
another two years, and then she came up again and said
her address for the moment was uncertain and she'd either
call or send for the money as it fell due. As a matter of
fact, she did neither. The next letter we got, following on
the heels of her last instructions, was to say she wanted
to realise her capital. We got her about nineteen hundred
pounds, and I supposed naturally that she'd bank the
greater part of it. But if she did, it wasn't with us. She
came up and collected the money in cash, and drove off
in a cab. And that's the last I heard of her till there was
all this how-de-do in the papers."

During his explanation the various documents for which
he had sent had been brought by a messenger, and now
Holt drew up for his visitor's benefit a neat table showing
the exact dates of Fanny's instructions and counter-
instructions and her periodical changes of address.

"Did she come for the money herself?" asked Gordon.

"You bet she did."

"Alone?"

"That I don't know. I'll try and find out."

Fortunately a youngish clerk, called Jerningham, did
remember her coming in. It was unusual for a woman to
take so much money in cash in a receptacle so flimsy as an
ordinary attache case.

"Did you notice the case at all?"

"Yes. It was a pretty shabby one, largish, and it either
wasn't hers, or she'd been trading under a false name.

because she held the lid up while she stacked the notes inside, and I saw the initials. They were W. A. S. I suppose the fact that they made a word caught my attention. Anyway, I'd just been snubbed for suggesting that it was a bit dangerous to carry so much money about in a case any one might wrest out of her hands, and that made me think it would serve her jolly well right if she did have some accident. She struck me as being a bit nervous."

"And that was why she crushed you?"

"I couldn't say that. She looked a bit of a tartar to me. But she had a lot of trouble shutting that case, as if there was something faulty with one of the locks. She was all of a tremble."

"H'm. That needn't have been nervousness. That might have been, as you've suggested, because she was unfamiliar with the case; and the trembling might be due to suppressed rage; because few things make a man or woman look more foolish than trying to shut a case that won't shut. Can you remember anything more?"

"Yes. My desk is opposite the door, and that swings open most of the day, during banking hours, and in any case I can see through the glass panels. She went into a cab, and there was some one in that cab, waiting."

"Male or female?"

"I couldn't see. Didn't catch a glimpse. But as she stepped inside the door swung to. She had the case in one hand and she was holding on to the frame of the taxi with the other. If you're alone in a cab, you have to turn, if your hands are occupied, before you can shut the door, but hers were closed and the cab had moved off before she could have had time to sit down."

"I see. A pity you didn't catch a glimpse of her companion."

"I couldn't even see if it was a man or a woman," acknowledged Jerningham regretfully.

There was no doubt in Gordon's mind as to that point. Fanny was not the type to go about with a duenna.

The manager, who had listened with interest, here broke

in, " By the way, Mr. Gordon, there's one other point that may be significant. When she moved to Maida Vale, Mrs. Hobart asked to have her letters addressed to her as Miss Penny, care of Mrs. Browne. She said she was resuming her maiden name. The cheques were still made out to her as Mrs. Hobart. I explained there would be some alterations necessary if she wanted them payable to Penny; but she said that didn't matter. No one saw the cheques but herself. I suppose she didn't keep an account, just spent the money as she went along."

That, to Gordon, was the most important development he had had. It might, and eventually did, lead to astonishing results.

4

His first visit, on leaving the bank, was to Maida Vale. 9 Kings Avenue was the address Holt had given him, but when he knocked on the trim little green door, this was opened by a pleasant-looking woman in the middle thirties.

" Mrs. Browne? " hazarded Gordon.

She shook her head. "No. My Name's McNeil. Do you want the most original wallpapers in the country? No? But you may sometime. Are you married? Oh, well, if your wife saw these she'd fall for them at once. They're marvellous. I know what I'm talking about. I designed them."

Gordon drew back a step. " I'm so sorry to have disturbed you. I'm trying to find a Mrs. Browne who used to live here."

" Sure it was No. 9? There's a Bennett at 27 and a Brundon at 29. Might be either of those? "

" No. I'm afraid it's Browne I want, and the No. was 9. Do you mind telling me how long you have had this flat? "

" Nearly two years. Are you trying to trace some one who went off without paying bills? "

" Not exactly. I see. Thank you very much. By the way, I wonder if you could tell me the name of the agents? "

" Hurst and Winter. 44 High Street."

Gordon thanked her again and disappeared, smiling at her physical fitness and vitality. At Hurst and Winter he explained that he was a police officer attempting to trace a lady who had been a tenant of theirs some years earlier.

" When was this? "

" Well, I don't know the precise length of her tenancy, but she was here three years ago. The name was Browne."

The man turned up a huge book. " Browne? Well, yes, there was a Hubart Browne took a flat there some years ago. We let those flats on a yearly tenancy. This chap took his for two years but just before the end of the second year he said he didn't want it any more. Of course, he was responsible for the rent, but as this Miss McNeil was keen on a flat we gave her a new contract, and this Mr. Browne saved the last two months. As for the lady— well, she was only Mrs. Browne by courtesy, you understand. The man's real establishment is in Grosvenor Street—258."

" How large are the flats? "

" Just a couple of rooms and a kitchen. No one there keeps a servant. They pool a char. That's about the size of it."

" You don't know anything of Mr. Browne or the lady since then? He hasn't come looking for another flat? "

" Not he. Had his medicine, I should say. He was a big man, rather a nice-looking, easy-going chap, but my word, he was all in the day he came in here. I don't know whether his missis had tumbled to it and given him hell, or what it was, but it was as much as your life was worth to speak to him. Or, of course, this woman may have let him down." He spoke with the casual philosophy bred in him by life as he saw it. Gordon, who agreed with the last supposition, made no reply, but asked for a note as to the actual dates that Browne had leased the flat. Armed with these he looked up the man in the telephone book. It would be much pleasanter to see him at his office address, if he could find it. The telephone book assured him that the Paul Hubart Browne of 258 Grosvenor Street had offices at 199 Bishopsgate, and Gordon determined to try and make an appointment with him there. A clerk at the offices said Mr. Browne was busy, and Gordon said tranquilly that he would wait. He wrote on a slip of paper "Confidential inquiries" feeling certain that would disturb Browne sufficiently to grant him an interview. A few minutes later an inner door opened and a big, florid fair-haired man stood on the threshold. He stared at Gordon in unaffected surprise.

"What the deuce d'ye want with me?" he said.

Gordon stood up. "If you could spare me five minutes, sir, it's rather urgent."

Mr. Browne waved him into a very comfortable-furnished room and, without sitting down himself, repeated his question.

"I dare say you've seen all this inquiry in the paper as to the murder of Miss Florence Penny," said Gordon deliberately, deciding to strike first and strike hard. Browne's face changed; all the good nature went out of it. He looked angry and perturbed. Gordon knew what that fellow at Hurst and Winters had meant when he said silence was their game.

"May I ask what the devil that's got to do with me?"

"Nothing, I expect. But we're having a good deal of difficulty in getting details of her back history."

With a fierce movement Browne took a cigar from a box on the ledge of the bookcase and said, "Why d'you want it?"

"They've arrested a man."

"So I saw. Well, then I see still less why they want to go muck-raking."

"I'm employed by the defence. If this fellow's innocent, some other man is guilty. It's some one who knew her well. That's why we're trying to run to earth all the men who fit that bill."

"And you think I'm one of them?"

"We know you were one of them, which is why you may be able to give us some information."

There was a moment's silence. Then Browne said simply, "I like your cheek."

There was something so naïve, so unsubtle about the man that Gordon knew he would not be capable of prolonging an intricate deception.

" Shall I tell you how much we know? " he suggested. " And this, of course, won't go beyond these walls unless it's absolutely necessary. We know you kept her in a flat in Kings Mansions for eighteen months or more between two and three years ago. Then there was a break—and it's there that you may be able to help us. Why did you suddenly break with her? "

" Found her carrying on with some other fellow when she wasn't expecting me," said Browne, explosively. " Some damned slick-haired counter-jumping cad. Excused herself on the ground that she'd known him for years, and she'd tried to be loyal. Loyal your grandmother! She couldn't have spelt the word."

" I see. You don't happen to know his name? "

" I know his bloody first name, if that's any help to you. Walter. That's what she called him. ' I've always cared for Walter,' she snivelled."

" W. A. S.," thought Gordon. " Thanks very much. Yes, it does help. Was that the last time you saw her? "

" The very last. I told her she could clear out with her snivelling, oily, beetle-backed, flannel-footed oaf as soon as she pleased. I was going to put the flat in the agents' hands. I gave her something to clear out on, and that's all I heard of her. First time I tried that sort of game since I married, and, by God, it's the last. Once bitten . . ." Gordon believed him.

He murmured, as though to himself, " She'd been very attractive."

" Oh, she was, though the Lord knows why. It wasn't her looks. It was something; made you feel you were missing things. Like bein' tight, you know. A lovely feelin' to begin with, and then you start getting over it and wonder what you saw in it."

Gordon nodded again. " By the way, where did you meet her? "

" Oh, just picked her up. In a bus it was. Empty,

except for us, and she asked me something, if I knew some street or other, and we got talking. I asked her to come out to dinner; at a loose end myself—my wife was away with the children at her mother's, and I felt a bit bored at the thought of the chaps at the Club. Well, she talked a bit. Said she'd been badly let down by some chap who had gone abroad, and she'd lost her job on his account and didn't know where to get another. All the usual stuff only she put it over better than most of 'em. Well, there it was. She was attractive and I was a grass widower, *pro tem*. And taking a girl like that isn't like taking an inexperienced girl, friend of your wife's or anything of that sort. At first we just had dinner together and so on, and presently I wanted her, didn't like the thought of some other chap havin' her—y'know how it is, kind of drunk, as I said before, and I took this flat. They're cheap," he added with gloomy and vast cynicism. "Dessay most of the people there had some one else's name on all the cheques they cashed. It was all right the first year; she didn't make a lot of demands and she kept up that sort of exciting air. Then it began to wear off. I was gettin' sick of makin' excuses, and there was the chance of some one findin' out—my wife wouldn't ha' stood for it for a minute—decent women don't understand that kind of thing—and what with one thing and another—and she was gettin' too sure and makin' more demands, wantin' money and money was tight. And then, as I say, I found this chap, and that's all I know about her."

"Except that she's been murdered."

"It seems a thunderin' shame they're goin' to hang a good feller for that kind o' goods," remarked Browne, indignantly.

"He may not be a good chap."

"What? Oh, I was thinkin' of this Hobart chap. By the way, what a liar the girl was. Married all the time and pretending he had put her in the cart and left her there. I s'pose she thought if I knew there was a husband in the offing she wouldn't have had her flat. And she wouldn't."

Gordon, who found such egoism tedious, only said,

" Can you tell me what you were doing on the night of the 26th? For formality's sake, it's a question we're bound to ask . . ."

All Browne's complacency and philosophy slipped from him. " Good Lord, you don't mean to say you're going to bring me into this? Why, my wife would get to know, and the boys . . ."

" I've assured you we shall do nothing publicly that can be avoided. You've only got to produce an alibi for that night—I've no doubt you can. It was Wednesday, the 26th March."

Browne had a diary in his pocket, and this he now consulted. Then he showed Gordon the entry. " Seven forty-five. Dinner. Carter."

" I can give you the chap's address, if you want it," he went on aggressively. " He'd back me up."

" What time did you get away? "

" About three in the morning. Some absurd hour. Went to this new night club all the fellows are talking about. The Painted Butterfly. Damned rotten, if you ask me. And as for the champagne, I'll swear those bottles were born with red labels. It was Mrs. Carter's birthday and that was her idea of a good time."

Gordon noted Carter's name and address, and asked a final question. " Did you ever see this man, well enough to recollect him, that is? "

" Saw all I wanted to, thanks. A nasty slimy underbred oaf . . ."

" Would you know him again? "

" My Lord, no. Looked like all the rest of these emasculate pub-crawlers . . ."

" Did you notice if he was dark or fair? "

" Dark as a Dago."

" Dark-skinned? "

" Looked as if he washed—when he washed at all— in mutton-fat," was Browne's vicious retort. Not the sort of fellow you could rely on in the witness-box, reflected Gordon, with a sigh. But it was better for him that it should be like that. Otherwise he might be called up for identification, if this man " Walter " could be shown to have any connection with the crime. As a matter of fact, it seemed to Gordon increasingly probable that the man who had wrecked Charles's home was the same man as Fanny had allowed to make love to her at Kings Mansions, though as yet he had no notion how to trace the fellow. His first task now was to test Browne's story, and this proved easy. Realising that so soon as the office door had closed behind him Browne might well ring up Carter and get him to pledge his assistance, he himself entered a telephone booth and rang up 258 Grosvenor Street. Mrs. Browne was out, but was expected back shortly, so Gordon took a bus to Victoria and loitered in the neighbourhood until he saw a youngish, candid, gay-looking woman of about eight-and-thirty approach the gate of No. 258. He thought her precisely the type for a clumsy but well-meaning fellow like Browne.

Assuming the part of a bewildered and rather indignant foreigner, he stood at her side, before she could enter the house and receive a message from her husband, and embarked on a voluble and unveracious account of an appointment with Browne.

" But not here? " said Peggy Browne, in astonishment. " My husband doesn't make business appointments at his own house. He's probably expecting you at 199 Bishopsgate." And to herself she added, " This is too rich to be true. What does he want? A loan, or is he trying to levy blackmail? " For, contrary to her husband's convictions, she knew there had been a woman a few years back, and was equally sure that that trouble was over now and wouldn't prove recurrent.

The pseudo-Frenchman explained, gesticulating frantically. " At first, you understand, I was to see him on the 26th. And then he said—No. Impossible. Why was it impossible? " His indignant gaze raked hers.

" We had another engagement," said Mrs. Browne, convinced now that he was in earnest but quite cracked.

" Ah! " It was like letting off a squib. " Another engagement? I understand. It was that cochon—du

Boisson, n'est-ce-pas? He has—how do you say it?—led me by the nose—no? "

An enraptured parlourmaid, watching the scene from the dining-room, thought, Ain't she sly, her looking so devoted and all? Good thing the master ain't here. Well, that chap's getting a bit of his own back, if you ask me. And, hearing the housemaid outside, she called softly. " Here, Floss—I say, Flossie . . ."

Meanwhile, shaking with laughter, Peggy Browne disillusioned her fiery litle companion.

" No, no, no," she said emphatically. " He was out at a dinner-party with me that night. Yes, all the evening, until three the next day. He couldn't make appointments for three in the morning."

The stranger, calming down, agreed that he couldn't. And, having made an agreeable spectacle of himself to women and passers-by, disappeared. By telephone, he verified the name of the club whence they had repaired after dinner; and here an official agreed that Mr. Carter had brought a party with him that evening, booking a table by 'phone. One of the men corresponded to Browne's description, and the observant manager added that he had a wife, slim, tall, dark, with a vivacious manner.

" So that settles Browne," decided Gordon. " Now for the next item on the programme."

CHAPTER IX

1

GORDON spent the evening reviewing his facts; with a pencil and note-book he went through all the information he had been able to gather, and upon re-reading it was struck by an important fact. Both Charles and Browne, speaking of X, the intruder, had declared that Fanny had excused her conduct on the ground that she had known the man before. Assuming, as he must for the sake of argument, while he was still working so much in the dark, that this man could help them in their search, if he didn't prove actually to be the criminal, then it was obvious that she had met the man either at her father's shop or before that, when she was working away from home. So that the next step was to get into touch with her relations and work backwards.

He went first of all to Sally Welling, realising that he would learn from her what her husband either would not or could not divulge. Mrs. Welling was a broadfaced, strongly featured woman who just escaped being handsome on account of an expression of permanent sullenness that spoilt the regularity of her features. At his first mention of her sister's name, it was clear that she had neither forgotten nor forgiven Fanny for the spell she had exercised over Arthur Welling. She greeted Gordon's questions with undisguised hostility.

" The more folks talk about it, the worse it is for the rest of us," she protested.

" And if we don't talk about it at all, think of what it means for Mr. Hobart."

But her bitterness prevented her from being just to that unhappy creature.

" I don't feel a bit sorry for him," she said fiercely. " And even if he didn't kill her himself, he left her on her own when any decent husband would have been looking after her, so he's as good as guilty. You can kill a baby by not feeding it, just like smothering it," an analogy that did not seem to Gordon particularly adequate. " And," she added hastily, before he could speak, " I don't doubt myself that it was him. Oh, she gave him cause, I dare say, but that's his fault. He didn't have to take her off to Brighton like he did. And if he had, then he shouldn't have gone leaving her about while he went away and pretended not to be married. It isn't fair to other women, a girl like that. Why, she was always a little slut, if I am her sister that says it, carrying on with the boys even when she was at school."

Gordon tried to find out if there had been some other man besides Charles at that time, who would square with the knowledge he had concerning the mysterious W.A.S., but Mrs. Welling thought he was probing after her husband and refused to help him. She would not even give him the name of the distant relative for whom Fanny had worked, until he remarked that he would get the information from her husband. Then she sulkily gave way.

" It was a Mrs. Ticehurst, a sort of cousin of mother's," she acknowledged. " Not that she'll be over-pleased to see you. Fanny treated them rotten bad, and I don't suppose Milly's forgotten it yet. They say she won't let any one so much as mention her name."

Gordon obtained the address, and found that a motor bus service connected Cambridge with Burton St. Lawrence at leisurely intervals. The distance was about twenty miles and it took an hour and a half to reach its destination. Even so it was less easy than Gordon had expected to get information. The landlady of the inn where he booked a room had only been there for two years; she remembered hearing about Fanny at the time of her death, but had not been interested. She said simply that she had no use for women like that, and thought it a pity to make a fuss about them. The inner drama of the affair, the correlation of worthless life with others less ignoble, the way in which her influence had spread like ripples on a pool until she united such dissimilar men as Browne and Charles Hobart, all this was lost upon her.

At three o'clock Gordon set out for " Balmoral," where he found Mrs. Ticehurst and an elderly companion-help with a grim face on which life had marked deep ruts and hollows. The companion opened the door, looked at him without sympathy and said she would ask her employer. Gordon waited in a neat, refined, desperately uncomfortable sitting-room with glass tulips stuck in a bowl of sawdust, and detachable cushions of pale striped velvet laid at impossible angles on the arms of two chairs and a chester-field.

It was the kind of room to cast a chill on the most ardent spirits, and by the time Mrs. Ticehurst appeared Gordon felt depressed and convinced of the futility of his errand. She was a big heavily-built woman, suspicious but intrigued. She had a pale unsmiling face and a flabby hand. In her mind were several guesses as to his identity; the man to speak about the new gas stove, the leaking gutter, someone from the chapel, the representative of an insurance company or someone collecting subscriptions. She had not for a moment connected him with Fanny, and at the bare mention of that name her demeanour froze.

"I am not disposed to discuss her," she repeated to everything Gordon could say.

But he was as inflexible as she. "It's most important for us to be in possession of all possible facts before the trial opens," he told her. "I understand that Mrs. Hobart worked for you for some time before her marriage."

"Three years," acknowledged his companion.

"And then you dismissed her?"

Mrs. Ticehurst folded her hands over a solid phalanx of stomach. "I have nothing more to say."

"Why did you send her away?"

"I thought it would be a good thing for her to go back. Girls get a little above themselves."

But in her voice was something more than mere contempt or boredom; it was shaken by an inward anger so great that it almost eluded her control. Something desperate had happened at that house before Fanny returned to Cambridge, and somehow he had to discover what it was.

"She was getting herself talked about in the neighbourhood, perhaps?" he suggested.

"I dare say. She was a showy sort of girl. Some people's choice, no doubt, though I've always thought anything that happened to her was her own fault."

"A bit careless?"

The old woman's face was bitter with loathing. "Careless you call it, do you? Well, that isn't quite the name I'd have given to it. A thief, that's what she was. Couldn't leave men alone. She nearly spoilt her sister's life, as she's spoilt the lives of heaps of men since. She was bad all through, and I knew it. I blame myself for letting her stay, but I couldn't see how it would be."

Nothing he could urge, however, would persuade the

old lady to tell him the story. In the hall he turned to the companion. " I fancy you could tell me a good deal, if you liked," he remarked keenly.

Terror sprang to her eyes. " No, no—I couldn't really. I'm in Mrs. Ticehurst's confidence. You must see I couldn't."

" Because you're afraid she might be angry? "

" She would send me away. And I shouldn't get another post very likely. And I haven't saved. I never could. It's quite impossible."

· " Have you forgotten Charles Hobart? "

She shook her head and clasped her short wrinkled hands.

" No, I haven't. I can't. That's what makes it so dreadful. Because if he didn't do it . . ."

" Don't you think he should have the benefit of the doubt? "

" Yes. But I can't see how, telling you something that happened here so long ago, that naturally Mrs. Ticehurst would rather forget, can help now."

" I think it might. In any case, we've no right to leave any stone unturned. Were you here at the time of the trouble? "

" I'd just come. You see, Miss Ticehurst was expecting to be married, and Mrs. Ticehurst would want some one . . . and it was arranged that I should be here for a month before the wedding to get into Mrs. Ticehurst's ways."

Gordon began to see his way more clearly; but he saw, too, the impossibility of hearing the story on Mrs. Ticehurst's doorstep. So he asked, " Do you ever get off, for half a day or anything? "

" As a matter of fact, it's my half-day to-morrow."

" Then take the bus that passes the door to Dunning Point, and I'll meet you there, and we can talk things over at our leisure." He gave her no time to refuse, but left her trembling in the hall, a little with fear but chiefly with an awful suppressed joy at the prospect of being for a few minutes the central figure of what she thought of as a dramatic scene.

128

When Mrs. Ticehurst asked her what Gordon had asked and what she had replied, she said that she hadn't told him anything. Yes, he had asked a lot of questions, but they had remained unanswered. The very course of the deception, she found, added to its perilous delight.

2

"As I've said, I was only at Balmoral for the month before it all happened," explained Miss Riley in a soft agitated voice. "Miss Ticehurst was expecting to leave home, and I was getting into her mother's way of doing things. Well, of course, I couldn't help noticing Fanny. She wasn't so pretty but she had a kind of bold air, and she used to laugh a lot, which no one else did. Though I must say her manner towards Mrs. Ticehurst wasn't quite suitable for a girl of her age. And Mrs. Ticehurst, too, if I may say so, wasn't so wise as I should have expected. She seemed to forget how young Fanny was; one learns wisdom as one goes on. You know that it's a wonderful thing to have a home behind you, to be sure of that, but when you're the age she was then you only look forward. And that was what she did. She didn't expect to have to swallow anything they might say in return for being fed and housed and given a little money. And they used to let everyone know she was a poor relation they were helping, and often, especially towards the end, they talked to her as if she wasn't a relation at all, but just a servant girl. She used to answer back, and more than once there was some talk of her leaving them. I know Mrs. Ticehurst used to get very upset about her. There had been trouble, I gathered, about a man called Burgess who used to deliver the milk at one time. Fanny used to—to flirt with him, I think, and Mrs. Ticehurst was afraid of people talking. But that was some time before Miss Ticehurst, Marigold was her name, was engaged to be married. Of course, people talked; said he only wanted her money. He was younger than she, rather a nice-looking man, a little foreign-looking, dark hair and a little dark moustache. He smiled very nicely and made a good deal of fuss over Marigold, but you could see his heart wasn't really in it. I only talked to him once, and then he asked me if the Ticehurst's always treated Fanny like that. He meant shutting her out from the family circle, if you know what I mean, and he said what a shame it was. I'm afraid from the beginning I foresaw trouble, but oh! I did hope that they would be safely married, and then, of course, they would have been all right. I tried once giving Fanny some advice. I'd seen her in the garden, you see, with this man, and it didn't seem right when he was going to marry Marigold that he should be kissing her like that. And her face when she came in—all laughing and rosy and happy. And then I felt it was a shame she should have to work like that when she looked really pretty and ought to have some fun. She wasn't a bit like her relations, and they thought she should be. Always on to her to be joining some Bible Class or going to some service. Mrs. Ticehurst and her daughter did a lot of that kind of thing, but they seemed to take it naturally. And Fanny didn't. If you'd seen her then, you would know what I mean. You couldn't imagine her in a Sunday School. I must say, even when I was most afraid, I couldn't help liking her in a way. She seemed so merry and—well, cheeky, is the only word I can think of, but it seemed to make her attractive. I thought how dull and plain I had been at her age. I did rather like her, in spite of everything. And then it all came out, how she was meeting this man on the sly, and—well, I don't quite know what had happened, but Fanny was sent away in disgrace at once. I'm afraid she really had done something rather dreadful, and of course, Marigold broke off her engagement. She was absolutely furious for some time, wouldn't see Mr. Sharpe . . ."

" Sharpe? Do you know his christian name? "

" Walter. Walter Sharpe. He travelled in motor accessories, I think. He was very keen indeed on motors, always talked of what he would do when he got the chance. People said that he was marrying Miss Ticehurst because she was his chance. But after Fanny left the worst storm of all broke. It turned out that Mrs. Ticehurst had been trusting him with some of her money affairs, and he had embezzled some of the money. Of course, they took it for granted he had wanted it for Fanny, and he may have done. He didn't bring Marigold anything very showy when he came, just a handful of flowers, and not roses or carnations at that; and perhaps a few chocolates. But he bought Fanny lovely things. I caught her gloating over a silk shawl once; it was beautiful. Though I can't think when she'd wear a thing like that. Of course, they must both have been perfectly mad to dream of such a thing."

" There was no talk of their marrying? "

" Oh, no. Well, they couldn't, could they? I mean, there was all this trouble about the money and Mrs. Ticehurst called in the police, and in the end Mr. Sharpe got two years' imprisonment."

" And was that the last you heard of him? "

" Oh, yes. Miss Ticehurst went away; she said she wouldn't be the laughing-stock of the place. She wanted her mother to move, too, but Mrs. Ticehurst said she had been here too long, and collected too many things round her. And anyway she wasn't going to have it said that she had been driven out of her house by a slut of a servant girl."

" And Fanny went home, and you've never heard any more since then? "

" Not till just lately. Oh, there was a terrible scene when Marigold accused her of being a common thief, and Fanny said that at any rate she never took anything without paying for it, and Marigold said that everyone knew the way she paid for things, and really I thought they would fly at one another's throats. As a matter of fact," she hesitated a moment, then went on courageously, " I did hear afterwards that this man wasn't any too good a lot. They said he used to get women to lend him money and promise them handsome interest, and of course, they never saw their money again. But that's only what people say. I haven't heard anything of him since then."

3

After hearing Miss Riley's story Gordon had a sudden rush of hope that he might learn more of Sharpe from Scotland Yard. They would certainly have his record there, and there might be a history of later convictions. However, it proved that the two years to which he had been sentenced for embezzlement of Mrs. Ticehurst's funds was his sole offence, so far as authority knew. Gordon delved into the records and read the brief account of the man's appearance before a magistrate, and his sentence by Mr. Justice Warner. Then it occurred to him that the prison officials might know something of him. He was informed, however, that Sharpe had been a model prisoner, had obtained full remission marks, and had not been heard of since his discharge. The Prisoners' Aid Society could not help, and Gordon applied to the chaplain in the faint hope that he might remember Sharpe. He must have been a plausible beggar from all accounts, wheedling money out of women for a livelihood, as he seemed to have done.

The Rev. A. W. Clary, however, proved another disappointment. He was a very tall spindly man of about five-and-forty. His eyes twinkled as Gordon explained the position.

" My dear sir, what d'ye take me for? A miracle-worker? I don't believe in these perfect convicts. If they're so perfect what are they doing in prison at all? Besides, it's healthy to grouse, like perspiring. Gets the damage out of your system. And did he grouse? He did not. He'd done wrong, he knew it, he regretted it deeply, but he'd learned something in prison he'd never learned outside it. You couldn't call it all a dead loss. My dear fellow," he laid a hand on Gordon's arm, " do you know what I wanted to do with that man? Follow him all round the grounds with a toasting-fork—with five prongs. Yes, five prongs. Keep up with him afterwards? Of course I didn't. I tell you what I did do, though. Wrote to the D.P.A. and warned 'em against him. I should think Satan must have looked rather like that chap when he came smarming up to Eve, poor lady, with the apple in his jaws."

" You told them not to help him? "

" Of course I did. Not that he'd be likely to apply. They'd have suggested something too much like hard work. Would you have me send him to them with a letter of recommendation? Of course you would. Because it would help you to trace him, not because you're concerned with any ethical point. And you're quite right, quite right." He clapped the astonished detective on the shoulder " I like a man to be keen on his job. It ought to come first, beyond any other consideration. But what about my point of view? Send him round there and say ' Here's a penitent man ' and then he takes the watch out of the secretary's pocket, and all your intelligent people hold up their hands and cry: ' Lord, what mugs these clergy be? How long, O Lord, how long shall we put up with 'em trying to teach us our business? ' No, I don't expect to see the gentleman again unless and until he returns here professionally. Good-afternoon. Not at all. Pleasure is entirely mine, I assure you."

The chief thing that Gordon had gleaned from this wearisome process of investigation was a photograph of Sharpe. He was certainly a handsome fellow, and if his tongue were as glib as his features were plausible there seemed no reason why he shouldn't continue to live on credulous old ladies. Gordon felt a moment of ruthless loathing for him. Rotten to the core, without a redeeming spark, according to all accounts. It would delight him to be able to nail him down for this particular crime.

4

It was not particularly easy to follow up the trail. Gordon obtained the name of a one-time employer, after a good deal of investigation, and went to see this man, a certain Marcus George, a motor accessories salesman. George proved to be a short swart man of uncompromising speech and aspect.

" Sharpe? " he said. " Yes, I remember the man. Up to no good. It wasn't that he wasn't keen. He was too keen in the wrong way. He never thought of anything but what he could make out of things. No *Esprit de corps* at all. And I wasn't sure he was honest. He had left my employ about a year before there was all this trouble."

" He never wrote to you after he left prison? "

" Well, he did. But I shouldn't dream of giving a chap like that another chance. He didn't pull his weight, and that's unpardonable."

" Have you the letter by any chance? It would be of great assistance to know his address at that time. We might be able to follow him up."

George produced a sheet of cheap white writing-paper, stamped with an address in Putney. Gordon asked if he might keep the letter for the purpose of having it more closely examined. An expert might even be able to tell whether the man who wrote that had also written the note found on Fanny's table.

A visit to Putney merely told Gordon that Sharpe had only stayed there a few weeks, and had moved on without leaving an address. The landlady, who had taken over the good-will of the establishment during the past eighteen months, knew nothing of him, but obligingly offered to ask Miss Larkin, who had been there most of her life, the woman added, " and God knows that's long enough."

Miss Larkin was a small resolute woman with an outstanding chin and an invincible determination to be different from the rest of the world and always to be in the right. The chin rose an inch when she heard Gordon's business.

" Certainly, I remember Mr. Sharpe. A most pleasant young man who had had great trouble."

" Did he say what sort of trouble? "

" A woman. His wife, he said. One of those women that go gadding about and never in when a man comes back tired from work. Always out for money. Money, money, money. Couldn't be happy in the sort of home he had made for her, but wanted clothes he couldn't buy her. He'd got into trouble on her account, he said."

Gordon lifted his expressive brows. He hadn't expected Sharpe's candour to reach this pitch.

" He told you that? "

" Yes. And that no one would employ him because of it. He had heard from his old firm that morning, giving him the cold shoulder. Of course, his wife wouldn't have anything to do with him. So that was why he wanted to start in business on his own account. No need for references, you see."

Gordon thought, " Well, the fellow was a crook all right, and nothing would surprise me less than to hear he was blackmailing this girl, but he had some sense of character." It had been a bold move to acknowledge his misfortune, but nothing less would have stirred the indignation and aroused the championship of this obstinate downright woman. He could fill in the rest of the story for himself, though for form's sake he asked, " And you helped him, perhaps? "

" Yes. I was proud to help him."

" With money? "

The small arrogant figure stiffened. " Is that anyone else's concern? "

" I'm afraid it is."

She said scornfully, " I suppose you're another of them, hounding him to perdition. Have you no human feeling? Hasn't he suffered enough? "

Gordon remembered the innumerable criminals who by the gentleness of their pleading and the dignity of their bearing have aroused in cultured and reasonable people a deep sense of compassion and an eagerness to assist. Sharpe had read this indomitable little creature easily enough, though she would be horrified to learn how well he had played her.

" Have you been in touch with him lately? " he asked.

" I haven't heard from him, but as soon as he starts making profits he's going to repay me."

" Do you know the nature of the business? "

" Something to do with motors. But businesses aren't built up in a day. They take a lot of foresight and patience and faith. 'He warned me of that. No one could have been more honourable. He said I might have to wait, and he wouldn't take a penny until I assured him I didn't need the money, and it would simply be lying idle at my bank. After that, of course, he agreed to take it because as soon as he starts making profits I shall be getting excellent dividends, and of course, the bank rate is shamefully low."

" But he hasn't repaid anything yet?   It's four years ago."

" You don't understand," she repeated. " You have to work up a—a clientèle. I know that. I'm a dressmaker myself. And the patience it takes, and the bad debts and losses of one kind and another, through ladies that say they'd like a V-shape and next time they come pretend they said square, and there's the material all cut and spoilt and no-one else taking it because it's not their colour. . ."

He wondered if the flame of hope burned as brightly in her heart as she would have him believe. Probably Sharpe's path was dotted with Miss Larkins and their savings that they'd never see again.   But no amount of investigation got him a single step farther on and two days later, after following up a barren clue, he returned to London to report to Egerton.

CHAPTER X

1

" I'm afraid we're in a cul-de-sac now," acknowledged Gordon, frowning, as he finished his story.

Up went Egerton's fair eyebrows. " Even a cul-de-sac has two ends," he reminded his companion. " One may well be a blank wall, though I'm not even sure of that in this case, but the other always opens into a street.   It has to."

Gordon seemed perplexed. " I don't quite get you. I've had inquiries made wherever it seemed possible to learn anything. The only other point that occurs to me is to circularise the petrol-filling stations in the country on the chance that he's still in charge of one. .That wouldn't merely be a long job, it would be definitely dangerous. It would mean putting our friend on his guard, without our learning much. For if he was a principal he wouldn't answer anyway. And we can't very well go round in person asking for him."

" And we haven't actually any proof that he ever was in charge of a filling station, beyond what he told Miss Larkin, and possibly Miss Ticehurst. In both cases there's very little to go on. And it's five years ago, and since then he's had the opportunity of running through Charles Hobart's money. He may be still interested in motors, but we haven't a shadow of proof for any of our assumptions."

" And how the deuce we're going to link up the fellow after five years of complete blank," murmured Gordon, and fell silent without finishing his sentence.

When he looked up he found Egerton's gaze fixed full upon him. The young man was smiling, but Gordon imagined a faint gleam of contempt in the ironical curve of the lips.

" Aren't you forgetting the other end of the cul-de-sac? " he asked. " There's going to be a good deal of significance in cul-de-sacs in this case, if I'm not wrong."

" I don't understand you."

" What was that taxi doing in the cul-de-sac that night? " Egerton asked. " You, of course, have considered the affair in all its aspects. And so, no doubt, like myself, you've been struck by the presence, practically on the scene of the crime, of what appears to be a useless feature. I don't much believe in these useless details, and I certainly don't believe in discarding them until you're convinced they play no part in the scheme. And here I think it is useful to remember that everyone speaks of Sharpe's passion for cars and motor accessories."

Gordon looked incredulous. " Are you serious about the taxi? Why, the fellow wasn't even sure it was a taxi; admitted it might have been a private car."

" He was sure it was a taxi till he was questioned so often he might have mistaken his own name. I don't believe that a man who drives a taxi for a livelihood could mistake one for a car, any more than, if you're accustomed to drive one car, you can go off by accident in another, even though they may appear identical."

"Why shouldn't it have been there for some reason completely divorced from the murder? " Gordon inquired.

"No reason at all, but by the same token it wasn't there without a reason. And no one can discover what that reason was. It wasn't hired by any one in the corner house; no one had a visitor who came by taxi; and, in addition, all the lights were out. I made a point of walking down Menzies Street at eleven o'clock last night; it was a fine clear night, clearer probably than the night of the murder. I put my car in the cul-de-sac, turned off the lights and walked up the road. As I came past it was no more than a shadow. The house on the opposite corner is tall and throws a deep shade over the road, and you might quite well pass that corner without realising the existence of a car. I should say the taxi-driver who brought Charles back to Menzies Street only saw the taxi because of his own lights. Now, we'll dispose of this mysterious taxi if we can. It would hardly be put in a cul-de-sac if it had been brought to the road by a visitor for some house on the other side; in fact, I find it almost impossible to believe that any man coming to Menzies Street wouldn't dismiss a taxi as soon as he arrived there. You can always pick them up in the main road and in these days of press publicity even a fool knows the tremendous value of blackmail. No, the taxi was where it was because it had been left there by its driver, and the lights were out because he hoped it wouldn't be seen. He may have been in Menzies Street for private business, but a man who has to get a living with a taxi doesn't generally go to that part of the world for that type of relaxation. I think our next point is to discover whether Sharpe is known, either in his own name or some other, by any rank or private garage."

"Which sounds easier than it is. As you observe, he may well have changed his name; he could easily change his appearance and his handwriting."

"But there are certain things he can't change. Fingerprints, for example."

" And we are to get the finger-prints of all the taxi-drivers in England? "

" No, I hardly think that will be necessary. To begin with, we may fairly assume he was the driver of a London taxi. There's the chance that he owns his own vehicle; if so we shall take a little longer to find him; that's all. There's the even remoter chance that a private person may have hired a taxi to drive himself on that night, but I think we may practically put that out of court. It would be so much less conspicuous to hire a car."

" Of course, he may have invested Hobart's money wisely and be running his own garage," speculated Gordon. " Then he could go out in any of his own taxis and no one would be any the wiser."

" That's perfectly true, and a point we must take into consideration. Fortunately we have plenty of time. You'll need some help but I take it you can provide yourself with that? Good. We ought to set the ball rolling without delay."

They settled down to draw up a scheme for circularising every garage proprietor with a description of the wanted man and his photograph. As they were making a police matter of it, it was probable that they would get replies in most cases, and where they only met with an obstinate silence they must go down in person and emphasise the importance of receiving an answer.

" Or it might be better to go round in person and insist on seeing the managers," suggested Gordon. " If this man, Sharpe, is one of them, we should be giving him an excellent opportunity to give us the slip. As it is, he may be going about disguised since the time of the murder."

" I doubt it," said Egerton, judiciously. " He's no fool, believe me. And that's the surest way to call attention to yourself. I know there are a number of people going round London (and elsewhere) saying ' No one knows me,' but that isn't true. You may know no one else, though that's most improbable, but people do know you. The woman who keeps your house, the neighbour who's keen to find out what your husband really died of, or even if he really existed, tradespeople, lodgers in the same house, perhaps the postman and more than one policeman on the beat. And if X changes his appearance suddenly, those people start putting two and two together. They say 'X hasn't been here for some days' and start asking questions. Then the news goes round, 'X is gone, but Y has come,' and presently some intelligent busybody says, 'It's odd, if you come to think of it (which, of course, no one has done hitherto) Y arrived at the precise moment that X disappeared,' and other people start discovering similarities that X himself doesn't dream of. A manner of walking, of moving the body or twisting the fingers. It's practically impossible for a man to adopt a new identity in a place where he's known. And if he disappears suddenly people draw the obvious conclusion. No, I'm not afraid of his vanishing. Only in a city of teeming millions, as the press hath it, it's easy for him to be overlooked."

"And, I suppose, when none of the managers prove to be the man or know the man—yes, we'll certainly go round in person, and then when the manager obviously isn't our quarry we can produce Sharpe's picture and pursue inquiries on the spot—then I suppose we start hunting up the individual owners of taxis. After all, every taxi driver must be licensed, so eventually we shall track the last one down. By the way," he grinned at Egerton, "the trial is supposed to be taking place this summer, isn't it?"

"They'll postpone it if we can show that we're raking in further evidence," was Egerton's imperturbable reply.

"And supposing—just for the sake of argument—that when we have done all that, we still find we haven't nailed our man?"

"Then I think we may assume the taxi didn't play any part in the murder; when we've tried all the garages and all the private owners and examined each man under the microscope to discover if he hired out his taxi that evening, we may safely assume we're on the wrong track. But not till then. After all, elimination is the first law in detective work."

2

Gordon set his men to work the next morning, and that night examined his harvest. It might have pleased Egerton, since it definitely put out of court all the men hitherto interviewed. Wherever there was a shadow of doubt a ruse was employed to obtain the suspect's finger-prints and a specimen of his handwriting, a simple enough thing to do, since the discovery that iodine vapour will bring up finger-prints on paper. Gordon bought the services of a man called Anstey, author, as some readers may recall, of a famous treatise on finger-prints, particularly well received in France and Germany, to examine all dubious imprints. Without him, the long tedious work of examination and cross-questioning would be useless, for the most sensitive amateur could frequently detect no difference between two similar points.

" It's deuced interesting," said Gordon, carried away by the scientific excitement of the process, and examining through a powerful microscope a number of impressions that had seemed to him identical, " eight hundred and eighty ridges on the ball of the thumb, or eight hundred and eighty-six seem all the same to me."

Anstey stood up, yawning a little. He had had a tiring day. " There are far more wonderful things than that," he observed. " Do you know how many teeth a snail has? Over fourteen thousand."

Gordon secretly confirmed that in an encyclopædia before he went to bed. When he found Anstey was right, he murmured, " Great snakes, what a life! " and lost a little of his interest in Fanny.

The second day was a repetition of the first; more impressions were brought in, since Sharpe was a not uncommon type, and it was not possible to say whether or no he was clean-shaved. Parsons had spoken of the pseudo-journalist as wearing a small black moustache, but that might have been assumed for the occasion. Gordon asked if there was any possibility of two identical prints being received, and Anstey said in his dry voice that the chances were one in sixty-four thousand million, adding that prints did not change with the years, but that the print of the baby merely increased in size with its growth, without changing in any other way.

It took five days to get through the garage proprietors, with every man Gordon could spare working on the job; and the results were negative.

"Not at all," corrected Egerton. "Think of the enormous number of possibles who are now impossibles."

They had inquired about the licence and had been furnished with a list of men named Sharpe licensed to drive cabs. All these had been run to earth and interviewed on one pretext or another, and none proved to be the missing man. However, they had been prepared to learn that he had changed his name, since his prison record would doubtless be against him. Egerton still held to his theory that they would find him as his own master; he had been obviously in desperate need of funds, since he had pressed Fanny so hard, and that argued private ownership, assuming that he needed the money for business purposes. Gordon thought Egerton took a good deal for granted, but neither hints nor downright incredulity made the slightest impression on the young man. What faced them now was enough to deject the most optimistic. Every private taxi-owner had to be traced and seen. For some days the search continued without result. And then Gordon himself ran their quarry to earth.

Early one morning he called at an address in the Mews off Lillie Road, Fulham. This mews overlooked a double row of private garages while the houses themselves faced the narrow street. The man himself was out when Gordon called; the slovenly woman who answered the door said that Mr. Blount had a job on with the cab. He only had one cab and employed no help. Not, she added, that he was in a position to pay more wages, since she had the devil of a drive to collect her own. In fact, she said she only came because she was so sorry for a man that would let a house go to rack and ruin sooner than lift a finger to keep it straight.

" And you're here every day? "

" Jest for an hour or two. That's all. I got other jobs."

" Do you have your own key or does Mr. Blount let you in? "

" Lets me in if 'e's 'ere, and if not leaves the key under the mat."

Gordon asked if he might come in and wait, without any idea that his tedious search was practically at an end. He was shown into a small sitting-room, furnished on the hire-purchase system, the labels of the warehouse still clinging affectionately to the legs of the chairs and the arms of the bamboo what-not. The place looked unkempt and unlived-in; dust on the mantelpiece, the clock was twenty minutes slow, and propped against it were a number of envelopes, mostly with halfpenny stamps on them. Old circulars lay about everywhere; the orange envelope of an ancient tele-gram was thrust among other equally old correspondence in a fake brass letter-rack on the table; the waste-paper-basket needed emptying, and the ashes of a three-days cigarette lay in an ornate tray on one of the chairs. Gordon thought that if this fellow was remiss about wages, the woman couldn't earn many. He walked round the room, staring down into the narrow cobbled mews and thinking how intolerable noisy it must be when the cars were being brought in and out.

The woman was moving about overhead, clattering china and slapping wet cloths over the floor. It was nearly an hour before Blount returned, and at the sight of him Gordon's heart lifted once again. He mightn't be the man, probably he wasn't the man, but there was a chance. He was of average height, dark-haired, clean-shaved, rather blue about the jaw; a good-looking man in a rather common way, with brown eyes set too shallowly under the thick brows; and he was running a little too fat, though insufficiently as yet to be disfiguring. His voice was pleasant as he greeted his visitor, and apologised for the delay. Gordon followed up his normal procedure and treated the conversation as a business interview. He repre-sented a Miss Curteis, he said, who was anxious to hire a cab to drive her to Waterloo on the following Thursday. She wanted an estimate and an assurance that the cab was safe. She suffered from nerves, Gordon explained.

"Oh, quite," agreed Blount. "I know them." He considered for a moment. "What time would you want it? "

"Pretty early, I'm afraid. About half-past eight in the morning. She has to catch the 9.7 to Frickham."

"What's the address? "

"Monkswood Hotel. You know it, of course, the big hotel at the end of the road. She's afraid an ordinary taxi may be reckless."

"That'll be all right," said Blount, and named his price. Gordon said in his turn that that would be all right, and asked for the figure in writing.

"A regular nerve case," smiled Blount, scribbling on a slip of paper. And then Gordon asked if he might see the cab. He had to assure Miss Curteis that it was perfectly comfortable.

"She once ordered one by telephone, I believe," he explained, "and got a ramshackle affair that nearly sent her through the roof in the first mile."

Blount had just put his car round the corner of the garages, without actually unlocking the door. He invited Gordon to come and see her, and Gordon's heart went down to his boots again. The car was the colour of a Jaffa orange, and he remembered the driver saying that " it was just an ordinary taxi "and certainly not an orange one. You could have sighted this one all down the street.

Blount had opened the door and was thumping the cushions. "I think the lady will find this comfortable enough," he said. " I've only just bought it."

"When? " asked Gordon mechanically.

"About a month ago; I had an accident with the other, and a smart appearance counts for a good deal in private work. Ladies like to think the car they hire is their own, and for some reason these orange ones do specially well. Something new, if you ask me, that's all."

"Do you do well? " Gordon asked conversationally,

having agreed to hire the taxi for the following Thursday.

Blount laughed. "Like that fish you always get at the seaside boarding-houses, with its tail in its mouth—just make two ends meet. But I'd hate some of my fares to see my shirts."

Odd, reflected Gordon, walking back to the tram-lines, that a man who could buy a new taxi couldn't buy shirts or pay his charwoman regularly. Or rather, odd that a man who couldn't do these things, could buy a taxi. Besides, there had been all those unpaid bills on the mantelpiece, and Blount's tacit admission of his financial straits. There was his own explanation of the accident and Gordon could do little until he knew more about that. He would have to move warily. His first step was to book a room at the Monkswood Hotel in the name of Miss Curteis, in case Blount rang up on any excuse and discovered he was being tricked. After some consideration, he thought his best plan would be to circularise the taxi-cab agencies; no doubt Blount had given the worn-out car as part payment for the new one. It was the usual procedure.

The taxi had clearly been a new one, not a good second-hand imitation, so that Gordon could narrow the field of his inquiries to such firms and agencies as sold new taxi-cabs. While he was waiting for his answer he got Anstey's assurance that Blount and Sharpe were one and the same man. He called to see Egerton on the strength of this information, and the two made an appointment to see Arbuthnot the following day.

"Now we have to connect this fellow, Sharpe—let's decide to call him by his own name; it will avoid complications—with the affair at all. We're at a disadvantage in this; if we were the police we could question him openly, but being merely private people we shall have to go very canny. We don't want to put him on his guard."

"And we don't want to find ourselves in a libel action," contributed Egerton. "We shouldn't, at the present time, have a leg to stand on."

"As things stand at present we can't even begin to ask him where he was on the night of the 26th," added Gordon,

Welling grumbled that it was Sunday.

"I know. But we have to get on with our job whatever the day of the week. What are the etchings like?"

"Oh, just what you'd expect. The church and the pump and cows in a field. As if the folk living here want to buy pictures of what they can see for nothing any day of the week."

"Does no one buy them?"

"We've sold a few of the smaller ones," Welling acknowledged, "but not to the people here. But folk passing through. We're a sort of exhibit, we are." His smile was bitter. "It's the church that does it. Regular museum that is. And there's a house here dates from 1600; supposed to have one of the oldest stained-glass windows in the country. That's older than the house by a long chalk; taken out by its owner and buried for God knows how many years, and then dug up again. One bit of coloured glass looks the same as another to me, but there's folks with so much money, in a country where there's thousands starving or living on the edge of it, to pay to see a bit of glass like that."

"You say you have some etchings, but you don't know the man who did them. Did you buy them outright, then? If not, what about the artist's commission?"

"I didn't buy them, and I don't pay any commission either. I haven't been here above four or five years. I took these over with the stock. The small ones we did manage to sell, but the big ones no one wants. I put 'em in the back of the window. Fine Original Etching—that sort of thing."

"Who had the shop before you did?" asked Field.

"My father-in-law. But after he had his trouble he turned it over to me and Sally. Said it was worth a lot. Well, it gives me a job, and now we sell pottery and medals and such like it pays its rent. But if it wasn't for my wife having the tea-shop at the corner, we wouldn't make two ends meet. But folks like their stomachs better than their minds, so she does well enough. You'd hardly believe how many people she can get in the season. Too they were mutually agreed. " There's an impulse in human nature," he added, " that makes the meanest of us shudder at the thought of another creature going through our particular hell; people are even superstitious about it, think that if they refuse help when the chance offers, they will one day have to endure it themselves."

Then they went on to discuss their future procedure. It would be necessary for the sham Miss Curteis to take up her abode at the Monkswood Hotel the next day, to allay suspicion. Arbuthnot was not disposed to cancel the engagement on some trumpery excuse.

" The point is," said Egerton, " could we get hold of some one to act as passenger who would identify Sharpe for us? What about this Miss Riley you interviewed at Burton St. Lawrence? Could she be persuaded to fake some excuse and come to town for a night? She would have to arrive on the Monday evening, and she could be back at her job by midday Tuesday. She saw the man frequently, and could probably recognise him again. I don't know of any one else, except Miss Ticehurst herself, and even in our present straits we can't very well appeal to her."

" I can try," said Gordon. " She'd jump at the chance, if she can pluck up her courage. She's terrified of the old lady, but I dare say Mrs. T. wouldn't sack her, for fear she went blabbing round the neighbourhood. Besides, she's probably got her for a song. I'm hoping to-morrow to hear about the taxi. It will be a nuisance if he bought it under a false name and disposed of the old one in the same way."

" Even so the difficulties wouldn't be insuperable," remarked Egerton, who didn't think difficulties ever were. " We should simply have to track down every man who had bought an orange taxi in the past month or so. We should get him eventually."

" Even when you've got him you're going to have your work cut out to prove a thing," observed Arbuthnot, agreeing with Gordon's estimate of Egerton's high-handedness. " We can't approach him direct on the information we've got."

" We must wait for the odd card," replied the politician. " Fate always has one up her sleeve, and we must trust she'll play it on our side. D'you remember the Penge murder? Two men brought a woman to a nursing-home in Penge, dying of starvation. They went into a neighbouring post-office and chanced to speak to one another on the subject, and a sailor standing by realised that they were speaking of his sister. From that sprang their subsequent arrest and trial, when she died shortly afterwards. Now you could hardly stretch the arm of coincidence farther than that, for a man whose trade takes him all over the world to be in a Penge post-office at that particular moment and overhear that particular conversation."

" And we're to wait for a similar miracle? "

" Or work it ourselves. I've no especial preference."

CHAPTER XI

1

DESPITE Gordon's anticipations the morning post brought no reply to his inquiries; he determined, however, to spend the morning at the hotel whose address he had given in his circular, on the off chance that some man, who distrusted putting pen to paper, would call in person. His action was justified, for soon after midday he received a visit from a rather aggressive, stocky man of middle-age, called Poynter, who wanted to know what was in the wind.

Gordon explained without giving his case away, but succeeded in satisfying Poynter's dubiety, for after a few minutes he talked readily of the transaction.

" Yes," he said, " I remember this fellow, Blount. We sold him an orange taxi on the 31st March. He brought the old cab with him, tried to kid us it was in quite good condition; I suppose he thought we were such mugs we shouldn't see he'd just painted it over to make it look a better article. If you ask me, seeing he swears he's only had it a little over a year, it was second-hand when he got it."

" How could you be sure it had just been repainted? "

" Oh, easy enough; it's quite an old dodge; you use ordinary paint, but you ' flat ' it with turps instead of oil, and it'll dry in about an hour. But it dries uneven. I mean to say, some parts'll be glossy and others dull. You mightn't think so much about it, p'raps, if you weren't always coming across fellows who want to take you in. It's quite an old dodge."

" Did you point all that out to him? "

" I did."

" And he said? "

" Said it was just an accident; he'd scratched a bit of paint off the cab and that was the only reason he'd repainted it. But he didn't take me in. It was a ram-shackle old car; he said himself he'd been wanting to buy a new one for some time, but times were hard."

" He paid for the new one? "

" So much down, y'know; the usual thing; and there was a bit—not much—on the old one. He'll go on paying in instalments . . ."

Gordon nodded. " Yes. That's what most of them do, isn't it? Wonder what percentage of traffic on the roads has been paid for. I dare say we should be surprised to know. One more point. What happened to his taxi? "

" One he brought? It's still in the yard, I expect. Couldn't hope to sell that again."

" What do you do with it? "

" Oh, send it out on hire. We hire out cabs, different rates, you see, and this will do for one of the cheaper ones."

" Could you tell if it had been used since it came into your possession? "

" Well, pretty sure to have done. We've had it the best part of a month, you see. And we're getting orders all the time."

" Would it be examined by any one when it first came in? "

" It 'ud be cleaned and swept out and washed."

" Could you find out who did the job? "

" You mean, which feller? I couldn't promise you that. I'll ask if you like."

He borrowed Gordon's telephone, and after a longish pause announced that a lad called Wilkins remembered the car. Gordon promptly asked why. Poynter shouted another inquiry into the mouth of the 'phone, and presently looked up and said, " It's called the Pink Pearl car by the men. Sort of a joke, I suppose."

Gordon didn't look as if he thought it at all amusing; instead, he asked whether he could come back with his companion and see this lad, Wilkins. Poynter looked surprised but resigned, and said he supposed he could if he wanted to. So they returned by taxi to Upper Beaumont Street together. Here Gordon was offered a private room, and here a few minutes later he was joined by Wilkins, a tall rather sheepish fellow, who had been called away from his job of mending a puncture.

" Mr. Poynter tells me you remember this taxi particularly," Gordon began, " and that you've got a nickname for it. How's that? "

Wilkins looked a little foolish. " Well, sir, you know how it is. Things aren't any too exciting and any little thing makes the fellows laugh. I was doing out this car, and we were talking about it's being repainted and saying what a fool the chap must be to think there were any flies on the boss, when we found a big sort of pink bead, squashed up, among the mats. That's all, sir. We just called it that, said it looked as if he'd been squeezing her a bit . . ." he shuffled his feet and fell silent.

" Do you remember where you found the bead? Inside the body of the cab, or by the driver's seat? "

Wilkins stared. " I couldn't tell you that, sir. I just happened to see it when I shook out the mats and swept round a bit. All I know is it came from the cab."

" You're quite sure you didn't notice what part of the cab? It's more important than you can realise."

" Well, I s'pose inside. Drivers don't go about carrying pink pearl necklaces in their pockets."

" I wish I were equally sure of that," muttered Gordon,

bitterly disappointed, but abandoning his examination of the lad.

On his way back, however, he realised that no jury would have convicted Sharpe on such flimsy evidence, even if the boy had been prepared to swear that the pearl was under the driver's own mat. They'd say that a man's life is a serious affair and must not be allowed to suffer jeopardy without something more solid in the way of evidence. It did, however, convince Gordon beyond all reasoning that Sharpe had murdered the girl, and it keyed him up to a particularly high state of tension and a determination to contrive the arrest, whatever means should prove necessary for the achievement.

2

His next step was to see Sharpe again and satisfy himself, if possible, precisely when the painting episode had occurred. It was not difficult to think of an excuse to call on the man. Disguised as a commercial traveller, dealing in silk goods, he went down in a small unobtrusive blue Morris saloon, with a stock of printed cards in his pocket, and samples in the back of the car. His story was a very simple one; he was expecting to be quartered in the neighbourhood for some time, and required a garage; Sharpe's house overlooked a double row of these, and he proposed to assume that one was vacant. On his arrival, he first of all searched the Mews in case the names of the lessors was anywhere in evidence, but fortunately there was nothing to show how the garages were leased. Gordon had no fear of being recognised as the man who had booked the car for the pseudo Miss Curteis; a slight moustache, a bright brown wig, and rimless glasses with clear lenses altered his appearance completely. He put his car outside Sharpe's house and rang the bell. Sharpe himself answered the door, and his irritated air changed to one of suavity when he saw a possible client.

" I'm so sorry to trouble you," said Gordon chattily, " but I understand there's a garage to let at the back here, and I can't find the name of the owner. I'm greatly pressed for time; I've got to go back north to-night, and I wanted to get things fixed up before I went."

" I didn't know there was one to let," returned Sharpe uncompromisingly, " they're generally pretty full. Where did you get the notion? "

" I asked at a shop I was in just now if there were any cheapish garages going round here, and I was told to try for these, as the fellow believed there was one vacant. He said they're cheaper than at that big garage in the Lillie Road."

" Oh, they are," agreed Sharpe. " That's why there's such a run on them. Well, the agents are Kingham and Bruce, but you won't be able to do anything to-night. This is the early closing day in this district."

Gordon, aware of that, having, indeed, timed his visit to coincide with the occasion, looked dejected.

" I say, isn't that bad luck? And it sounded just the sort of thing I could afford. They're fair-sized, aren't they? "

" Oh, good enough, unless you've got a Daimler."

" Well, you can see for yourself the sort of bus I drive. A chap in my position can't hope for anything better till times mend. Do you know these garages? "

" I rent one of 'em. I must say they're quite convenient."

" H'm." He appeared to consider. " It's asking a good deal of a stranger, I know, but it would be extremely kind if you'd just let me have a peep at yours. If you're not too awfully busy. Then I should know whether it was worth while writing to Kingham and Bruce."

Sharpe hesitated, then said " Oh, all right," and taking down a key, led the way to the back of the Mews. He unlocked a painted door to display a bare and rather cramped shed, in which stood the orange taxi.

" This yours. Nice cab that. Find a lot of business about here? " Under pretext of examining the fittings in the farther corner, he squeezed past the cab and saw on the ground two stained drums, one empty, the other still

containing a little dark brown paint. Also, on a wedge of
newspaper, was a large brush, and, with the appearance of
stumbling over this, Gordon touched it. That convinced
him that it had not been used very recently, since it was
quite hard, but then he reminded himself that it was almost
a month since the painting of the taxi had taken place. He
contrived, however, to read the name of the local oil shop
where the paint had been procured, which would definitely
fix the date of the purchase, though he had little doubt in
his own mind as to when this had been.

He walked thoughtfully back to Sharpe's side. " Do very
nicely, I think. I hope I have the luck to get one. I shan't
be down for a week or two, but perhaps when I am we
might see something of one another. Travelling about isn't
such a bad life, but you can't settle. It's here to-day and
gone to-morrow; you meet a chap one night and then he
goes out of your life. And I'm a companionable sort of
man. I like to be matey. Still, we must look on the bright
side. Remember what that chap, Whatsisname, said about
commercial travellers? That theirs were the most successful marriages, because they only met their wives at week-
ends, so didn't have time to get bored."

Sharpe made a casual and rather coarse rejoinder, and
the two men parted. Gordon went straightway to the
premises of Messrs. Peterson and Son, the oil and colour
merchants who had sold the paint, and found, as he had
expected, the shop blinds down and the door locked. It
seemed possible, however, that Mr. Peterson lived over his
shop; certainly some one was there, for the gas had been
lighted, and he could see shadows on the blind. He rang
the private bell two or three times before he got any
answer; then an elderly man, bald and a little slow in his
movements, opened the door a crack and asked what he
wanted. It took Gordon some time and a great deal of
tact to persuade the old man to let him in; only the fear
of the old-fashioned respectable tradesman of being concerned in a police case finally won him over. And he
agreed to look up his order book and see if he could trace
the sale.

" March 28th," he said presently, looking up from the records. " Two drums."

" Did he often buy paint here? "

" He couldn't have done, because I see he was charged for the drums. A man that's had them before returns the empties. They add quite a bit to the cost."

" Did he buy anything else at the same time? "

" Turps. He wanted to use the paint at once for an urgent job, and that makes it dry quicker than oil."

It seemed to Gordon highly significant that the suspected man should have bought the paint so soon after the murder, and then have got rid of the taxi, as it might have seemed conspicuous.

It might, of course, be pure coincidence, but he was inclined to scout that possibility. Things were fitting too neatly into place. What they still lacked was a motive; a man of Sharpe's calculating abilities did not murder a woman who was financially useful to him without some very strong reason. Gordon did not believe the crime could be explained by passion, not passion based on affection. That Sharpe had lost his head and in the violence of his mood committed the murder was probable. But why? Perhaps the worm had turned at last, had told him finally that he need expect no further assistance, had, even, perhaps, hoist him on his own petard, and threatened to have him arrested for blackmail. Very likely there had been letters that would prove her case in court. Or she might have told him that all she wanted now was to be acknowledged as Charles Hobart's wife, a position that would raise her out of his reach; in either case he would be left stranded, and Gordon thought that possibly very discreet investigation might discover the actual facts of the case. If he could show that Sharpe must have money immediately, he would be one step farther on.

While Gordon had been engaged in tracking down his man and laying plans for future conversations, should the necessity arise, the real Miss Curteis, one of his female staff, had gone to Burton St. Lawrence to interview Miss Riley. She had had a good deal of difficulty in persuading her to accept the suggestion to spend a night in town and identify their quarry, but good fortune arranged that she should receive a letter from a distant relation who lived in London, and who was seriously ill, so that Miss Riley squared her conscience and agreed to fall in with Gordon's scheme.

So much settled, Miss Curteis went on to Hinton St. Lawrence and had tea at Sally Welling's Blue Bird Cafe. There was practically no one else there, and Sally herself was working in the tea-room; Miss Curteis contrived to entice her into conversation, and presently the talk turned on Fanny. Mrs. Welling had no idea that her customer had been arguing cleverly for a quarter of an hour in order to manœuvre this subject into their conversation; she didn't, of course, bring up the name of Fanny crudely, but worked round to subconscious fears, inventing one for herself, and drawing Sally out, until the latter said quite casually, " I had a sister who was simply terrified of being shut up alone. When she was small it was the only way you could get the better of her; the ordinary punishments were like water on a duck's back; but that broke down her stubbornness."

It appeared, too, that Mrs. Penny had not been slow to appreciate the value of such a penalty, while Fanny had struggled desperately to maintain her pride in the face of the family's ready scorn. That fear, never openly acknowledged, breeding a deeper shame as time drew on, had obtained an irremediable hold over her by the time she was twenty; and the bare notion of being imprisoned would be sufficient to drive her frantic with alarm. So that, supposing all their assumptions to be founded on fact, Sharpe had found the ground very well prepared for him.

4

It had been arranged that Miss Riley should adopt a little disguise in the shape of tortoise-shell spectacles, in place of the harsh steel-rimmed ones she normally wore, and allow Miss Curteis to use a little make-up for the purpose of changing her appearance. Indeed, though she did the minimum, the change was enough to alarm Miss Riley.

Gordon, however, knew that at all costs Sharpe's suspicions must not be aroused, and though it seemed improbable that he would remember a woman he had only seen occasionally several years ago, the issues at stake were too grave to take any hazards. In point of fact, the test went off without a hitch, though Miss Riley's excitement was so great that she almost gave the game away. She recognised Sharpe at once as Marigold Ticehurst's whilom lover.

" He hasn't changed anything to speak of," she assured Gordon, in a loud stage whisper, as Sharpe disappeared with a battered hand-case and a bundle of rugs. " I should know him anywhere. And prison or wherever else's he's been doesn't seem to have troubled him much."

They had some difficulty in keeping her sufficiently calm to behave in a normal manner. Gordon, who had foreseen this crisis, had taken care to impress upon Sharpe his client's nervous and excitable temperament, and he hoped that the man would put down her rather extraordinary behaviour to this source. At Waterloo Gordon paid his man, hinting that he might want him at a later date for a similar errand, and, when the taxi was out of sight, had the luggage taken to the cloak room, where it could be called for later in the day.

" Why do you do that? " Miss Riley wanted to know. " You could just as easily put the things on another taxi and take them away."

" The drivers and porters might wonder what was up," said Gordon. " We have to sustain our parts."

He arranged for the boxes to be delivered to his address in Kingsway by carrier that evening, and settled down anew to the problem of proving a recent association between Sharpe and the dead woman. It seemed to him that if he could put his finger on some one who had known the man during those hidden five years he might be able to pick up the thread and trace him back and forth and see where Fanny and he coincided. He knew nothing of Sharpe's life since he left prison, except for the two or three casual details he had managed to elicit; the fellow appeared to have no relations and no friends. Then it occurred to Gordon to wonder if he were married; a wife might simplify matters a good deal. There was no sign of a woman at the Mews, but she might have discovered the type of husband she had taken, and have left him. He could ascertain this by making inquiries at Somerset House. Presumably Sharpe had been a bachelor at the time of his engagement to Miss Ticehurst; thereafter he had served two years' imprisonment, so that it would only be necessary to search the records for the past five years. Gordon put a man on to this at once, with a result so astounding that even Egerton was jerked out of his normal composure.

In May, 1928, Walter Alfred Sharpe had been married to Florence Hilda Hobart, widow of the late Charles Hobart of Kenya, and daughter of Frederick Penny, sometime of Cambridge!

" Well, that tells us one important thing," said Egerton warmly as he and Gordon discussed the position with Arbuthnot, " we know now the hold he had over her. Bigamy's a punishable offence, and I don't think she could have put forward a ghost of proof that she really believed Charles to be dead."

" It's even more to the point whether Sharpe believed it," the lawyer observed. " Of course, if the question is ever put to him, he will swear he thought he was marrying a widow. But did he know? And what was her motive in marrying a man who couldn't support her, and whom she must have known was untrustworthy? "

" Pure affection, I think," said Gordon. " I honestly believe she did care for this rascal; in spite of everything she seems to have stuck to him year after year, though he could never have been anything but a millstone round her neck. Perhaps he was cooling off, and she thought the only way to hold him was to have him legally. It's a pity that she can't tell us the facts of the case from her point of view; for certainly he never will."

" What about the date? " asked Arbuthnot. " H'm. Within a fortnight of her dismissal by Browne. It looks uncommonly as though we were going to fit things together, after all. What date did she withdraw her legacy? "

" Three days before the wedding," said Gordon, who had kept a note of all these details. " As you say, sir, it fits in uncommonly well."

" I wonder what happened after the marriage," Egerton speculated. " Did they live together openly? and if so, for how long? For they'd abandoned any such situation long before her death. Or did he marry her and proceed to live on her? Was she helping him financially during her association with Browne? I shouldn't be surprised. We've got to get more information. We could try the address from which he was married."

But this effort proved abortive. Sharpe had only spent a week or two there, and no one remembered him. Nor could Gordon trace the couple in any way. There appeared to be only one solution, and that was to tackle the man personally. With this notion in mind, Gordon had already prepared the ground on the day of his visit to overlook the garages. Messrs. Kingham and Bruce regretted that they had no vacancies at the moment, but Gordon put up his modest little affair at a larger garage close by. Then he waited his opportunity and one evening casually joined Sharpe as the latter turned into the Mews.

" I was wondering if I should run against you," he observed jovially. " Often thought of you while I've been north. I couldn't get that garage, had to go to the Cullompton Garage. Know it? "

Sharpe did. He asked Gordon if he were interested in cars.

" Matter of fact, I am. I can't tell how it makes me feel to have to go round with all this footling silk-wear; I'd like to travel in cars." He was, in fact, no mean technician, and he broke into a spate of conversation that delighted his audience. He soon recognised that Sharpe had always represented himself as a man keen on automobiles for the simple reason that that was the truth. He was fanatical in his zeal; he seemed to forget that he scarcely knew his companion; he insisted on discussing and arguing and speculating, while Gordon kept him at white-hot pitch knowing that every moment his own chances of success drew nearer. Let Sharpe overwhelm the natural barriers between men meeting for the second time, and he would turn quite naturally into more personal channels.

" I wonder you don't go into management for yourself," he said jocularly, as Sharpe paused for lack of breath.

" Tell you the truth, that's what I'm going to do. .I'm going to have a fleet of cabs all with the Pocock Brake. That's the newest thing there is. It's expensive, but it's fine. And presently cost of production'll come down. Know this chap, Pocock? "

Gordon said he didn't.

" I met him up at Merston at the time of the Motor Exhibition there. Go to that? "

" No, I missed it. Couldn't get away."

Sharpe tapped his teeth with the stem of his pipe. " Ah! Pity that. It was a good show, though I think they were crazy only to run it for a week. It 'ud have run a month, easy."

" You went up? "

" Yes. I wouldn't make any appointments for that day. The 26th March it was, and I'd been promising myself that treat for a long time. That's where I saw the brake. It's good, you know, amazingly good, though it's too expensive at present. But one of these days I'll have a fleet of taxis all fitted up with it. It will be necessary to experiment until we can find a way of cheaper production; of course, that'll come automatically as the demand increases; at present it's in the experimental stage. But I like it—— " there was no doubt about his sincerity; he was carried away by his own enthusiasm. " I like it very much. I saw Pocock, but he's a stand-offish sort of chap. It's no use his inventing a thing we can't afford to use; but he seemed to think that when he'd invented it he'd done everything necessary."

" How long did you stay up at Merston? " Gordon asked casually. " It wasn't much of an exhibition, I heard."

" Wasn't it? " defended Sharpe, warmly. " First-rater show I thought. But then, I never miss 'em if I can help it. People talk of what the motor industry has done; nothing to what it can do and will do. And I'm glad I went, just for this brake."

"I suppose you can't recommend me a decent hotel?" Gordon went on. "I've got to go up there on my next journey out, and it's a help sometimes to know a place where the beds are comparatively healthy and the food fit to eat."

"Well, don't go to the Four Feathers," Sharpe advised him. "I went there and a fouler place I never want to see. I suppose they thought they could play fast and loose because there was such a crowd there wasn't room in the town for all those who wanted beds. Every place was full, and I suppose I was lucky to be able to share a billiard room with about six other chaps. Food was bad, too. I complained about it. And on the top of everything else they had the cheek to charge us full price. Seven-and-sixpence for a place on the floor and some half-cooked ham! I believe the place to go to is the Coach and Horses."

"I suppose that was full up?"

"Absolutely. The town was packed. It was an odd place to choose for that sort of exhibition, except that they've got the show-space. That was magnificent. But the accommodation's very limited."

"You hadn't booked a room in advance?"

"No, I didn't mean to stay the night. I thought I should see all that was necessary in the one day; I started early, the 9.7 from Waterloo; that's the first train there is, bar the milk train which goes about five. But when I saw this brake I thought it was a golden opportunity to see Pocock. I sent in asking for an appointment, but he said he was too busy. He could see me in the morning. At first I thought I'd let the whole thing rip, but presently I changed my mind, and let the 6.8 go to London without me. By that time, all the decent rooms were booked; as I say, I suppose I was lucky not to be sleeping out-of-doors."

Gordon laughed. "And I expect you thought it was worth it."

Sharpe agreed. "That's a fact. A motor show hypnotises me, like a rabbit faced with a snake. You interested in cars?"

"Mad on them," lied Gordon. "And I like what you told me about the brake. Funny I hadn't come across it."

"It's only just been patented. Here." He opened a drawer and pulled out a bundle of pamphlets. "I've got a diagram here. See?" He was explaining eagerly, almost vehemently. "Pocock gave me these. They're confoundedly interesting. I'm only sorry the thing isn't feasible at once. Pocock's a bit disappointed, I think. Doubt if he booked half the orders he'd expected."

"Well, that's most interesting," observed Gordon a little later coming to his feet. "We must have another yarn sometime. I expect to be kept down here for a bit. Come and dine with me one night, will you? I'm staying at 68 Drummond Road."

"Thanks very much. Yes, I'd like to. Fix a day? Well, not Tuesday. Tuesdays I go round to see my fiancée. Yes, getting married one of these days, I suppose. She's keen on cars, too; I believe in husbands and wives having something in common."

"Going into partnership with you?" suggested Gordon jocularly.

A little to his surprise Sharpe remained grave. "Well, I shouldn't wonder. It takes time and money to build up a business and I'm ambitious; I don't want to trail along as a taxi-driver, if it is my own taxi, for the next fifteen years. And there's not so much in it as you might think."

The taxi was standing outside the door, and Gordon observed affably, "Nice affair, that. New, I see."

Sharpe repeated his story of the accident at the end of March though he named no specific date.

"Must have been a nasty jar," remarked Gordon, "that you had to get a new cab."

"Well, the other had done good service; matter of fact, I messed things up a bit, trying to be in too much of a hurry. And I have to be careful. That Mrs. Mordaunt, for instance, I was driving the day it all happened, she's got an eye like a vulture. Likes to think she owns the cab when she's out, and when she saw the slash on the paint she was on to it like a knife. ' What's happened? ' she asked. I'd taken her up to town to meet some friend of hers at the Criterion, and I cruised about a bit during the afternoon, picking up odd fares, because I had to take her back at five o'clock. Well, I couldn't explain to her there'd nearly been an accident. She's one of these old ladies all nerves at the sight of a cat on the roof. Well, I said I was going to repair the damage, because she's been very useful to me. Got me no end of recommendations. And, as I say, I tried to make too quick a job of it, and mucked it up. However, she's so pleased with the new one she goes out oftener than ever."

" You couldn't have got the other car to stump up something? "

" Not likely; they'd argue that a slab of paint was nothing to matter. I don't even know whose the lorry was."

CHAPTER XII

1

GORDON exercised his wits for some time as to the best and least conspicuous way of approaching Mrs. Mordaunt, whose testimony he needed both for confirmation of Sharpe's story and for the actual date of the alleged accident. Eventually he decided to adopt the pose of a man setting up work in the neighbourhood as a private taxi-driver, and soliciting a trial. His appearance and the persuasive quality of his tongue won him an interview, but immediately he began to explain his errand Mrs. Mordaunt, a stout, hypochondriacal old lady, cut him short.

" Oh, no, no, no. It's quite out of the question. If I'd realised that was what you had come about—I have a most reliable man—really, if he were my own chauffeur I couldn't be more satisfied. So careful and considerate. My heart, you see . . ." she vaguely indicated her ribs. " I have to avoid any excitement or danger. I used to employ a man called Kelly, but really, the way he would rush through the traffic, and the language he used if people got in front of him. . . . Really, my man, I used to say, you're not running a Marathon . . ."

" Didn't know there was another man here like that," said Gordon sharply, as if he suspected her of inventing the whole story.

She bridled with some indignation. " Indeed, there is, as many of my friends will tell you. I send them all to Blount, and they are all delighted with him. I'm afraid that there isn't much room for another man."

" I've got a new cab," suggested Gordon, insinuatingly. " The kind of car a lady might be proud to drive in."

" Blount has just bought one of these charming orange cabs. A very stupid driver scraped a lot of paint off the other one; I had him hired that day, as it happened; he took me to town and was to call for me later in the afternoon, and as soon as he drove up I saw there had been some kind of a collision. However, he assured me it was nothing serious. If it had been any one but Blount, I'm afraid I should have felt nervous, but he is so careful and so good that I was sure I could take his word for things. And the next time he called for me he had this new car."

" Still, mine isn't a three-weeks old. I dare say this orange one . . ."

" Can't be much older. The accident only happened on the 27th of March. It's really most hard on him, because he says the insurance company will do nothing. Though I must add," she broke into an astonishing scald-crow of laughter, " his loss is our gain. The new cab is most comfortable."

" Well," thought Gordon, leaving the house, " if the rest of Sharpe's story is going to be as handsomely substantiated as that, it'll put the kybosh on Master Scott Egerton's theories, and then we shall all be at sea, for we haven't another idea between us."

It mightn't, he reflected, be so simple to prove the Merston side of the evidence, in a crowded third-rate hotel; no one would be likely to remember a man who shared a billiard room with six others on an over-crowded night. If, however, it could be proved that Sharpe was actually out of town that evening that would clear him of the imputation. Gordon decided that the best thing would be to attempt to pump the old woman who did his chores and though it was too late to accomplish anything further that night, he telephoned to Sharpe's house, asking for an appointment for the taxi-cab the next morning early. Sharpe, however, said he was sorry but he was booked up until half-past twelve; and that being all Gordon had wanted to know he said civilly that he was sorry and rang off.

He spent the evening at a music-hall to clear his mind of the impressions of the day, and was up early to make sure that Sharpe did really leave his premises as he had said he would. There was nothing spurious about those engagements; watching from a secreted corner, Gordon saw the orange taxi drive off a few minutes before nine, and a few minutes after the clock at St. Thomas's had struck the hour, he rapped on the narrow painted door and asked the old woman if her employer was in. When he heard that Sharpe was not he looked thoughtful, and said, tapping his teeth with a pencil, " H'm. I'm sorry about that. Know when he's coming back? I suppose you don't sleep on the premises."

The old woman said she didn't, and Gordon went on in the same speculative tone, " I was afraid not. You might have been able to help me. It's a matter of a car robbery, took place late one night or early the next morning, we're not sure which. And if you'd been sleeping here you might have heard something of it. Oh, well, I suppose I shall have to come back when Mr. Blount is in."

" What date was this? "

" The 26th March—or early on the 27th. I've told you we aren't sure which it was. He might remember something . . ."

" Not likely," she said derisively. " Why, he wasn't even here that night."

" Are you sure? "

" Am I sure? Well, seeing it's the first bit of luck I've had since I took up me job here . . ."

" Why was it lucky? "

" 'Cause I didn't get in meself till nigh 'alf-past eight, and me time's 'alf-past seven. And a rare stew me lord gets into if I'm a bit behind me time. Never makes allowance for nothing, he don't, and me sister havin' twins in the night quite sudden-like and a nour and a half between the first and the second, which is enough to upset any woman, and me bein' up with 'er, havin' had eight of me own, if they didn't all live, the whole blessed night, wouldn't seem to him a good enough reason for bein' a bit late the next day. I tell you, me heart was in me mouth as I come hurrying up the road. And then I come in and he ain't there."

" Sure he hadn't come in and gone out very early? "

She put her hands on her skinny hips and jeered. " Ho yus, likely, isn't it? And I s'pose that's why 'e left all 'is supper on the table, and the telegram in the letter-box and his bed unslept in. Lay on the floor, p'raps, and used his boots for a piller? Oh, likely."

" All right, all right," Gordon soothed her. " Well, of course, if he wasn't here, he can't help me."

" You going all along the road here asking questions? " she demanded sharply, and Gordon, seeing it was inevitable, said Yes, he was.

" Well, I 'ope you 'ave some luck," she remarked, but not as if she meant it. " Did you think he might have took it? "

" Who? Mr. Blount? Of course not."

" And why ' Of course not? ' I wouldn't put it past him; wouldn't put nothing past him if it comes to that. Like these ladies that don't steal pearls—oh, no, they're ladies, they ain't thieves, but they're kleptomaniacs, the kind of thing a lady can be and snitch anything she fancies and not get put in jug for it. Can't help it, they say, see what they like and just take it. Well, I wouldn't be surprised to hear Mr. Blooming Blount was the same. Fair crazy over cars; you'd think they was children, though Heaven help any child that got too near 'im. A narsty, fierce temper 'e's got, and so I'm telling you."

" Still, you can care for cars and even have a fierce temper, without stealing them," Gordon pointed out reasonably.

" Well, 'e's a queer sort of fellow. Always talking of when he'll have a lot of cars of 'is own, and plannin' and workin'. Lot of cars indeed! When he owes money on the furniture and it's all I can do to get me wages. Of course, I suppose 'he's thinking of this Miss Yates. Beats me why she doesn't see through him."

" Is she a relation of his? "

" Going to be soon, relation by marriage. Yes, he's after her money, though she don't see it. As proud as proud she is, telling every one that'll listen that she's goin' to be a partner. Partner indeed! Pay off the money-lenders more like."

" Is he in their hands then? "

" How should I know? You don't s'pose he'd tell me, do you? He thinks he's a gentleman. But what about his bills— and what's he marrying a woman old enough to be his aunt for? Well, I didn't have a blooming angel for a husband, though according to all accounts 'e may be one now, but I'm sorry for that fool of a woman. Little she knows what's comin' to 'er."

" Still, she's presumably old enough to know her own mind . . ."

" I should say she is. Thirty-seven she calls 'erself— and a bit, m'dear, and a bit. But 'er father's glad enough to see 'er married to any bit of dirt that comes round to the house. Jest waiting to get her out o' the way to take up with a girl younger'n my youngest—the old toad! And of course, she's half-crazy to get a man at all. Lady Marion Yates—and 'er second-'and car-shop, what she'll pay for and 'e'll profit from—'cause there'll be profits off of 'er money—'Is Nibs'll see to that."

Gordon appeared to recollect his business. " Well, if neither of you was here, I'm afraid I shall have to write this house down blank. When did he come back? "

" Some time Thursday, I s'pose. I go at ten; and 'e was 'ere on the Friday when I come. Matterfact, I know he was back on Thursday, cause I saw him walking with that Miss Yates in the evenin'. I will say," she added grudgingly, " 'e knows 'ow to make 'imself look smart. Never guess he was just a taxi-driver to see 'im go off to Merston that day all in his black coat and trilby 'at and 'e 'ad 'em on on the Thursday night, too. There's plenty thinks 'e's a good-looking man, but 'andsome is as 'andsome does, I've always said."

" So perhaps Miss Yates isn't as much to be pitied as you thought just now."

" Oh, well," the old woman picked up her duster and made a half-hearted dab at a dusty table, " I always say meself it's better to have a man than not. Gives you a sort of cachou, as they say. And it's a matter of chance, say what you like. They're pretty much the same when it comes to living with 'em. Their looks is the most different thing about 'em."

Gordon came away from the interview curious and exhilarated. The revelation of Miss Yates was a further proof of Sharpe's need of money; since he had failed to get it from Charles Hobart's wife, very likely he had turned to the woman he proposed to marry. He could not, yet, however, spare time considering Miss Yates; she might not come into the case at all. First of all he must continue his inquiries along the Mews, and this would not be time thrown away, for sooner or later he must learn whether any one recollected seeing or hearing a car pass down to the garages at about one o'clock on the fatal morning—and then he must go to Merston and see what confirmation he could get of Sharpe's story.

There were twenty-eight houses in the Mews, and Gordon called at each one. He had not, from the outset, any very great hopes of learning anything fresh; unless something particular had happened on the night of the 26th there seemed no reason why any one should remember it. And investigation showed that practically no one did. Only at one house did he learn anything fresh, and that was one more scrap of news that just fell short of being of any value. A tired-looking woman in a black dress came into the narrow hall of No. 7 to speak to him, and hearing the date of the inquiry quickened a little into a faint interest.

" Ah, I remember that night," she said quietly, and told him her story. She had been sitting up with her husband who was dying in great pain; all she desired for him was sleep, for he had been unable to rest all day; it was no longer possible for him to take food, and for three days she had known there was no hope. So intense had the pain been that she was praying agonisedly he might slip into unconsciousness and never return. At about one o'clock in the morning, when he seemed a little more quiet, the silence had been broken by the sound of a car turning into the Mews; her taut nerves ashiver she had cursed the driver for coming at such a moment; the car was being driven hard, and she heard it turn the corner in the direction of the garages. Fortunately, the dying man was too far gone to hear anything, and she herself never dreamed of moving. She had no idea what type of car it was, and had not caught a glimpse of it from her place by the bed.

Gordon, in the sad circumstances, could say nothing, but inwardly he raged at the futility of her evidence. There were not, probably, many taxis lodged in these garages, and if Mrs. Probert could have given him proof that a taxi had been driven into shelter at that time on that particular morning, he felt it would greatly have strengthened his case. There was, however, nothing more to be learned, so he pursued his patient, unprofitable round until he had seen the tenant in each house and learned nothing at all.

2

He was travelling to Merston on the 9.7, the train by which Sharpe claimed to have travelled. It would not be possible to prove whether he had actually done so; the train was a popular one and likely to be fairly full. Probably on that occasion it had been crowded, and certainly no individual porter or guard could be expected to remember a casual passenger. In any case, it did not seem to Gordon that the point was an important one. As soon as he arrived at Merston he telephoned to Pocock, a local man, asking for an appointment. Mr. Pocock was very much engaged, but could spare a few minutes at half-past twelve, which gave Gordon an opportunity of starting his inquiries at the Four Feathers. This proved, as Sharpe had said, to be a third-rate inn, slovenly and unattractive and none too clean. Probably all Sharpe's complaints were justified, the detective thought, grinning wryly, as he attempted to break down the coquettish hauteur of the red-haired young woman who allotted him a room.

" Nice view," he observed brightly, looking with some distaste at the stained walls and shabby floor-covering. " I'm in better luck than a man I know who was staying here for the Exhibition in March. He couldn't get a room anywhere, and had to share the smoking-room with several others."

The girl tossed her head. " If he was one of that lot it was more than he deserved. Folk that want rooms should come and book 'em at the proper time; and then to complain when he's charged in the usual way—leastways, one of 'em did, I don't know if it was your friend. Cap on the back of his head and all. The sauce of it. We didn't ask you to come, says Mr. Farmer—he's the boss—what's more we didn't want you, and we told you so. But since you would stop now you can pay and no more hollering for a reduction, because you won't get it. And they didn't. He saw to that."

" A bit of a rough house? " suggested Gordon sympathetically.

She nodded, wrinkling a snub nose. " That's what I don't like about this place," she confided. " Too much argy-bargy. That sort of thing wouldn't have happened at the Swan or the Coach and Horses. Not likely. If they'd crowded in there and wanted rooms and not been able to get them, they'd have come out again as meek as Moses when the house closed. But here the young fellers think they can do anything they like."

" Have you been here long? "

" Six months. But I shan't stay. Wouldn't lead anywhere, and the sort of fellow you meet in a place like this
isn't worth knowing. A girl can always tell. I shouldn't
of come here to start with. Oh, yes, I know that now.
It's all these low-class commercials. Don't never seem to
have heard of manners. Think if they wink at a girl or
slap a kiss on the back of her neck they'll keep her awake
all night with excitement."

" How foolish of them! I hope you didn't have too
difficult a time the night of the Exhibition."

" Me? Well, I always say a girl who's worth her salt
knows how to keep a man in his proper place, which is
down there." She stamped emphatically on the dirty
linoleum with a shabby patent shoe, with $2\frac{7}{8}$-inch heels.
" When this bunch of fellows came flashing in asking for
rooms I told 'em we hadn't got none left. You'll have to
go somewhere else, I said. They'd been everywhere else
and every place was booked. And they wouldn't go. Ever
hear such cheek? Six or seven of 'em wanting beds, and
the last room booked at eight o'clock. And that isn't what
I'd call a room either. Cupboard is what it 'ud be called
at the Swan or the Coach and Horses."

" Still, you made a profit on them, didn't you? I mean,
you got the last laugh on them. Did they stay to breakfast? "

" Yes. And one of 'em had the impertinence to complain that the food was half-cold, and he hadn't been able
to get a bath."

" Unreasonable! " commented Gordon, smoothly.

" Unreasonable you call it? Well, I said, and do you
have to come all this way to get a bath? Cheaper for
you to stay behind and take one in your own house, if
you've got such a thing, I said. And anyway, I tells him,
nobody asked you in here. And he just laughed and said,
' Steady, Gert. Steady, old girl.' My name's not Gertie, I
told him. It's Alysse, and I spelt it for him. Oh, he said,
and how do you spell barmaid these days? Angry? I tell
you, it was lucky for him the bar wasn't open. I'd have
soused him proper, yes, if it had to come out of my wages

170

and all. I never did like these plus-four chaps; makes 'em sidey, if you ask me. Then he started saying I reminded him of his mother. I tell you, when all them chaps went on laughing and saying what a handsome fellow his father must have been, I got real mad. Why don't you go to Buck'n'm Palace? I asked him. We don't expect noble lords sleeping on the floor here. Let alone that some one'll have to scrub the place out now, and it not being due till Saturday. Oh, he said, this is a great day for the hotel, and then they made no end of a fuss, scrabbling like a lot of rats, and sticking their silly names in the Visitors' Book. I looked at his after he'd gone—Mr. Walter Blount he calls himself. Well, he may be Blount but he seemed to think he was sharp enough."

" But not so sharp as you," Gordon complimented her. " You got his money, after all."

"Mr. Farmer saw to all that. Stood by that door and watched 'em as they came out. One of 'em said he was going to buy some tobacco, be back in a minute or two. You pay before you leave my house, said Mr. Farmer. I wouldn't know you again from Adam and you could easy swear you hadn't been here. I'm going to see the colour of your money before I budge."

Gordon came down the stairs, and glanced idly through the visitors' book that lay on a table generously besprinkled with dust. There, under the date of the 27th March, he saw the entry " W. A. Blount " and then five or six names following it. He was something of a hand writing expert, and there was no doubt in his mind, even if all the evidence had not pointed in that direction, that the man, Sharpe, had really been here that day. So far, so good—for their suspect.

It was striking noon when Gordon left the Four Feathers and walked leisurely down to the offices of Messrs. Pocock and Shelly in the High Street. Specimens of the brake were exhibited in the show room window, but Gordon saw Mr. Pocock in a smallish room at the back. He was a tall business-like man, fair-haired and excessively neat. He had a brisk though courteous manner, shook hands in an impersonal way and waited for Gordon to explain his visit.

The detective began by asking the inventor to regard the conversation as strictly private, and went on to say that he was conducting inquiries in connection with a criminal trial shortly to be held.

" I understand on the 26th March, the day the Motor Exhibition opened, a man called Blount from London asked for an interview. . . ."

Pocock's quick brows drew together. " Well, really, it isn't possible for me to corroborate any statement so vague as that. Probably several hundreds of people asked me for interviews. Did I see him? I don't recall the name. I'm sorry to seem unhelpful, but you must realise that you're asking the practically impossible."

" Only because we're perpetually being asked for it ourselves," returned Gordon, with a keen smile. " But perhaps we're more accustomed to it. Yes, you saw Mr. Blount, but not on the 26th. You offered him an appointment on the 27th, that he at first refused; but subsequently he decided to spend the night here and saw you early on the morning of the 27th. He was interested in your new brake for taxis. He's in the business himself, and is proposing to enlarge it shortly. He added that he thought your invention excellent, but apt to be costly for the small man."

A gleam came into his companion's alert grey eyes. " I begin to recall him. He has a fleet of private taxis, he said, and is very keen to keep up with the latest improvements. He certainly is a good engineer and knows what he's talking about, and I had at one time hopes that he might place a substantial order. But I soon realised he wasn't in a financial position to do that, and when he began to talk about the great additional expense, I got rid of him with a bundle of literature. One's time is really too valuable to be taken up with conversation that is coming to nothing."

" And you are sure of the time and the day? This is really very important."

" As a matter of fact, I have a note of it in my office diary. He sent in a card twice during Wednesday after-

noon, I remember, but it was quite impossible for me to
see him. You will realise that in the course of a single day,
the first day in particular, it is out of the question for me
to see every one who wants to talk about my brake. I said
I should be happy to give him an appointment on Thursday morning, if he could wait so long. I really didn't
expect him, but I got a message the next morning saying
he'd stayed overnight after all, and would be glad if I
could see him. It would have to be early, because he had
an appointment in London that necessitated his catching
the 10.31 train. I suggested 9.45 and he arrived very
punctually. He spoke, I remember, of the crowded condition of the town and the discomfort he had himself
experienced at his hotel. Then we talked about the brake;
as I say, I soon realised he didn't mean business and got
rid of him."

" Would you know him again? "

Pocock looked doubtful. " That's rather a hard question
to answer. One sees so many people, and he wasn't a
particularly noticeable type."

" Would you recognise him from any of these photographs? "

He spread several on the table, and Pocock, evidently
a conscientious man, examined them with care.

" That's the most like him," he said at last, picking out
Sharpe's portrait. " I wouldn't swear, of course."

Gordon came away feeling the evidence was conclusive.
He returned to town the bearer of what must be to
Hobart's defence extremely disquieting news.

3

Egerton had been summoned to his Yorkshire con-
stituency, and Gordon did not feel that at this juncture
there was anything to be gained by consulting Arbuthnot,
so long as he had only negative evidence to offer. A murmur of their suspicions against Sharpe would lay the
foundation for a pretty slander charge, and they could not
risk losing a single point now. But regard it how he

would, it did seem to Gordon that the evidence of the girl at the Four Feathers and of Pocock substantiated Sharpe's story. Their only chance was to put the alibi out of mind for the moment and concentrate on the crime on the hypothesis of Sharpe's guilt. It might be possible to discover some man or woman who recollected seeing Sharpe on the Wednesday evening; perhaps entering his house or putting away his taxi. He even toyed for a short time with the notion that the murder was the work of two men, reminding himself of the famous case of John Franklin, a matter of impersonation that had baffled the police for months. There the alibi had seemed impregnable. The man in question had been, not an hundred miles away but three thousand, at the time of the crime, and only by acting on a supposition of his guilt had it proved possible to formulate a case against him, on the strength of which he had ultimately been convicted.

The first step to take was to interrogate all the men who hired garages in the Mews, and the following morning Gordon obtained a list of their names and addresses from the agents, after presenting his credentials, and started on his wearisome task. He met with surprise, coldness and suspicion, and endeavoured as well as he could, without betraying himself, to allay a great deal of curiosity. The majority had no reason for remembering the date, and those who could place it had either locked up their cars at a far earlier hour or had not taken them out that night. No one seemed to have seen Sharpe, so far as Gordon could discover, and there was nothing to prove that the solitary car heard by the woman in black had belonged to him. After some consideration Gordon decided to visit Miss Marion Yates and see if he could learn anything useful from her.

She proved to be a woman of three—or four-and-forty, tall and spare, rather deliberately girlish, eager and shy. Her body was lank and she had difficulty in controlling her movements; she jerked her arms and shoulders in little futile nervous gestures while she talked. She looked like a woman who has been palpitating on the shelf for years, almost beyond hope, who cannot actually believe that she has achieved sufficient personality to attract attention. Gordon represented himself as a journalist interested in women's enterprises. He said he had heard that Miss Yates proposed to enter into partnership with her husband in a motor concern.

" Yes, indeed," said Miss Yates proudly. " He thinks very well of my business capacities. Of course, I always tell him I'm not a patch on him. He's got an unusually good business brain. And he can make rapid decisions. I do admire that so much in a man. Look at the way he settled this affair; the opportunity came and he snatched it without any hesitation. I must say, Mr.—oh, Mr. Raymond—I did feel flattered at the way he immediately got into touch with me and asked me to co-operate. No shilly-shallying, he said, there's no time. The successful people in this world are those who know what they want, and are prepared to take risks and grasp it when the chance comes. Chances don't come more than once, he says. He's got the courage of his convictions, and I must say I do think well of a man who isn't afraid of other people's opinions. If it weren't for him, I should defer sometimes to what neighbours or relations thought, but he's shown me that's wrong. If you're going to forge ahead you must take chances and you must be prepared to seem rash. It's the only way. I must have seemed rash when I said Yes, go ahead, I'll stand in with you, but I'm glad I did it. I trust Mr. Blount, and I haven't any doubt that I shall soon be able to prove how wise I was not to hesitate. I hope, if you're going to put this in your paper, you'll say something about his resourcefulness and energy. He's got enterprise, and that is so admirable, I always think."

" Suppose you tell me about this ' rash ' scheme in more detail? " suggested Gordon diplomatically. " I really don't know much more than that you are going into partnership with your husband. I didn't know the scheme was actually in progress."

" Well, we haven't set up yet, but it's started. We shall open quite soon, I think, but you can't do these things like waving a wand, can you? We had been talking about it for a little time, but nothing definite had been settled until he went to a big Motor Exhibition a month or so ago. And there he met a man called Dyson, who was going to set up a big concern, but wanted a partner who could put up a thousand pounds. Well, money is difficult to come by these days, and it so happened that it wasn't convenient for Mr. Blount to find so much. So as soon as he got back to town he telephoned to me, and asked if I would care to come in, putting up half the amount and he'd put up the other. I was very flattered, of course. He said he thought of me at once. He does not care for too many people to be running a thing, but he is sure he and I would see eye to eye in business matters. Of course, I should rely on him, though I don't say I shouldn't use my own judgment, if I thought it best. But wasn't it a compliment, really, ringing me like that from the station the minute he arrived? He was going on to see this Mr. Dyson and had to give him his reply at once."

" And you've put in your share already? "

" Yes. I had a cheque waiting when Mr. Blount came that evening."

She continued to talk of the venture as though it were some tremendous game; she had no notion of business and would, Gordon realised, always be easy to defraud, provided you had first won her confidence. It was some time before he could take his leave and then he was pursued by tiresome queries as to when the interview (or article) would appear, and in what paper, as she would certainly require several copies. He felt a momentary spasm of remorse as he got away, almost running down the street in his thankfulness to escape from that irritating voice, for having raised a flood of futile hopes, but a moment after his attention was riveted once more on the problem before him. All that Miss Yates had done was to enclose Sharpe still more securely from suspicion.

When he reached his office Gordon took pencil and paper and began to make notes in pretty full detail of the itinerary Sharpe must have followed if he had, in fact, committed the crime. He claimed to have left the house in time to catch the 9.7 from Waterloo, and here he was backed up by Mrs. Parr. Supposing him not to have spent the night at Merston there was the question of the train that brought him back. He hadn't taken the 3.15, because Pocock said that he had sent in his card after four o'clock; there was a 4.43, but that was a very slow train that did not reach London till almost 9. The next, the one he had originally intended to catch, was the 6.8 that got into Waterloo at 8.16. Presumably he was aware that Fanny was spending the evening with her husband, and was trying to dun him for five hundred pounds. He wanted to hear how the affair had gone, so he went up to Menzies Street, saw her, learned that there was no chance of getting the money, and in ungovernable fury strangled her. That must be their case. But if so, he hadn't spent the night at Merston. And if he hadn't, what of the testimony of Mrs. Parr, the girl at the Four Feathers and William Pocock? He certainly hadn't slept in his bed, hadn't touched his supper, had been seen at the hotel where he had made himself rather conspicuous, offensively so in fact, and had kept his early appointment with Pocock. And even if he had come back on the 6.8, how on earth was Hobart's defence going to prove that? No one at Fulham seemed to have seen him. In his absorption Gordon began to walk up and down the room, his hands behind his back, re-examining in his own mind every scrap of evidence he had accumulated. Now he went over not merely the incidents he had proved but every jot of conversation, in case a chance word should give him the clue. It was useless to hope for identification by any one who travelled with him. He looked very much like other people; and he agreed with Mrs. Parr that he didn't look like a chauffeur. It was no wonder that Mrs. Mordaunt thought so highly of him: not even much wonder that he should be so successful with wretched women like Fanny and Miss Larkin. Even Mrs. Parr must have a soft corner for him, or she wouldn't go on working when, on her own testimony, she had such a job getting her wages. Her face had changed to a less spiteful animation as she spoke of him, " looking quite like a gentleman . . ."

Gordon came to a dead stop; a rush of excitement flooded his being. He'd got it; after all this cogitation and twisting of clues and theories he had got it at last, the unshakable proof that, however he had managed and whoever he had suborned to support his story, Walter Sharpe had, in fact, returned to London on the night of the 26th and had travelled back to Merston on the morning of the 27th.

" Now let's see how we can make hay of the yarn he's put up," reflected Gordon light-heartedly. " He'd have to go on the milk train, of course. There might be some chance of identifying him. I doubt if a great many casual passengers take that. But it won't do to count on it. Then I must get in touch with Pocock again, though it's ten to one he won't be able to help me. And I must somehow manage to get inside Sharpe's house to make doubly sure that I'm on the right track at last. I wonder what sent him pell-mell to Fanny that night, or if he intended to go, anyhow. He put up a very good defence, all things considered, for he had precious little time. But there were some things he couldn't guard against. He said he determined to stay the night before the 6.8 left Merston, but we have evidence that there were beds at the Four Feathers up till eight o'clock, so he didn't try and get a room there that evening. And though he had come to that decision he didn't ring up Pocock for an appointment till the next morning. Now, if he'd been at Merston that night he wouldn't have run things so fine. He had luck about the hotel. This chap, Farmer, on his own showing, couldn't recognise any of the bunch of fellows who slept in his smoking-room or whatever it was, so it would be perfectly safe for Sharpe to class himself with them. It wouldn't occur to any one, of course, that he'd want to pay for a room he hadn't slept in. I wonder how the train runs, what time it gets in."

He rang up the inquiry office at Waterloo; this was going to be a matter of minutes, and he didn't dare risk the slightest inaccuracy. He learned that the milk train left Waterloo at 5.49 and reached Merston at 8.10. He could find out from the Four Feathers what time they served breakfast; it would not be hard, with the town so full, for a sharp man to guess the position and pass himself off as one of the overflow guests of the previous night. No one could conceivably identify him, and wasn't his name written large in the Visitors' Book for every one to see? Luck had favoured him again in making the early interview with Pocock feasible. Certainly it provided an excellent excuse for the unexpected night at Merston, contrary to all he had told his charwoman, and his own intentions.

" I'd better follow Charles Kingsley's excellent advice and do the job that's nearest, I suppose," he reflected. " What would be the best make-up? I might go as a workman. I wonder whom Sharpe employs—or rather, his landlord— for outside jobs? Better not take any chances, and it shouldn't be hard to find out. But that rig gives me a chance of getting into his room, and I ought to be shot if I can't get rid of the old lady for a couple of minutes while I go through his wardrobe."

CHAPTER XIII

1

HE had to wait some time the next day for Sharpe to leave the house, and he was on tenterhooks lest the old woman should go first, which would mean a wasted day. In spite of his disguise, he wished to avoid seeing Sharpe; the man had keen eyes and might tumble to the actual position. At about ten o'clock, however, Sharpe walked round to the garages and brought out the orange taxi. As soon as he had disappeared, Gordon, looking warm, smoky, and dressed in a shabby, paint-stained suit, knocked at the front door. (There wasn't any other, a position Gordon didn't care about; two doors made your task much simpler, and eliminated a lot of risk.) The old woman seemed in a very bad temper; she came banging a bald old broom on the passage floor, and stuck herself in the doorway while she asked the visitor's business. She was just going, she said ungraciously, and couldn't wait for no man, not if he was ever so.

" I've come from Berridges to see about the leaking gutter," said Gordon, promptly. " Shan't keep you more than a minute, Ma."

" 'Ere, who are you calling Ma? " she asked wrathfully. " And if it comes to that, we ain't got a leaking gutter."

" I know you haven't," said Gordon to himself, but aloud he only said, " Your mistake, Ma. I got me orders. Mr. Berridge has had the complaint. . . ."

" Mr. Sharpe didn't say nothing to me about it."

" Forgot, I s'pose. Can't expect a busy man to remember everything."

Still grumbling, she led him upstairs to an oblong room furnished as a bedroom.

" Don't know what people are coming to," she said bitterly, leaning on the handle of the broom. " A drop of water is more than they can stand now. Leaking gutter, indeed! "

Gordon swept the room with his eye. It was obviously a man's apartment. A woman would have placed the mirror under the window and wouldn't have left the wardrobe with its long glass in a corner where it would get the least light. It was this wardrobe that was his objective, but he had no opportunity of examining it until he sent the old woman scurrying downstairs under pretext of an imaginary bell. The instant she turned he swung open the wardrobe door to display a very shabby mackintosh, the dark suit admired by Mrs. Parr, some flannels, a suit of brown plus-fours, an odd coat and two rather bright striped cardigans, one with sleeves and one without. There was time for a hasty examination of the pockets of the various coats, but these yielded nothing; then Gordon opened the other half of the wardrobe, that was ranged with shelves, on which were some poorly-darned underwear, socks, handkerchiefs, a bowler hat, a chocolate-coloured homburg and another, a cheaper one, in dark grey. A collection of ties caught his eye for a moment; obviously Sharpe believed himself to be a ladies' man. Those would go down very well with the type of woman he was most glad to enmesh. Then feet sounded on the stairs, and Gordon swung the doors to again. He took no notice of the old woman's rage at finding there hadn't been a bell after all. Unless it was them dratted boys. . . .

" I'd swear I heard one," said Gordon blithely, having discovered what he came to learn. " But I'll tell you what you are right about. There's no leak here. Mr. Stammers'll have to give us more particular details. You're sure it was this room? "

" Mr. Stammers? Who's he? "

" Well—your employer. Funny, not knowing his name." He laughed heartily.

" My—'ere," she flourished the bald-headed broom. " You think you're funny, don't you? Well, I'll show you."

Gordon dodged the broom. " Not funny a bit," he protested. " This is No. 21, isn't it? "

" Thirty-one. Mean to say you've kep' me all this time looking for a leak in the wrong roof? Well, I— I——"

Gordon left her to it.

2

" That's that," he reflected with some satisfaction as he left the house; but before he had gone far that glow faded. He still had nothing he could take into court. What was an old woman's evidence, particularly one as unreliable as old Mrs. Parr?

" No, I've got to get more than that," he decided. " The fact that she says he went off on Wednesday in a dark suit and a homburg and he was seen at the Four Feathers on Thursday in plus-fours and a cap, isn't enough proof to any one but ourselves that he did actually return home and change his clothes, presumably to avoid recognition."

But no matter how slight the evidence seemed, he must get it confirmed in as many directions as possible, so he put through a trunk call to William Pocock.

" You remember my coming to you about a man, Blount, whom you saw on the morning of the 27th March. Can you recall what he was wearing? "

He expected no help here, but to his pleasure Pocock returned, " As a matter of fact, I can. They say all business men have their foibles, and that's mine. That is, I do expect a man to be suitably dressed for his job. And while I shouldn't expect a clerk to turn up for an appointment in tails, equally I don't expect a man on a business appointment in plus-fours. And I do expect him to have shaved."

" Do you remember the colour of the plus-fours? "

" I should imagine it would be difficult to forget it. The most virulent brown I've ever seen. Bought off the peg, too, which struck me as strange, because his hat was a good one. I know something about hats, and I'm never mistaken. He didn't get that under two guineas."

" It sounds peculiar to wear that type of hat with cheap plus-fours."

Gordon could imagine Pocock's shrug, though he couldn't see him. " Oh, well, that's the sort of fellow he was. Not the type I'd care to do business with. Unreliable, I should say, and precious little sense of proportion. Oh, and he was carrying a mackintosh, a foul old thing, stained with tar. A nasty piece of work altogether, I should call him, since you ask me."

Gordon remembered quite definitely the girl at the Four Feathers speaking of Sharpe as wearing a cap that he had pushed on to the back of his head. So that for some reason he must have bought the chocolate-coloured homburg now in his wardrobe, after leaving the inn and before he met Pocock. Why he should do this puzzled Gordon a little, but he came to the conclusion that in an excess of caution Sharpe was trying to cover himself at every point. If any one remembered a man in a ginger-coloured cap and plus-fours to match going north by the milk train, the man who travelled south a few hours later must present a different appearance. Hence the hat and the mackintosh. Besides, there was always the chance that some one had seen the plus-fours at the Fulham end of the trail, and that person or persons must not be allowed to identify that figure with Walter Sharpe, returning in a hat and a mackintosh. That meant another journey to Merston to try and trace these articles.

So Gordon went to Waterloo and asked if it would be possible to see the driver of the milk train on the morning of the 27th March. By great good fortune he was on the premises, a big wild red-haired man with a tremendous fist and a mouth like a letter-box.

" Like to make a bit? " asked Gordon. " Well, d'you remember a man travelling up on the milk train one morning towards the end of March? I don't suppose you'd recollect the date. A chap in plus-fours and a golfing cap."

" Oh! " grinned the driver. " Beautiful bouncing Bert. I remember 'im all right. So does me mate. You doin' a bit of dirty work for the wife? "

" I beg y'r pardon? "

" Well, there was something wrong with him all right. Coming home with the milk, he was, and didn't want no one to know it. I on'y thought p'raps his wife caught 'im, after all. You don't get many fellers like that coming up on the milk train, and there's usually trouble later, if you do."

" It seems to me a long time for you to remember him," objected Gordon. " D'you remember the colour of his suit? "

" Rather. A nice tasty ginger. That'll give the girls a treat, I says to my mate. Tell you how we remember 'im so well. 'E was so afraid of us seein' 'e was there. If you ask me, I believe 'e'd 'ave gone under a seat if 'e'd 'ad a chance. I remember we tried to pass the time o' day with him, and he jest pulled 'is cap over 'is eyes and wouldn't say a word. Bit of a head, I shouldn't wonder. That what comes of spending a night on the tiles," he added virtuously. " For meself, I don't think there's nothing like a bed."

" Was he clean-shaved or had he got a little ginger moustache? "

" Well, 'e'd lost it by the time we met 'im. No, 'e was clean-shaved, on'y 'e 'adn't done it that morning, if you see what I mean. Well, don't s'pose 'e'd 'ad a chance."

" And do you remember where he got out? "

" Got out at Merston. Went tearin' past the ticket-collector, too, as if 'is wife was at 'is 'eels. No, I didn't see where 'e went, but I dessay 'e was in an 'urry. Got a job, p'raps, and 'ad to 'ave a shave and breakfast and be in at nine. To say nothing of the missus."

" Would you know him again? "

The driver instantly looked nervous. " Well, I couldn't say Yes to that, sir. Bit too much of a risk. Y'see, what with 'is cap bein' over 'is eyes and all . . ." He was shown a photograph, but wouldn't commit himself further than to say it was very like.

" You're sure it was a cap he was wearing, not a homburg? "

" Dead sure. Why, mean to say it's the wrong gent? Well, all I can say is, it's the only gent we've 'ad on the milk train for a long while back. That's why we remembers 'im, that and the fact that a fellow we know 'ad got 'imself into a nice mess with some gal or other, and we thought this one was in the same stew. Made us talk about 'im a bit."

Gordon paid him handsomely, and inquired the next train to Merston. It appeared there was a quick one in twenty minutes' time, so he decided to take that. He wanted to learn whether Sharpe had bought the hat on the morning of the 27th, and what had happened to the cap, since he had seen no sign of it at the Mews.

Since he had been wearing the cap at the Four Feathers. and there hadn't been any opportunity for him to buy a hat before he reached there, it seemed reasonable to suppose the shop lay somewhere on the road between the inn and Pocock's office. The road was almost a straight one, and there was only one hatter in it. Not, reflected Gordon, the type of hatter to which Sharpe was accustomed. You could imagine him strolling nonchalantly into some big branch shop and examining those ghastly coloured hats that were being put on the market this year—blue and yellow and scarlet, making their wearers look like a lot of very inferior macaws. But Dobson stocked only hats by known makers, and you certainly wouldn't get anything here under a guinea. Sharpe must have been seriously perturbed by his appearance, or the impression he wished to make on Pocock, to have gone in at all. He was able to see the manager, and thereafter it was a simple affair to turn up the books and learn that on the 27th March a nameless customer bought a homburg hat for thirty-seven-and-sixpence. The assistant who had sold it was interrogated, and after a little prompting recollected the sale.

" It was your saying he wore brown plus-fours that reminds me," he explained, " and a cap. We remember that cap here. He came in early, not longer after we'd opened, though I'm afraid I don't remember the day of the week or anything. But that's all in the bill. We never have an undated one. Didn't want to give as much for the hat; I should think the cap cost about two-and-eleven. We asked him if we could send it on or if he'd have it in a bag, and he said, ' Oh, you can keep the cap.' "

It appeared to have become a standing joke among the assistants. Whenever any argument arose, one side or the other would say derisively, " Oh, you can keep the cap," and that usually ended the discussion. Gordon asked if it was still on the premises, and fortunately it was. As Carew had said, it probably cost about three shillings originally, and bore the name of a Fulham outfitter. The detective asked gravely if he might borrow the cap for a few days, and immediately brought down on his head the inevitable rejoinder.

His inquiries after the mackintosh were less successful. There was a small side-turning, known as Bunters Alley, a short distance from Pocock's office, and here second-hand coats and mackintoshes in every state of disrepair were sold for the proverbial song. But the elderly man who kept it could give Gordon no satisfactory reply, and he was forced to abandon that line of investigation.

3

Travelling back to town Gordon's mind twisted this way and that seeking a tangible thread that would give him a straight clue to the mystery. For all that he had discovered, he had still not the ghost of a case to take to a jury; he had not yet established a connection between his suspect and the dead woman. He had the carriage to himself, so that he could move about as much as he liked. Like Field, he believed that movement helped the working of the brain. The track was constantly bent by angles in the line, so that the sun fell first at one end of the carriage and then at the other. Gordon, who disliked sitting in strong sunlight, was perpetually changing his position from one seat to the other, and possibly this persistent movement accounted for the idea that suddenly flashed into his mind.

" Of course! " he exclaimed. " What a double-barrelled fool I am not to have thought of it before. The notes! If we could trace any of those to him we'd be a long way on our road."

He was thinking of the hundred pounds Charles admitted giving to Fanny; fifty of these had been paid into the Post Office, but he had assumed that the other fifty had been kept against current expenses. A recollection of the room and its contents, however, assured him that no money had been spent on it for some time, while with the exception of the blue coat and frock, there were no new clothes in Fanny's wardrobe. It seemed more than likely that the fifty pounds in question had gone to Sharpe, to keep him quiet while Fanny played her husband as a not too skilful angler plays a fish. Unless she had been greatly pressed for the money she would scarcely have taken a step that, above all others, would alienate Charles's sympathies.

Arrived in London Gordon rang up Arbuthnot and obtained an appointment. He explained the progress he had made and the information the lawyer could get from Charles. Arbuthnot was going to see the young man the next morning and undertook to telephone to Gordon's office. His information was interesting. The hundred pounds had been paid over in five notes of ten pounds each and fifty notes of one pound each. The notes had all been very crisp and new, and Charles could not remember the numbers of any of them. He said, however, that before parting with them to Fanny he had had occasion to settle an account of a trifle over eight pounds. The only ten-pound note in his possession was a rather creased one with the name " R. Underwood " and an address in West Kensington on the back. Hesitating, for some reason he did not pause to diagnose, from giving that note in ex-change for his bill, he had substituted it by one of the five notes intended for Fanny.

" So," wound up Arbuthnot, " if we can trace that note back to Sharpe we can at all events prove that he was dunning her for money within a few days of her death."

It would not be difficult, as Gordon knew, to get news of the note in question. The press would give all the assistance it could, and no doubt information would shortly be forthcoming. But such publicity involved warning Sharpe of their suspicions, while, if the note remained in his possession, he had only to destroy it and ruin their hopes. So he made out a list of the most likely people to whom Sharpe would have given it, surmising, quite rightly as it turned out, that Fanny had kept the single notes for herself. A clerk at the Post Office where the account was opened recollected a girl paying in fifty pounds in single notes quite recently; there had been some discussion as to whether she had paid in too much, two of the new notes having clung together. The clerk added that she had been surprised that some one dressed as Fanny had been paying in a lump sum of that amount. Gordon's list ran:

> Landlord
> Kingham & Bruce
> Petty (tailor)
> New Post Furnishing Company
> Rate Collector.

The first three inquiries proved abortive, but the New Post Company remembered Sharpe's paying with notes to the value of ten pounds on the 20th March. There had been some trouble with this particular customer, who had allowed his payments to fall considerably into arrears. He had been plausible when called upon and had promised substantial settlement in the near future. They had been prevailed upon to give him extended credit, but shortly before the money was paid over they had been compelled to warn him that they would call and take the furniture away if they were not paid immediately. That had had the desired effect. Sharpe had come in and paid down twenty-seven pounds in three ten-pound notes. They had asked him to sign all these, and the assistant remembered seeing a name on the back of one of them. By good fortune the note had been given as change to a man well known to them and further inquiries became possible. Eventually, after some difficulty the note was produced, and a neat table was drawn up to show the hands through which it had passed since Charles gave it to Fanny. There was no loophole for doubt; Sharpe had been blackmailing the dead woman six days before the murder.

"That's half our job done," he reflected with the satisfaction of a tired man, "now for the next half." It didn't occur to him any more than it did to Egerton that, having come so far, they might be compelled to retreat.

4

He saw Egerton that night. There was a note waiting for him at his office, inviting him to dine with the young politician, if he could spare the time. Gordon, feeling justifiably pleased with developments, went straightway. His own voice took on a tinge of excitement as he explained the present position, seated in Egerton's study, but Egerton was so cool he might have been arranging a dinner party. Even his hands, clasped on a blotter in front of him, were as steady as Time.

"So far so good," he said, as the story came to an end. "Do you know, Gordon, what amazes me most in every criminal case I've ever known? The one factor you don't seem able to eliminate? That is, the desperate effort after security made by the criminal. Nine times out of then they sign their own death-warrants, men who might well have escaped even suspicion if they'd had the sense to stand still. They're like women pursued by wasps; they flutter and squeal until they arouse the wasp's dander and then they get stung and blame the wasp, poor thing. If Sharpe had had the steadiness of nerve to stay put, I doubt if we should ever have got a finger on him. He was wise to obliterate the marks of his presence in Fanny Hobart's room, but he should have stopped there. That placing of the necklace in Charles's cigarette-box; the buying of a new taxi on such a flimsy pretext; and now this insane vanity that convinces him he'll be singled out from a crowd, none of whom probably have noticed him, all those will convict him in the end. There's another thing, too, that for all his experience of women he doesn't seem to have learned; and that is that when you ask a woman to describe a man she may begin with the colour of his hair, though she'll very likely give you a vague description; but she'll certainly tell you what he was wearing. Mrs. Parr did; the girl at the Four Feathers did. And unfortunately for Sharpe, they noticed he wasn't wearing the same clothes. He wanted to look as different as he could, in case any suspicion against him put up its head. And he put his neck into the noose."

" We're not out of the wood yet, though," Gordon reminded him.

" We're not. But we've plenty more material to work on. To begin with, we have to remember all this part of the action was unpremeditated; and it only took place at all because he was absolutely desperate. Now, he wasn't desperate when he went to Merston on Wednesday morning; so that something happened between say eight o'clock, when he reached town, and midnight, when Fanny Hobart was murdered. Now what? Oh, we've got our answer all right. Mrs. Parr gave it to us."

" The telegram? "

" Of course. Telegrams aren't sent casually, particularly to men who have a telephone. It must have been something very urgent, and I think we may assume it was a demand for money. For without pausing for food, he went straightway up to Menzies Street. I'm convinced that was never part of his plan. Both Fanny and he were anxious to get Charles into a trap from which he'd never escape. He was to be persuaded to go to Menzies Street, into the house itself, with Fanny. What took place after he got in, or whether anything took place at all, was beside the point. It would be simple to urge that men don't go to Menzies Street for a cup of tea and a chat, and certainly not to a house with a reputation like that of No. 39. If Fanny's plan had worked, they'd have been in a position to black-mail Charles successfully to the end of his days. So that Sharpe certainly wouldn't have run any risk of breaking in upon them."

"There's just this point," suggested Gordon. "After all, it would be only her word against his. Mightn't Sharpe have meant to go up there anyway, to be an additional witness?"

Egerton considered that. "He might," he conceded. "But would he have left his meal untouched, gone off in such a hurry? My idea is that he got the telegram, that it contained bad news, probably a demand for money to be paid immediately, and it was so urgent that he forgot every-thing except the need for touching money, and went straight off to tackle Fanny. She presumably told him he could abandon hope, and then he lost his head and throttled her. When he realised what he'd done he went round blotting out all evidence that he was there that night, and settled down to plot an alibi. And on the whole he did it rather well, with a bit of luck here and there. But he's a type that, as Pocock says, is unreliable. If you examine his record, his house, you'll find that there's nothing enduring, nothing you can bank on. He isn't methodical, or at least only up to a point. He can plan courageously, but he can't go beyond a certain line. After that anything may betray him. And he made a very serious blunder here. He rang up Miss Yates from Waterloo and asked for money immedi-ately. According to his own story he had only just returned after twenty-four hours away from London; he wanted money and he wanted it at once. There was no time to hesitate. Now, you and I, Gordon, know it's all my eye and Betty Martin pretending that this fellow, Dyson, had to have not only an answer but also spot cash within a few hours. That's not the way men enter into agreements. They consult a lawyer, they spend time discussing pros and cons. They don't settle it all in a rush over a telephone. But Sharpe knew that was the one way to get the money he had to have. He rushed Miss Yates off her feet with stories of a glittering chance they mustn't miss. Then he went round and collected the money. I wonder what really happened to it. That he needed it to pay off some creditor is obvious, and from his terror I should say it was something more considerable than an ordinary debt. After all, he'd done crooked things before and there's no reason to suspect a change of heart. He may have got himself into a criminal mess. He wasn't so terrified of imprisonment as Fanny was, but he'd had enough for a lifetime. He didn't mean to go through that again. A good deal of that is pure supposition. What we have to do is prove it. Can you get hold of this Dyson man? You'll very likely find that he sent the wire. Could Miss Yates help you, do you think? Pretend you want a little more information about her enterprise. She might let on where the mysterious Dyson lives. And somehow we've got to trace that telegram."

Gordon said slowly, " There was an orange envelope on the table in his office when I first called there. I should say it might stay there for six months."

"We must get hold of it," said Egerton, without hesitation. " I could do that, or you could put one of your men on to the job. I don't think it's safe for you to go down there again. I don't for a moment expect the telegram will be inside, but if we're right, and Sharpe opened it on Wednesday night, while Mrs. Parr discovered it in the letter-box on Thursday morning, he would have to re-seal the envelope. The probability is he wouldn't use the same kind of gum as is supplied by the Post Office; we can get an expert to tell us if it's been gummed for a second time. That would all be to the good. But we must learn

what was in the envelope and who Dyson is—unless he's
an invention of Sharpe's brain. But I think that will see
us nearly home—when we've cleared up the telegram
mystery."

"Even then we shan't have proved that he was in
Menzies Street."

But Egerton only smiled and lighted another cigarette
and said that, like the famous pilgrim of Newman, they
must be content with one step at a time.

CHAPTER XIV

1

IT was easier to trace Dyson than he had anticipated.
Miss Yates gave him all the information he needed. She
was, she said, very much surprised and disappointed that
the article had not yet appeared in the press, but was
mollified to learn that Gordon did not consider it complete. The name of Sharpe's pseudo-partner, she told him,
was Dyson, W. A. Dyson, and he lived at Nottingham,
where he had a motor business. He wanted Sharpe to open
a London office, while she herself was to be the sleeping
partner. But she meant to learn all about it and help
wherever she could, she added. Gordon obtained a Nottingham telephone directory, and looked up the name of
Dyson; there was half a column of them, and none of them
had initials " W. A." Either Sharpe was completely hazing
his fiancée, or the man wasn't on the telephone, at all
events, not in his own name. There was, however, a firm
of motor engineers called Dyson, and Gordon took the
afternoon train to Nottingham and called at their office.
He asked for a sheet of headed paper to write a note to
the senior partner who, he was informed, could see no one
without an appointment at that hour. The note-paper contained a list of the partners; there were five, three of them
Dysons, and the last of the three had the initials " W. A."
Gordon asked if he could see this man, but was told to

make an appointment for the morning. He arranged to call again at ten o'clock, and leaving the premises went down to the Post Office. Here he obtained an interview with the postmaster, to whom he confided that he was a police officer engaged in tracking down a blackmailer. A telegram signed Dyson had been despatched on the 26th March and it was very important to know its precise contents. The postmaster was impressed and had the necessary inquiries made, with the result that a facsimile of the telegram was produced. It read:

To-morrow is your last day. Dyson.

Gordon instituted further inquiries among the clerks in the hope of getting some information as to the man who despatched it, but no one recollected him. Gordon must, therefore, trust to chance, and see what could be gleaned from to-morrow's appointment.

Dyson kept him waiting a quarter of an hour and even then seemed irritable and ill-at-ease. He was a rather short man with a square pale face and very small brown eyes. He listened in silence while Gordon explained that he had come in connection with the affairs of Mr. W. A. Blount of the Mews, Fulham, and then asked " Why come to me?"

" Because of the telegram you sent him on the 26th March." Dyson's small eyes flickered. " Well? "

" I'm afraid this is all part of a very unsavoury criminal case. We don't want to drag more people into the court than is absolutely necessary, but we've got to get the affair straight. I understand that Mr. Blount owed you money recently, and has just paid off his debt. That is, if he's paid it all off. We know he paid you five hundred pounds."

Dyson laughed curtly. " Then you know more than I do. He only paid me two-fifty. That's all he owed me— since you like to put it like that."

" We should be more than glad to hear your version of the story," Gordon assured him. " His is too fantastic to be credited."

Dyson was silent for a time. Then he said, " How long have you known Mr.—Blount? "

" Long enough to realise that isn't his right name."

" Precisely. What's your game, by the way? Are you trying to come it over me for demanding money with menaces or anything of that kind? Because, if so, you're barking up the wrong tree."

" We're not," Gordon said mildly. " We simply want to get the actual facts, and we're not satisfied that we've got them from Blount himself."

" I'll be shot if you have. The chap's a thorough-paced rotter, but he's so damn' plausible he could coax a hippopotamus out of its pool on a hot day. And knows how to act! When I told him I'd prosecute he turned green—literally green. ' I'd put myself under a train before I did another stretch,' he said. You knew, I suppose, he'd done two years for another little forging job? "

" Yes. This was forgery, too, was it? "

" That's right. He came to us for a job, oh, a little over a year ago—say, eighteen months. A good man, knows his work, I'll say that for him. But he knows too many other things, too. Well, we were pleased with what he'd done, and I suppose we were a bit casual. We didn't know about the prison record, then, and one day I found he'd put my name to a cheque for two-fifty and cashed it. Goodness knows what he did with the money. He was an extravagant sort of chap, no notion of the value of money; and he spent a good deal on himself, I should think, one way and another. When we got him we told him we'd prosecute, and then, as I say, he threatened to put himself in the river or somewhere, and swore he'd pay it back, if we gave him a chance. Well, there was no likelihood of our ever seeing a penny if we prosecuted, so we gave him three months. And, of course, he just vamoosed. We couldn't trace him anywhere. He changed his name and went to London, and there one of our travellers happened to see him about six weeks ago. We were so busy with this exhibition coming off that none of us could rush down to London, but I wrote telling him we'd got him under observation, and that he had a fortnight to find the money. The 27th was the last day of the fortnight. And I sent that wire on the 26th to assure him that we were in earnest."

" And you got the money? "

" He sent me a telegram on the 27th, promising the money the next day. I can't say I believed him, but I waited till the next morning, and then I got a cheque. I still had my doubts whether it would be passed but it was."

" Have you the telegram he sent you? "

Dyson opened a drawer and searched among some papers. " I thought I kept it. Is it very important? "

" Probably the most important piece of evidence we shall have, tangible evidence, I mean."

Dyson opened another drawer and this time he was successful. He handed the flimsy sheet to his visitor. Gordon was not interested in the message itself. He knew what it would be. But he looked eagerly both at the time of sending and the office whence it had come. He had been right when he told Dyson it might prove the most significant piece of evidence they would produce. Here at length was actual proof, that the most hard-bitten jury could not resist, that Walter Sharpe, despite all his protestations, must have returned to his own house on the 26th. For the telegram had been despatched from Waterloo Railway Station, 12.7 on the morning of the 27th. Sharpe's train would arrive a few minutes before the hour. He had to get in touch with Miss Yates before he dared send a wire; but he hadn't had time to go near his house that day. And so he must have returned on the Wednesday night and read the telegram then.

Having obtained the name of Sharpe's bankers, Gordon went down to see them. They acknowledged, after some pressure, that a cheque signed M. J. Yates, to the value of five hundred pounds, payable to Sharpe, had been received on the 27th March. The next day Sharpe had drawn a cheque to the order of W. A. Dyson for half that amount. Sharpe had managed it all rather well, Gordon thought. He must have pointed out to Miss Yates the folly of sending two cheques; indeed, it would be impossible. He wouldn't want his partner-presumptive to know that he was unable to raise the necessary capital. Oh, he could talk her round easily enough. But what struck Gordon most forcibly was the coolness with which he had obtained from the woman double the sum required. Similarly, he had (one supposed) instructed Fanny to follow the same tactics.

But even now he had, if he were to satisfy Egerton, to provide irreproachable proof that Sharpe had not merely been at Merston that night, but had definitely been at Menzies Street, and turn which way he would he still could see no light in that direction.

2

A final iota of proof awaited him at his office. Paine, one of his best men, had been down to the Mews, had obtained entry to Sharpe's house on a spurious errand, and had come away with the envelope of the telegram in his pocket. It was easy to show that this had been torn open and then sealed with a different kind of gum; and a sample taken from a bottle in Sharpe's office was proved to be identical with the second kind.

3

For three days the proving of Sharpe's guilt presented an apparently hopeless problem. Egerton insisted that if a crime had been committed the clue to that crime must eventually be forthcoming; if they couldn't find it, they must persuade the murderer to give them the final clue; and he added, with perfect truth, that if they brought a case against Sharpe that they could not substantiate, he would doubtless escape for life, and even though they succeeded in arousing sufficient doubt to get Charles acquitted, he would bear the stigma of possible murder to the end of his days. "And I don't precisely care that my brother-in-law should be branded as a man who was lucky enough to foozle the judges," he wound up dryly.

Nevertheless, Gordon at all events could see no clear way out of the tangle. He followed up one or two minor suggestions but these advanced him not a jot. On the fifth morning Egerton rang him up.

" A rather peculiar development has occurred," he said. " I have got a request from Sharpe for an interview."

" The devil you have! " exclaimed Gordon. " That means mischief, I'll be bound. He must somehow have realised we were after him."

" Must have," agreed Egerton, cordially. " I've asked him to come along this afternoon. I shall be free about four o'clock. Can you make it convenient to come as well? I think it would be best to have an additional witness."

" What the deuce are you staging? " Gordon wanted to know.

" I'm staging nothing. I'm not going to do the talking this afternoon. I'm going to leave that to Sharpe; and sooner or later he'll give us what we need to know."

" If he thinks we can formulate a case against him, he may give us the business end of his gun before we can stop him," observed Gordon, dryly. " It might be as well to be prepared."

But Egerton only laughed and rang off.

4

When Gordon arrived at Eaton Square that afternoon he found Egerton in his library, a square, comfortably-furnished room that contrived to retain an air of austerity in spite of its deep chairs; there was a recess at the back, covered by a curtain, and Egerton asked the detective to remain there during the interview with Sharpe.

" For several reasons," he explained. " Firstly, if he does give himself away, we must have another witness. Secondly, because, if there's to be dirty work, I should like to feel I've got you at my back; and thirdly, in case he acts as hastily as we believe he once acted before, when we should need some one to bear witness to the truth."

" You're running a considerable risk," exclaimed Gordon, but Egerton only said that he was generally supposed to be a cautious man but there were limits even to his schemes of self-preservation. He seemed to think this was his opportunity and that if he failed now to rescue his friend the fault would be his. He looked, indeed, something like the young David in the wilderness of En-gedi when he was informed that his enemy was even now delivered into his hand.

He had barely finished explaining matters to Gordon when some one knocked in a precise manner on the front door.

" That'll be our bird," suggested Gordon, preparing to conceal himself, but Egerton said, " No, that will probably be Bremner."

" We want some one official to back us up," he added. " We aren't the police force; we can't do anything definite. Bremner will be our shield and buckler."

Bremner came in, shook hands with Gordon, asked Egerton a question or two, and then said, " Nuisance we can't smoke, but it's too big a risk. A clever man can distinguish the fumes of different tobaccos, and though I don't suppose Sharpe is as versatile as that it doesn't do to take chances."

5

Sharpe came on the stroke of the hour. He was, not precisely nervous, but obviously anxious and perplexed. His manner was quiet and collected, and he achieved a dignity for which none of them had been prepared.

He came to the point at once. " It's good of you to see me, Mr. Egerton, considering the way you feel about me. I hadn't realised till just lately what your game was. I don't know how you got on to me at all. Perhaps I gave myself away somewhere? " He paused, looking at Egerton inquiringly, but Egerton didn't speak, and Sharpe went on, " It wasn't till I got these letters that I saw where you were trying to put me. But you're wrong. You've got a lot of right on your side—I admit that—and things won't look any too well for me—but you're wrong for all that. Here are the letters."

He passed two typewritten sheets of poor paper across to the young politician. Egerton took them in silence and appeared to master their contents without for an instant removing his eyes from his visitor. He was quite as aware as Gordon could be of the danger in which he stood. If Sharpe was going to be put in the dock he'd make sure he got a full run for his money, and a second murder seldom appears such a serious affair as the first.

The letters ran:

(Undated.

No address.)

" DEAR SIR,

" I think you ought to know that you are in some danger. When you are gone out of a morning people come to your house asking questions. They are trying to get you for the murder of Fanny Hobart. Ask Mrs. Parr how many men have come to the house wanting you. I tell you this because I think you ought to know that you are in danger. I do not know anything about things, but they are trying to get you, I am sure. I do not give you my name because they might try and get me, but I give you this warning.

" A WELL-WISHER."

" DEAR SIR,

" They are still after you, though you may not know it. You had better beware. If you do not believe me, ask Mr. Scot Egerton, because it is he that is doing it all. They have found out everything about you and are trying to ruin you.

" A WELL-WISHER."

Egerton handed the letters back. " A pity your friend doesn't know how to spell my name," he observed " Did those come through the post? "

" Yes. I didn't think to keep the envelopes, but they come from my district. I got one the day before yesterday, and the other this morning. I thought first it was just a plant, because I didn't see how you could have got on to me, but when I got the one this morning I tackled Mrs. Parr, and she told me there had been men looking at the roof and asking strange questions, and I thought if there was anything in it, it would be better for me to know."

" Know what? "

" Just what your suspicions are."

Egerton said coolly, " We think you murdered Fanny Hobart, who was your mistress."

Sharpe displayed no surprise. " I thought it was that, and if it all comes out, all you've learned about me, it'll be my ruin. And it seems to me it's likely to come out when they bring Mr. Hobart up for trial. Understand, I don't blame you. You want to save him; he's your friend; and it's reasonable enough. But you're clever enough to pile up a lot of bits of evidence against me, and make it sound all of a piece, when really I know no more about Fanny's death than you do. At least, not who did it. But I'm coming to that. I'd like to tell you everything, and see if that doesn't make a bit of difference; because, however much you want to get Mr. Hobart off, you don't want an innocent man's life smashed up into the bargain, and if people get to know my record it means the end of everything I've worked for since I was a boy. I shouldn't stand a chance against you."

Egerton, quite unmoved by this special pleading, said, " I ought to warn you that anything you may say will be used against you when the time comes. I haven't asked you to come and tell me your side of the case; but I shouldn't hesitate to make use of anything I could learn from it."

Sharpe said quietly, " I quite see that. It's only natural. But the truth is so different from what you think. It's— ghastly. You'll realise that when you hear what it is. And I believe you'll listen fair and give me a square deal, though you may believe I'm a murderer."

" Well, I've warned you," said Egerton, briefly. " I don't regard this interview as confidential; but, that being understood, I shall be glad to hear anything you may have to say."

" That's quite understood," said Sharpe. " You've got a lot at stake, too. Not as much as I have, because, in spite of the highfalutin' people, a man does value his own life above his friend's. But I want to make you believe that, though all the appearances are against me, I didn't kill Fanny. I better begin at the start. I don't know exactly how much you know; you can pull me up if I'm only telling you what you'd found out for yourself. I don't mind admitting there's a good deal I'd like to keep dark. It means the end of everything for me if all my past is going to be made public."

" To save time, I might say we know about your engagement to Miss Ticehurst, and how and why it was broken off. We know about your two years in prison, and we know that you found Mrs. Hobart when you came out and have kept in touch with her ever since. And we know that you ' married ' her two years ago, in your own name."

A spasm, his first sign of emotion, twisted Sharpe's face. " Yes; I hadn't changed it then. Oh, I was a fool, of course, to dream I could live down my past, but I meant to. I'd had my lesson, and I thought if I went straight it 'ud be all right. It wasn't, of course. My Lord! I reckon these judges don't know what they're doing when they give a man two years. A life sentence would be nearer the truth. Not that you can blame 'em altogether," he added, in less strained tones. " They don't know what they're doing. They haven't been through it themselves. I didn't know at first. But I soon learned it isn't enough to turn your back on the past. There's always some one turning up that used to know you, or was in the next cell with you, and wants a bit of temporary help. And it would have ruined me if it had come out that I'd done time. That's why I wrote to you; I didn't want to, but I've got on my feet at last, after all these years, and I don't want to be tripped again."

Egerton, still unsympathetic, asked him to get on with the story.

" I quite appreciate your motive for asking for the interview," he added. " Now go ahead."

Sharpe began with the story of his engagement, his visits to the household at Burton St. Lawrence, his first meeting with Fanny and his gradual enslavement to her charms. He explained his growing resentment at the manner in which the girl was treated by her relations, a manner that passed from the merely domineering to the openly discourteous, ending in giving the girl her meals alone, whereas hitherto she had had them with the family.

"That," said Sharpe, "got my goat more than anything. It was as if they were trying to show me she wasn't good enough for them. Well, I thought, if she's not good enough for you she is for me. And I suppose they began to notice that. I know that, for all my ambition, and I was ambitious—still am, for that matter—I couldn't pretend my heart was in things like it had been. Even the motor business Miss Ticehurst was going to help me set up seemed pretty small and dusty compared with her. To do her justice, she'd have coaxed the heart out of any man. Well, when they began to treat her like a brat in disgrace I got pretty mad, and next time I saw Fanny I told her how things were. I was for breaking off the engagement, and her and me getting married right away; but she said we hadn't any money for that—I hadn't got a job, not a regular one, at the time—and she didn't want us to start in that way. Well, you know what happened; then Marigold broke off the engagement herself, and Fanny got sent home. And then . . . ." he began to experience more trouble with his words, as if even now the memory of that old humiliation was more than he could endure, with composure.

"Oh, well," he went on, seeing Egerton was not disposed to give him a hand, " you know about the next two years. And then when I came out and went hunting round for Fanny, I found she'd married this Hobart fellow. It took me some time running them to earth, but I meant to do it. It was only the thought of her that kept me going at all during those two years' hell. When I found her—somehow I hadn't thought of her being married—I found that she was more than a bit disappointed. It was easy to see that, and to see why. If a man in Mr. Hobart's position chooses to marry a girl like Fanny he's no right to keep her mewed up as if he was ashamed of her, which I suppose is about the size of it. Anyway, she was glad enough to see me, and pretty soon we were back on our old terms. I wanted her to come away with me at once, but she kept putting me off. Then she told me he'd got a job abroad, and would be going any day, but if we were careful he'd have to make provision for her. I said I didn't want his money, and anyway he never seemed to have enough to go round, but you couldn't move Fanny once she'd made up her mind. And it's true I was finding it pretty difficult to get a job. I'd written to some old employers of mine, and answered plenty of advertisements, but nothing turned up. However, I managed to borrow a bit of money and got started with a motor repair place, and sold an occasional second-hand car. Used to buy 'em cheap, and paint 'em up and sell 'em at a little profit. It wasn't much but it was all grist to the mill. Mind you, I didn't know at that time that Hobart had left Fanny any capital; I thought it was just an allowance paid every quarter. That's what she told me. This garage affair failed, and for a time I was desperate. At last I got a job in the north as a commercial traveller, and though it meant leaving Fanny I couldn't refuse. She said she might get daily work in London, and then when we were together again we could have some sort of a home. I didn't do badly; I suppose if you're keen on a thing you're more likely to make another chap buy it than if you hardly know which way up it ought to stand. But I couldn't send Fanny much money. Then like a bolt from the blue I got a letter saying she was sick of waiting, and she hadn't been able to get a job, and she wanted a bit of security and a bit of fun before she was too old to enjoy it, or find any one to give it her."

" She had, in fact, found such a person? "

" Yes, a fellow named Browne. Picked him up on a bus. She told me afterwards she'd been trailing him for over a week, and thought he'd never speak. He went quite off his rocker about her for a bit, and took a flat for her in Maida Vale. She used to write to me—she'd gone back to her maiden name by then—and when my job came to an end I came back to London, and we met at her flat. By this time, I'd practically got to consider ourselves man and wife; Hobart seemed to have faded out of the picture. It wasn't much of a position for me, because Fanny was afraid of Browne finding out about us, and she wouldn't often let me come and see her. That first year I felt pretty desperate. I got work on and off . . ."

"And lived on Browne's money the rest of the time, I suppose?"

Sharpe coloured; the sudden rush of blood to his face that had hitherto been unusually pale was a little startling. But Egerton knew his man; he mustn't be allowed to go on in this calm way. He had so clearly prepared his statement, omitting everything that might give the other side a handle against him.

"I've said before that Fanny and I felt like married people, it didn't seem strange for her to be helping me a bit. Anyhow, it wasn't much of a position for a man. I couldn't have her to myself, I couldn't actually marry her, and I didn't want any one else. One day, though, I felt I'd got to the end of my tether." Egerton's gibe had done its work; he spoke more quickly, with less precision and composure. The words came fast from his lips; passion kindled in his eyes. "Either I must break with her altogether, or she must give up this chap and we must sink or swim together. I went round to see her; she couldn't understand my point of view. What more did I want? Hadn't we got a nice flat where we could meet, and she had plenty of money, and could always get as much more as she wanted? Browne was mortally afraid of his wife finding anything out, and Fanny could be a bitch when her temper was out. Well, by sheer bad luck, Browne came in unexpectedly that day and found us together. I hadn't meant to stop so long, but Fanny argued and argued, and I couldn't get away. I think myself the fool had been trying to find a way out for some time, and he jumped at this. He made a hell of a dust, and the end of it was that he'd give up the flat at once and never wanted to see Fanny again. Fanny didn't really mind once it was over. She said later she'd never really liked him much, but he had money to burn and was easily pleased, and you couldn't pick and choose if you were poor. Then she told me that we could get married, if we liked. Hobart had died during the past six months of a kind of fever, but she hadn't dared mention it to me in case I wanted to take her away from Browne at once. She hadn't known then, she said, that he would leave her anything; but now she'd heard that she was to go on having this hundred a year for life, and the capital was hers, too."

" You asked to see the documents, perhaps? "

" To tell you the truth, I was so staggered by the way she told me, I never thought of such a thing. We talked over the future, and decided we might draw out the capital or part of it, and start a business of our own. We started —cars, again, of course—near Kingston. I knew I'd never be any good at anything but cars; I've always gone to every exhibition there's been, and any trade show I could get a ticket for. For about seven or eight months we were in clover. We had a car we hired out, with me driving, and I got a man called Simpson to help in the shop, with Fanny, too, of course, and we did repairs and sold an odd car or so, and second-hand motor-bikes, and everything seemed well. Then it all came out."

" What came out? "

" About Hobart not being dead after all."

" How did you find out suddenly? He didn't write to her."

Sharpe looked reluctant, like a horse trying to find a gap in the hedge rather than take the leap. But no gap was apparent, so at last he confessed, " It was the usual thing; I suppose I ought to have expected it. But I was busy and keen, and Fanny seemed happy, and honestly it never went through my head. It was that hired man, Simpson. Couldn't leave her alone. She said she could't keep him off, but that's all rot. The truth was she didn't want to. It wasn't only him, either. There was a young chap was always coming in to have his bike attended to. And there may have been others. I don't know. Well, I found out . . ." He stopped again. Egerton forebore to comment that now he had some notion of what Charles and Browne had felt in their turn, when he had cuckolded them. " We had a ghastly scene, of course, and I said I wished to God I'd never married her. I might have guessed she wouldn't play fair. Then she got into one of her rages and said I could go as soon as I liked. She said that Simpson and Ellis had as much right to make love to her as I had. I asked if husbands didn't count at all, and she said I ought to know, remembering her husband, and then she told me he wasn't dead at all, and she'd only lied because she'd been sorry for me, and knew I wanted to marry her."

" And could she offer you any proof that he wasn't dead?"

" She couldn't show any proof that he was; and she said I could ask the bank and they'd tell me that the capital had been hers ever since Hobart went abroad. I didn't ring up the bank, but I found out about Sir Gerald, and I rang up his rooms and said I was a friend of Hobart's, had been at school with him, and did they know his address. I got a servant of some sort, and he said Hobart was abroad. He couldn't give me the exact address, but a letter would be forwarded."

" And you separated after that? " There was a derisive note in Egerton's voice that made Sharpe wince.

" It may seem incredible to you that I should mind so much, seeing there had been Browne already, and I dare say other men as well, but I'd thought of her as my wife all these months, and when I saw how things were and that she'd never change—perhaps she couldn't; some people are made that way."

" People who aren't responsible for their actions should be in lunatic asylums," was all the satisfaction he got from Egerton. " We maintain them for that express purpose."

" Well, anyhow, after that, I didn't even want to stay. I felt quite sick, crazy. I never wanted to see her again. The shop wasn't doing as well as it had been, and Fanny wouldn't put in a bit more capital when we had a chance of enlarging. I found out afterwards that Simpson had been helping himself; I suppose she knew that. She and he together kept the books. Anyway, she said she'd seen enough of her money pitched away on a lousy second-hand shop, and I could take the hiring-car and clear out. But I didn't keep the car long. I hadn't any capital, and soon I was looking for a job again. And I got in with Dyson. You know about Dyson? "

" Yes."

" But what you don't know," cried Sharpe in sudden passion, " is that he lent me the money. I didn't take it, as he says; it was a loan, but like a fool I had nothing to prove it, and I knew he could rake up the Ticehurst case, and I shouldn't get a chance. I'd be condemned before the first word was spoken. When he wanted the money back I couldn't get it for him . . ."

" So you disappeared and used another name? You were at Fulham all the time? "

" D'you really feel like that? Haven't you a heart at all? " demanded Sharpe. " P'raps you don't know what it is to have a man on your heels till you can't sleep o' nights wondering if he's under your window? "

Egerton disregarded that. Voice and eyes as cold as icebergs, he observed, " So when you say you changed your name because you couldn't get a job, you really mean you changed it to avoid being run down? You hadn't changed it when you went to Dyson? "

Sharpe looked this way and that like a beast seeking cover. After a minute's silence Egerton went on, " You couldn't meet his claims, so you thought of Fanny Hobart again. Is that it? "

" I met her by chance. She'd changed so much I hardly knew her. She'd come down in her world all right, but she told me she had seen her husband, and she meant to get something out of him for all she'd suffered all these years. He ought to have been keeping her fairly, not leaving her to get along anyhow. I told her I must have money; I'd got a host of other bills. They were threatening to take away my furniture. Fanny said she'd help . . ."

" After you'd reminded her that bigamy is a punishable offence? Go on."

Gordon, secure behind the curtain, thought, " My God! I wouldn't have believed there was so much concentrated bitterness behind that quiet mask." And he heard Sharpe say, "What a first-rate inquisitor you'd have made, wouldn't you? Well, anyhow, I told Fanny I'd got to have fifty pounds, and she got it for me. She said she hadn't been able to squeeze another penny out of him at the moment, but she would have another try." Like a small vicious ferret, thought Egerton, curbing his rage by a fierce effort of will, hanging on to the helpless Charles, drawing blood at every turn. "She said she'd help me further if she could, but you didn't live in Menzies Street for a joke. She'd had a rotten time since we parted; Simpson had swindled her right and left and chucked her out. Now he'd got just the kind of place I'd always meant to have, and it was flourishing—blast him."

"And she agreed to get the money for you to satisfy Dyson?"

"Yes."

"The whole two-fifty?"

"She said she'd fight for two-fifty, but she didn't know if it would be wise to ask for the whole lot at once. That was the Tuesday before she died. She was seeing Hobart again on Wednesday, and on Thursday she'd let me know what had happened."

"So it wasn't part of your original plan to see her on Wednesday at all?"

"No. She had Hobart that night. I was to keep out of the picture."

"And Dyson's telegram upset everything?"

A malevolent gleam passed over Sharpe's pale face. He was perspiring heavily now, the drops of sweat gleaming on forehead and lips.

"Is there anything you don't know? Yes, I got that, and I knew what it meant. I hadn't remembered somehow the time was so short. But I'd have put myself under a train before I let them give me a second stretch. And I thought my only hope was Fanny. I didn't stop for anything; I couldn't telephone, because there isn't a 'phone in the Menzies Street house; and it wouldn't be safe to telegraph. Besides, I felt I had to know that night. So I got out the taxi and drove up to Menzies Street. I could see at once that she wasn't in. It was only nine o'clock, so I settled down to wait. Her room was dark and the curtains weren't drawn. She was funny about lights, hated to sleep without a light in the room; and nothing would have induced her to go to bed or even sit in a room at night without the curtains drawn. I went back to my cab, stabled it in the cul-de-sac and switched off the lights. I didn't think any one would notice it there, and I didn't want to be seen hanging about. I had an idea that if she hadn't been successful she might not want to see me that night, so I kept in the dark. I had to wait till some time after ten, and then a taxi went by and stopped at No.39. I nipped out and stood at the corner to watch. And Hobart got out and she followed. There was some conversation and then the taxi drove away, so I took it for granted he was going in with her and I thought . . ." he stopped.

" You thought she'd got him on a string for ever now," supplemented Egerton urbanely. " Well, and then you found he wasn't going in after all. What happened then?"

" I'd gone back to my cab. I thought I'd better stay where I was because people were coming and going in the road now, and I thought I'd be safe for half an hour anyway. Well, Mr. Egerton, you're very keen on showing Mr. Hobart didn't kill Fanny, but she was killed by some one during those two hours. More than that, she was killed by some one in less than that. You say, because Mr. Hobart says it himself, that he never went into the house, but came past the end of the road a few minutes afterwards. Well, if he didn't go in with her some one else did. I never saw him go past the end of the road."

" Because you were inside the cab in the dark. You admit people were passing up and down."

" I didn't see him," maintained Sharpe, stubbornly. " I was in the cab and there I stayed for half an hour or so. And then I went to look at the window, and the curtains were drawn now but still there wasn't a light. I felt a bit bothered about that, because Fanny never forgot when she was a nipper being shut up in a dark cupboard. It nearly drove her frantic. I never knew her stay in a room without a nightlight or something.` Still, I didn't like to go up to the house, so back to the cab I went again, and wondered what I should do if he spent the night there."

"Oh, surely you'd have been waiting on the doorstep to greet him in the morning," suggested the smooth voice.

"You don't help a chap much, do yuh?" demanded Sharpe in aggressive tones, but Egerton only said unemotionally, "You can't run with the hare and hunt with the hounds; at the moment I'm with the hare."

"Well, I waited and waited till at last I began to get nervous. Then I thought I must have missed him with so many people coming and going. If he'd gone I didn't want to hang about any longer, because I wanted to find out what luck Fanny had had, but that black window bothered me. I thought perhaps she'd gone out, too, and that looked as if she hadn't got anything out of him. I felt half-mad standing there, not knowing what to do, and knowing that Dyson 'ud get them to issue a warrant next day, and I might find myself faced with another two years. At last I thought I couldn't stand the uncertainty any longer, so I followed some people up the steps of the house. A bit tiddley they were, but that was so much the better for me. They wouldn't know me if they saw me again."

"Why were you so afraid of being seen?" asked Egerton curiously.

"Well, would you like to be found in Menzies Street that hour of the night? I suppose you think because I'd had Fanny like that I didn't care? Well, I may have had her, but I stuck to her. Till the last break I didn't look at another woman and the atmosphere of that street made me want to vomit. And I was going to be married, too. It's a nice thing for an engaged man to find himself in that place at such a time. Well, as I say, I got into the house. There was a landing—you know the house?—no? oh, well, there is a landing, and from behind a curtain I could see Fanny's door. There was no light under it, of course, and yet I couldn't be sure. I didn't want a hell of a row, so I waited and waited, and thought that probably I'd got myself into a worse hash than ever."

"But what jam if Hobart had emerged and found you on the threshold," prompted Egerton encouragingly. "You could even have roused the house."

A wave of despairing rage passed over Sharpe's face. "Why do you suppose I'm telling you this at all?" he cried.

Egerton regarded him incredulously. "Surely not because you thought you'd benefit from it? You can't expect me to believe you're as naïve as that."

"I'm telling you because things have got to a pitch where the truth must out. I can't lie low any longer. If I do you'll have your way and I shall be in that damned dock instead of your friend and Fanny's husband. I'll get on. I waited behind that curtain till I couldn't stand it any longer, and I crept up the stairs—there was a little light from a wick floating in a glass bowl of oil; Pilgrims' Lights, Fanny used to call them—and I turned the handle of her door very softly. If it was locked I knew that 'ud mean he was with her still; but I thought most likely he wouldn't take the risk of being away all night. But the door opened. I tell you, I felt mad then. I was so sure that meant she'd gone out again, meant, too, that she hadn't got the money. And I didn't know when I'd see her again, and I had that two years—or more— hanging over me—and I felt like a rat in a trap. I had a little torch with me, I always carry one in case I have a breakdown at night and want to see some little crick in the machinery. I switched it on—I didn't dare put up the light in case the curtains weren't drawn quite close and some one might see me. And—oh, Mr. Egerton, it was awful. The beam fell right on her face where she lay on the bed!" He shuddered and buried his own face in his hands. The watchers behind the curtain stiffened; Egerton was immobile as rock; but Rosemary and Lucy would have recognised his reaction to that.

"Have some brandy," was all he said, and he moved towards the sideboard.

Sharpe took the tumbler with shaking hands and gulped the contents at a draught.

"Thank you. That was—generous. It was pretty

ghastly, I can tell you, to see her like that, with her tongue
lolling out and her face all swollen. It's haunted me ever
since, as if I should never forget. For a minute I didn't
know what I should do. I sagged against the door like
a piece of spent elastic: Then I put on the torch again,
keeping the beam low on the floor, and drew the curtains
perfectly tight. I'd begin to see my position and I wasn't
taking risks. It never occurred to me that any one but
Hobart had done it. Why should it? I didn't know how
long she had been dead, or when he escaped, but he
couldn't have stayed in the flat long. I'd been behind that
curtain half an hour, and it wasn't quite midnight now.
I felt I was caught, and I wanted madly to get out. If any
one had recognised me, if I left the slightest trace and they
brought it home to me, they'd soon ferret out our past
history. They'd discover about Dyson and the money I
wanted from Fanny; I shouldn't stand a chance. Even if
Hobart had been seen leaving the house, leaving her room,
even, that evening some one might come forward and say
I'd been seen later. The only thing to do was to rouse the
house, and I didn't dare. I knew I shouldn't be believed.
There wasn't any weapon, you see, and every man has a
pair of hands. Any jury would say I'd done it. And then
I remembered seeing a man on the stairs, a man in evening
dress. He wasn't sober either, but he might remember
seeing me here; anything might happen. I had to make up
my mind quickly, and not shift from my decision. The
smallest slip would probably mean death. The only thing
to do was to cover my tracks and make it appear impossible
that I'd been near Fanny that night. And the only way
out I could conceive was suicide. The beam across the
room gave me that idea. It was a crazy chance but my
only one. There was too much against the alternative of
slipping out and hoping no one would track me. I looked
round for some rope, and saw that piece round the box. I
untied it and fastened it round her throat. When I'd done
that I thought I'd done the worst there was to do. I loathed
touching her; she wasn't cold, you see, and yet she was
dead. And her eyes would stay open. I did try shutting

them, and they opened again slowly. I almost shrieked when I saw that. It was as if she was watching me. I picked her up and put the cord over the beam, and then very slowly let her down, inch by inch. I didn't want the rope to break. I put the stool there—I never thought of the imprint of feet that they'd look for—and then I started to write the note. It was worse than I had imagined. Every time I caught sight of her, the room seemed to be full of her, she had moved a little. I didn't know at what angle I might glance up and see those eyes fixed on me. It made me so nervous I kept botching the note, and I had to burn a lot of experiments; but I finished it at last, and then I looked through her things, and found a letter I'd written her, so I burned that, too. Then I had to go round the room rubbing up everything I'd touched, for fear of finger-prints; I had to move softly because of the people downstairs who might hear me, and I couldn't rid myself of the feeling that she wasn't dead. Once she touched me as I passed; oh, I suppose I went too close, but I nearly gave the show away then. At last I decided I'd done everything possible, so I slipped out and locked the door on the outside. I meant to throw the key away—as a matter of fact, I did throw it out of the window next morning on the way to Merston. It's somewhere in a clump of furze now and nothing but luck would lead you to the right clump. I couldn't pick it out myself. I went back and looked up the trains, and then I saw it must look as if I hadn't had that telegram, so I stuck it up again and put it in the letter-box where I'd found it. Then I changed so as to avoid being recognised and went up to Waterloo, travelled on the milk train, where a clumsy lout tried to engage me in conversation, and had a bit of luck in the way of making it look as though I'd spent the night at the Four Feathers. I fooled about and insisted on every one signing the visitors' book, and got a stamped bill as an alibi. I didn't think I'd made a mistake anywhere, but somehow you got on my trail. I don't know how. The taxi perhaps. I happened to hear that the police were making inquiries about taxis, and I got the wind up. I had an excellent

213

excuse—there was a genuine accident—and I sold mine. It's difficult to remember everything."

" Still you remembered a good deal," Egerton consoled him. " Even to asking Miss Yates for double the amount you needed for Dyson."

Sharpe looked up, bitter and contemptuous. " Well, you fool, what else could I do? I'd told her I was starting a company. I had to have some capital. I could tell her she'd got 500 shares, and it wouldn't convey anything to her if I made them worth ten shillings apiece. I had to do that. I was driven." Then, as Egerton said nothing more, he went on more calmly, " Do you see now how things are? You may think you can get me, but you can't. Your pal did her in all right. Understand? "

" There's one thing that puzzles me," Egerton acknowledged. " You admit you wrote the letter? "

" Well? That doesn't make me a murderer."

" Do you remember exactly how it went? " He took up a slip of paper from several documents that lay on the table. " I'll read it, shall I?

" ' I do this because I must. I have made my last appeal, and he has refused me. I know no one else to whom I can turn, and if I cannot find the five hundred pounds at once I am faced with worse than death. This is the second time he has failed me.   F. P.'

" You'd only asked for two-fifty."

" Yes. But she tried to get five hundred. She was going to keep half for herself."

" You knew she was going to do that? It was part of the plan? "

" No, it wasn't. I thought she was only going to ask for two-fifty. In fact, she was a bit doubtful about asking for so much. I must say I thought she'd ruined her own case by asking for five hundred."

" That's where my perplexity comes in. How did you know she asked for five hundred? " He had not raised his voice nor changed his position, but it was as if, with that question, a charge of electricity shot through the room; all the suppressed vitality of the man leaped into his expression. Not one that heard him but started and quivered as the reflect of that passion touched him.

Sharpe looked bewildered, alarmed, then blundered out, " She told me, of course . . ."

Egerton gave him no further quarter. " Told you, did she? But when? You didn't know before the dinner-party she was going to double your demand. What opportunity did she have of telling you afterwards, *if she was dead when you went into her room?* " He saw Sharpe's expression, trapped, fierce, terrible. But nothing could have stayed him now, not the most urgent consideration of his personal danger. " But she wasn't, of course. She was alive and bitter at her failure. And she told you that she couldn't raise the money. I dare say she didn't tell you very tenderly or pityingly. Perhaps she even laughed at your distress. Oh, she looked dreadful enough, I know, lying on the bed, and she may have made your blood freeze when she dangled from that beam; but I think the moment that she looked most ghastly was the moment when you realised what you'd done and what was going to happen to you."

He was interrupted by a movement behind him, and a quick warning, " Look out. The fellow's armed." But Egerton hadn't learned ju-jitsu for nothing. He had his man in an iron grip and the revolver fell to the rug, whence Bremner presently retrieved it. And it was Bremner, too, who noticed that Egerton was as white as paper and only kept on his feet by the strength of his indomitable will.

6

" I wonder who really wrote those," murmured Gordon a little later, when Bremner and Sharpe had gone, touching the anonymous letters that every one had forgotten. " A bit of luck that, getting him up here."

Egerton lifted his head. He really did look done to the world, Gordon reflected; a pretty grim strain for him, when you came to think of it. He must have known his danger. But all Egerton said, in a heavy voice, was, " A dirty trick; the sort of thing that makes decent men retch. But then we were dealing with such a dirty criminal, and it seemed the only way. I had to get him here and he must come of his own free-will. And having got him, under a disadvantage, since he was in my house, I had to bait him out of his cautious attitude. He might never have committed that blunder about the five hundred pounds if he hadn't been jockeyed into fury that made him lose his head. He was clever enough to see where I was leading him, and he only had to say that it had been pre-arranged for Fanny to ask for five hundred in the hope of getting half that amount for us to return to our position of stalemate." He picked up the letters and made a gesture as if to tear them across. Then he hesitated. "Better not, perhaps. Bremner may want these later. I could do with a small brandy, I think. Join me, won't you? "

EPILOGUE

THE posters that, not so much later, were to announce crudely, " Sharpe Executed " were emblazoned to-day with a legend that Egerton at all events found almost as deplorable. The picture papers shouted " FROM CELL TO ALTAR " all across their front sheets. You couldn't go into a newsagent without seeing a photograph of Charles staring up at you, with the bride inset in one corner. Or *vice-versa*. Even Sir Gerald, to his disgust, saw himself reproduced in the printed page now and again. As for Egerton, he had by this time grown too much accustomed to seeing his photograph in the press to pay any attention.

The only other person who did not mind, who was indeed quite appreciative of all this fuss and publicity, was Lucy Hobart. She said placidly, " Don't fuss, Charles, it's their job. And stand still for a minute or they won't get a proper picture and they'll probably get into trouble." And, when he attempted like a restive horse to get away from them all, added, " But I think it's nice of them to be so pleased; if you were a tenth as happy as I am nothing would worry you." She even posed especially for a latecomer and started her honeymoon followed by his blessing.

The crowd mobbed the church, mobbed the boat train,

surged on to the platform to peer at the conspicuous couple. A little group of working-girls cheered them, and an elderly woman observed to her friend, " My dear, I knew from the start it was all a mistake. He's one of the Shropshire Hobarts . . ." whereat Egerton suddenly grinned.

" Are you going to drive? " asked his wife cheerfully, as he and Rosemary got away from the crowd to their own car. " All right, I will. Oh, dear, what an exciting day. Don't you love weddings, Scott? "

" No," said Egerton with rather unnecessary violence, " and not even for you would I go through that a second time." Secretly he was amazed and rather indignant at the feminine capacity for endurance; he put down a good deal of it to insensitiveness. Then, trying to be just, he reminded himself that Charles was his friend and not Rosemary's. He was content for his wife to take the wheel and he lay back at her side deep in speculative thought. Even if women were less sensitive than men they had the most irrational faith that was always proving itself justified. Look at Lucy, for instance. After Gordon's departure he had gone up to her room and found her embroidering exquisite monograms on something made of peach-coloured silk. An open drawer at her feet was two-thirds full of other garments in every pastel shade.

" You're an extravagant young woman," he observed. " I'm glad I didn't marry any one with your tastes."

" Rosemary has just the same tastes as I have," Lucy told him tranquilly. " Only I don't suppose you ever notice. I don't expect Charles to. It's just a feeling women have when they're in love. They don't feel they can ever be quite nice enough."

He asked in an odd voice, after a moment's silence, " Do you mean you're sewing your trousseau? "

Lucy looked apologetic. " You did say there was nothing I could do, and I did want to be nice for Charles. I couldn't be under your feet all the time; it might only have put you off. And if you're thinking about extravagance, I'm a perfectly lovely laundress."

" I'm sure you are, but I'm not interested in your abilities in that direction. Do you mean you've been so sure all along the line? "

" Well," said Lucy, genuinely perplexed, " he had you."

" And suppose we hadn't managed it—what about all those fal-de-lals then? "

Lucy's small mouth widened into a smile that swelled to a laugh. " Oh, Scott, I never thought of that." She stood up and slipped one hand under his arm. " You know, Scott, but of course you don't, so I will tell you just this once and then you can forget it, if you like—if it were not for Charles, and the fact that your father and mine were the same, I might be a little envious of Rosemary."

Egerton roused himself for a moment. He thought he'd tell his wife that and see what her reaction was. But fortunately just in time he remembered his Scotch ancestry, that carried obligations, and he sank back again without speech.

》》 If you've enjoyed this book and would like to discover more great vintage crime and thriller titles, as well as the most exciting crime and thriller authors writing today, visit: 》》

The Murder Room
Where Criminal Minds Meet

themurderroom.com

www.ingramcontent.com/pod-product-compliance
Ingram Content Group UK Ltd.
Pitfield, Milton Keynes, MK11 3LW, UK
UKHW022316280225
455674UK00004B/323